To Sheila

Love

Madge + Bill   1968

A
Christmas Book

BOOKS BY ELIZABETH GOUDGE

Novels

ISLAND MAGIC
A CITY OF BELLS
TOWERS IN THE MIST
THE MIDDLE WINDOW
THE BIRD IN THE TREE
THE CASTLE ON THE HILL
GREEN DOLPHIN COUNTRY
THE HERB OF GRACE
THE HEART OF THE FAMILY
GENTIAN HILL
THE ROSEMARY TREE
THE WHITE WITCH
THE DEAN'S WATCH
THE SCENT OF WATER

Short Stories

WHITE WINGS
THE REWARD OF FAITH
THE WELL OF THE STAR
THE PEDLAR'S PACK
THE GOLDEN SKYLARK
THE IKON ON THE WALL

Novelette

THE SISTER OF THE ANGELS

Juveniles

SMOKY HOUSE
HENRIETTA'S HOUSE
THE LITTLE WHITE HORSE
MAKE-BELIEVE
THE VALLEY OF SONG
LINNETS AND VALERIANS

Non-fiction

GOD SO LOVED THE WORLD
ST. FRANCIS OF ASSISI
A DIARY OF PRAYER

Anthology

AT THE SIGN OF THE DOLPHIN
A BOOK OF COMFORT

Omnibus

THE ELIOTS OF DAMEROSEHAY
THREE CITIES OF BELLS

A Christmas Book

by
Elizabeth Goudge

HODDER AND STOUGHTON

*Printed in Great Britain
for Hodder and Stoughton Ltd.,
St. Paul's House, Warwick Lane, London, E.C.4,
by Richard Clay (The Chaucer Press), Ltd.,
Bungay, Suffolk*

CONTENTS

ACKNOWLEDGEMENTS

Material from the following books:

ISLAND MAGIC   A CITY OF BELLS
TOWERS IN THE MIST

is included in this volume by arrangement with the
publishers Gerald Duckworth & Co., Ltd.

The author and publishers are indebted to the
Executors of the Laurence Housman Estate and
Messrs. Jonathan Cape Ltd., for permission to
quote the poem on page 214 of this book.

PREFACE

IN the mid-winter gloom Christmas comes up over the horizon like a lighted ship homeward bound. The arrival has been prepared for and is expected, yet as the archaic shape draws slowly nearer and nearer, the lights of the lanterns reflected in the black water like moons and stars, the sails luminous as huge moth's wings in the dark, we feel profound relief. The great ship has not been wrecked. We, in its absence, have escaped destruction. It is to happen again; the landfall, the home-coming, the music of the ship's viols that is already sounding over the water, and the sight of the mysterious shadowed figures coming down the gangway to where the carpets have been spread, to keep the cold of earth's stones from their shining, soundless feet. The shadows never entirely veil the shining; they do not want to hurt our eyes with the extraordinary splendour of their love, but are not quite able to hide their shining feet.

The bells of the earthly city ring out as the ship docks. The shape of her belongs to legend, for she has come from far, from beyond space and time. It is strange how the moment she is with us her lanterns glow in a manner that makes her a veritable ship of light; yet the shining is gentle and meditative as candle-light and we wonder why it is that it should bring us such a deep sense of reassurance. Then we remember that the landfall has been within us, in our hearts, that we are always, if only secretly, much afraid, and that to faint hearts reassurance must come very gently. Such a blaze of light as flung the lion-hearted Paul of Tarsus to the ground for a few moments would fling us into eternity for ever, and we may not want to go there just yet. We would rather be gently reassured, Christmas by Christmas, that the land beyond space and time, where our ship has come from, is nothing to be afraid of.

There was always the Feast of Lights. Our forefathers, we believe, had stouter hearts than we have. As the wise animals do, they took disaster and death as they came. But they did fear the eeriness of mid-winter darkness. What if the sun did not rise tomorrow? What if spring never came back? What if they never

7

again heard the birds singing in an April dawn, or saw the flowers in the fields bending before the wind? And so our forefathers lit great bonfires on the hills at night to encourage the Sun God. He was growing weak. They could not have him dying. They could not live without the Light of the World. They reached out to him and received the reassurance they longed for. They were not to be afraid. Spring would come again. The birds would sing once more and the earth bring forth her fruits.

And so Christmas is still the Feast of Lights. So many of them. Once it was the yule-log, the burning brandy of the snapdragon game, and the flames round the Christmas pudding. Then it was twinkling wax candles on the Christmas-tree. Now the candles are mostly electric, and if safer are not so beautiful, and the blazing lights in Regent Street are rather garish. But it does not matter, for whatever they are they continue to be reflections from the light that at the beginning of all things moved upon the face of the waters, that in the fullness of the days was born to be the glory of Israel and a light to lighten the Gentiles, that in the ending of the days will shine out upon whatever chaos we have brought upon ourselves, and even then, amidst the tumbling and extinction of all earthly lights, will bring reassurance to the ultimate horror.

There is treasure in the ship's hold. The shadowed ones bring it ashore but they keep it hidden and bestow it as secretly as they bring it. We do not know what the gifts are; unless, in the midst of the Christmas turmoil, we suddenly find ourselves possessed of a tranquillity foreign to our normally agitated temperaments, or are astonished by an amazing visitation of joy, a singing in the soul, a new power of generosity, or insight, or endurance, or whatever the needs may be that we sometimes scribble on a list of "wants" and present to God with not much hope, even when we have written "hope" at the bottom of the list. It is strange that the list of temporal wants we present upon request to our relatives is offered with every expectation that something, the tin-opener if not the Jaguar, will be forthcoming. But with the other list we are astonished if we get what we asked for. Yet the gifts on the lighted Christmas-tree are no more than symbols of the other gifts. Without the unseen bestowals they would not be there at all, for there would be no Christmas. We think lovingly of the baby in the manger, once a visible gift to us, and the marvel of his beauty and innocence blind us to the fact that he is not any baby but one who "looks us through the lattice of our flesh and speaks us fair", bringing to us the supremely hidden gift of "God with us", the very meaning of existence since the dawn of light first brought life to the earth.

"Thou shalt light me a candle," said the psalmist. "Thou shalt turn my darkness into light."

Elizabeth Goudge

January, 1967

Christmas in the Cathedral

1

EVERY year, at half-past-five on Christmas Eve, Michael
lifted his great fist and struck the double quarter, and the
Cathedral bells rang out. They pealed for half-an-hour and
all over the city, and in all the villages to which the wind carried
the sound of the bells, they knew that Christmas had begun.
People in the fen wrapped cloaks about them and went out of doors
and stood looking towards the city. This year it was bitterly cold
but the wind had swept the clouds away and the Cathedral on its
hill towered up among the stars, light shining from its windows.
Below it the twinkling city lights were like clustering fireflies about
its feet. The tremendous bell music that was rocking the tower
and pealing through the city was out here as lovely and far away as
though it rang out from the stars themselves, and it caught at men's
hearts. "Now 'tis Christmas," they said to each other, as their fore-
bears had said for centuries past, looking towards the city on the
hill and the great fane that was as much a part of their blood and
bones as the fen itself. "'Tis Christmas," they said, and went back
happy to their homes.

In the city, as soon as the bells started, everyone began to get
ready. Then from nearly every house family parties came out and
made their way up the steep streets towards the Cathedral. Quite
small children were allowed to stay up for the carol service, and
they chattered like sparrows as they stumped along buttoned into
their thick coats, the boys gaitered and mufflered, the girls with
muffs and fur bonnets. It was the custom in the city to put lighted
candles in the windows on Christmas Eve and their light, and the
light of the street lamps, made of the street ladders of light leaning
against the hill. The grown-ups found them Jacob's ladders to-
night, easy to climb, for the bells and the children tugged them up.

Nearly everyone entered by the west door, for they loved the
thrill of crossing the green under the moon and stars, and mounting the steps and gazing up at the west front, and then going in
through the Porch of the Angels beneath Michael and the pealing
bells. Some of them only came to the Cathedral on this one day

13

in the year, but as they entered the nave they felt the impact of its beauty no less keenly than those who came often. It was always like a blow between the eyes, but especially at night, and especially on Christmas Eve when they were full of awe and expectation. There were lights in the nave but they could do no more than splash pools of gold here and there, they could not illumine the shadows above or the dim unlighted chantries and half-seen tombs. The great pillars soared into darkness and the aisles narrowed to twilight. Candles twinkled in the choir and the high altar with its flowers was ablaze with them, but all the myriad flames were no more than seed pearls embroidered on a dark cloak. The great rood was veiled in shadow. All things alike went out into mystery. The crowd of tiny human creatures flowed up the nave and on to the benches. The sound of their feet, of their whispering voices and rustling garments, was lost in the vastness. The music of the organ flowed over them and they were still.

But a few came in through the south door and Tom Hochicorn gave them greeting as he stood bowing by his brazier. Albert Lee had worked quickly, had come by some charcoal and had it lighted and installed by the time the bells began to ring. He had sat on the bench chatting to old Tom for a while and then, as people began to arrive, he took fright and was all for escaping back to Swithins Lane, but old Tom grabbed him and held on with surprising strength. "Go inside, Bert," he commanded.

"What, me?" gasped Albert Lee. "In there? Not bloody likely!"

"Why not, Bert?"

"Full of toffs," said Albert Lee. "'Ere, Tom, you leggo. I don't want to 'urt you."

"You won't see no toffs," said old Tom. "Not to notice. Just a lot of spotted ladybirds a-setting on the floor. That's all they look like in there. You go in, Bert. Not afraid, are you?"

"Afraid?" scoffed Albert Lee. "I ain't been afraid of nothink not since I was born."

"Go in, then," said Tom. He opened the door and motioned to Albert. "Look there. See that pillar? The one by the stove. There's a chair behind it. No one won't see you if you set behind that pillar. If you look round it when you hear the Dean speaking you'll see him."

He had hold of Albert by his coat collar. Albert didn't want to make a scene or own himself afraid. He found himself inside with the door softly closed behind him. Sweating profusely he crept to the chair behind the pillar and sat down on its extreme edge. Cor, what a place! It was like old Tom had said. No one didn't notice you in here. You were too small. Cor, this was a terrible place! It was like night up there. But the door was near, and so was the homely-looking stove. For a while his eyes clung to the door, and then as the warmth of the stove flowed out to him his terror began to subside. It was nice and warm in his corner. No one couldn't see him. He'd sit for a while. The bells were pretty but he didn't like that great humming rumbling music that was sending tremors through his legs. Then it stopped, and the bells too, and there was silence, and then miles away he heard boys singing.

They came nearer and nearer, singing like the birds out in the fen in spring. One by one men's voices began to join in, and then the multitude of men and women whom he could scarcely see began to sing too. The sound grew, soaring up to the great darkness overhead. It pulled him to his feet. He didn't know the words and he didn't know the music but he had sung with the Romany people in his boyhood, sitting round the camp fire in the drove, and he'd been quick to pick up a tune. He was now. He dared not use his coarsened voice but the music sang in his blood like sap rising in a tree. When the hymn ended there was a strange rustling sound, like leaves stirring all over a vast forest. It startled him at first until he realized that it was all the toffs kneeling down. He knelt too, his tattered cap in his hands, and the slight stir of his movement was drawn into the music of all the other movements. For the forest rustling was also music and that too moved in his blood. There was silence again and far away he heard the Dean's voice raised in the bidding prayer. He could not distinguish a word but the familiar voice banished the last of his fear. When the prayer ended he said Amen as loudly as any and was no longer conscious of loneliness. From then until the end he was hardly conscious even of himself.

There were not many who were. It was that which made this particular Christmas Eve carol service memorable above all others in the city's memory. The form of it was the same as always. The familiar hymns and carols followed each other in the familiar order, the choir sang "Wonderful, Counsellor, the Mighty God, the everlasting Father, the Prince of Peace", as gloriously as ever

15

but not more so, for they always put the last ounce into it, the difference was that instead of the congregation enjoying themselves enjoying the carol service they were enjoying the carol service. They were not to-night on the normal plane of human experience. When they had climbed the Jacob's ladders of the lighted streets from the city to the Cathedral they had climbed up just one rung higher than they usually did.

There was another difference. The form of this service was the same as always but the emphasis was different. Generally the peak of it all was the anthem, but to-night it was the Christmas gospel, read as always by the Dean.

Adam Ayscough walked with a firm step to the lectern, put on his eyeglasses and found the place. As he and Elaine had left the Deanery to go to the Cathedral he had been in great fear, for he had not known if he would be able to get through the service. Then as they crossed the garden she had slipped her hand into his and he had known he would do it. "All shall be well and all manner of thing shall be well." He cleared his throat. "The first verse of the first chapter of the gospel according to St. John," he said. His sight, he found, was worse than usual and the page was misty. But it was no matter for he knew the chapter by heart. He raised his head and looked out over the congregation. "In the beginning was the Word, and the Word was with God."

His voice was like a raucous trumpet, it had such power behind it. The people listened without movement, but though they had all come filled with thankfulness because he would be here to-night they were not thinking of him as they had thought of him on other Christmas Eves, thinking how ugly he was, how awkward, but yet how in place there in the lectern, looming up above them in his strange rugged strength, they were thinking only of what he was saying. "The Word was made flesh and dwelt among us." Was it really true? Could it be true? If it was true, then the rood up there was the king-pin that kept all things in perpetual safety and they need never fear again. To many that night Adam Ayscough's speaking of the Christmas gospel was a bridge between doubt and faith, perhaps because it came to them with such a splendid directness. He stood for a moment looking out over the people, then left the lectern and went back to his stall. His sight had been too dim to see them when he looked at them and he had no knowledge that he had been of service to them.

16

Nor, when at the conclusion of the service the Bishop and clergy, the choir and the whole congregation, flocked down to the west end of the nave for the traditional singing of "Now thank we all our God", did he know that his presence with them all was one of the chief causes of their thanksgiving. But when the Bishop had blessed them, and the clergy and choir had turned to go to their vestries, he did what no Dean had ever done before and moving to the west door stood there to greet the people as they went out. To break with tradition in this manner was unlike him, for he revered tradition, yet he found himself moving to the west door.

He had no idea that quite so many people as this came to the Cathedral on Christmas Eve. Surely nearly the whole city was here. Most of them only dared to smile at him shyly, as they passed by, but some bolder spirits spoke to him, saying they were glad he was better and returning his good wishes when he wished them a happy Christmas. To his astonished delight almost all those who in the last few months had become so especially dear to him, like his own small flock of sheep, were among those who gave him a special greeting.

Bella was there, in her cherry-red outfit, clasping her doll. "She would come," her grandmother whispered to him, "though it's long past her bedtime, and she would bring her doll. I knew it was not right but I could not prevent it." Mrs. Havelock was looking extremely tired and the Dean took her hand to reassure her. Bella, who had been looking as smugly solid as a stationary robin, suddenly became airborne and darted off into the night. Mrs. Havelock, abruptly dropping the Dean's hand, fled in pursuit.

Mr. Penny was there, not identifying the Dean in his robes with Lear's fool, and bowing very shyly as he passed, and Ruth with her wise calm smile and little Miss Throstle of the umbrella shop. Albert Lee was there, borne along by the crowd as an integral part of it and quite comfortable in his non-entity, and yet bold as well as comfortable for he was one of those who paused to wish the Dean a happy Christmas. Polly and Job were there, as he had known they would be, but they smiled at him as though from a vast distance, and he was glad of it. They were in their own world. Polly wore her bonnet with the cherry-coloured ribbons and her left hand lay on Job's right arm in the traditional manner of those who are walking out. She had left her glove off on purpose that the world might see her ring.

With them was Miss Peabody, looking not so much ill as convalescent. She was one of those for whom despair, to which she had lived so near for so long, had receded during the reading of the Christmas gospel. Yet she would have slipped past the Dean unnoticed had he not stopped her and taken her hand. "A happy Christmas, Miss Peabody," he said cheerfully, as though there had been no clock. "I am obliged to you for coming to-night. Much obliged. God bless you."

But the one he had most wished to see, Isaac, was not there. As he walked home he was deeply unhappy. Isaac and Elaine, he feared, he had loved only to their hurt, and he prayed God to forgive him.

Back in the Deanery again there were many matters to attend to and it was not until late in the evening that he went to his study to finish writing his Christmas sermon. He turned back to the beginning of it, to refresh his mind as to what he had already written, and as he read he was in despair. It was a terrible sermon for its Christmas purpose of joy and love. It was academic, abstruse, verbose. Why was it that he could write a book but could not write a sermon? He told himself that a sermon was a thing of personal contact, and in personal contacts he had always failed most miserably. Already, as he turned the pages of this most wretched sermon, he could feel the wave of boredom and dislike that always seemed to beat up in his face when he tried to preach, and he shrank miserably within himself. Nevertheless the sermon had to be written and it had to be preached and he picked up his pen, dipped it in the ink and began to write.

But presently he found to his dismay that he could not see what he wrote. He turned back to the earlier pages and found they were as blurred as the page of the gospels had been when he stood in the lectern. He realized that he was too tired to prepare this sermon, too tired to sit here any longer at his desk. Fear took hold of him. This dimming of his sight had not mattered this evening, for he had known what he had to say, but in the pulpit it would be fatal, for he had never been able to preach in any other way than by reading aloud from the written page. The gospel he had known by heart. "By heart." It seemed to his bewilderment and fatigue as though a voice had spoken. A great simplicity had come into his life these last months, a grace that had been given to him with the friendship of humble people. Could he tomorrow preach from his heart and not his intellect? Could he look upon his heart with

18

his inward eyes and speak what he found written upon it? A man's heart was the tablet of God, who wrote upon it what he willed. He took up the manuscript of his sermon and tore it across, flinging the fragments into the waste paper basket.

Then he lit the candle that stood upon a side table, put out the lamp and went out into the darkened hall. When there was much work to be done he often went to bed very late and by his command no servant waited up for him. He climbed the stairs slowly with his candle, and as he climbed the clamour of the bells broke out once more. It was midnight, the hour of Christ's birth. At the top of the stairs there was a window. He put his candle down on the sill and stood for a moment in prayer. Then he opened the old casement a few inches and the sound of the bells swept in to him on a breath of cold air. He closed the window again and saw that a snowflake lay on his hand.

2

He slept deeply that night, a thing he had not done for months past, then woke at his usual early hour, dressed and made his meditation. Then he left the house for the first service of Christmas Day. As he closed the garden door behind him he stood in amazement, for he had stepped not into the expected darkness but into light. It was neither of the sun nor moon but of the snow. The sky was a cold clear green behind the dark mass of the Cathedral, the wind had dropped and the stillness was absolute. The snow was not deep but it covered the garden with light. He moved forward a few steps and looked about him. The roof of the Cathedral, every parapet and ledge, the roofs of the houses and the boughs of the trees all bore their glory of snow. He walked slowly through the garden in awe and joy, thinking of the myriad snowflakes under his feet, each one a cluster of beautiful shapes of stars and flowers and leaves, all too small to be seen by any eye except that of their Creator, yet each giving light. That was why he always wanted a white Christmas. Almighty God had been so small, as small as the crystal of a snowflake in comparison with the universe that he had made. "Such light!" murmured the Dean as he opened the door into the Cathedral. "Such light!"

19

In the Cathedral it was still dark, for he was very early, as he liked to be, and only the lights in the sanctuary were as yet lit, but he could have found his way about the Cathedral blindfold. He went into the chantry of the Duchess Blanche and knelt down and as he began his prayer he found that light was in his mind and spirit. The darkness of yesterday had been taken from him.

3

After breakfast Elaine stood in the drawing-room, one hand on the mantelpiece, looking down into the fire, steeling herself for the moment between breakfast and matins when she and Adam always gave each other their Christmas presents. She never knew what to give him, for he had no hobbies apart from this recent rather ridiculous one of horology, and he was indifferent to what he ate. This year she had a book of travel for him which she had chosen at Joshua Appleby's bookshop. If he did not like the reading matter it was at least a book, and she believed that he liked books not only for their contents but for their shape and feel, for she had seen him touch and turn their pages as though each one were a unique thing of beauty, like the petals of a flower. She had only noticed this just lately, during his illness. There were many things about him that she had not noticed until just lately. But even more difficult than her gift to him was his to her. Once again she would have to simulate pleasure at sight of some trinket that she would never be able to wear. Her beauty being her *raison d'être* it was impossible for her to desecrate it by some jewel that was not in keeping with its perfection. Adam's taste in clothes and jewels was atrocious.

He came in and she gave him his book and saw that she had truly pleased him. "The Isles of Greece, Elaine," he said as he turned the pages. "You have remembered how I went there as a young man. My dear, I love you for it." She had not remembered but she smiled very sweetly at him and accepted his tribute. When sensitive apprehensions were attributed to her she was always able to appropriate them quickly. It was a part of her charm.

Adam laid the book aside and now it was her turn. Her heart sank. But he produced no jeweller's velvet case from his pocket, instead he said to her, "My dear, I have no real gift for you this year. I must tell you why." Then he told her about the celestial clock, describing its beauty, telling her that by some mischance it had fallen and been broken. "There is only the fret left," he said. "I am so sorry that it is all I have to give you."

He put it into her hands and she carried it to the window and gave an exclamation of pleasure, so delighted was she to find it was nothing she might be expected to wear. The Dean was startled. She stood in the wonderful snowlight, which could not dim her beauty but only enhance it, and on her face was the look of pleasure he had longed to see, called there by the fragment of a broken clock. Truly there was no understanding women. He did not try to understand. She was pleased and he was content to love her beauty and her pleasure.

'I am so sorry the clock was broken, Adam," she said, "but I like this fret. I shall use it as a paper weight." She looked at him with a smile. "It will help me not to lose my letters as I did Ruth's. The bells have started. I must put on my things."

"I'll wait here for you, my dear," said the Dean. "We will go together."

Waiting for her he had a moment of panic about his sermon but he put it from him. What a peculiar thing the mind was. Yesterday had been full of darkness and distress, both pressing sorely upon him, but to-day he was happy and at peace, and though physical malaise never left him now it seemed pleasantly relaxed, like a hand that has relinquished its grip though not its hold.

Elaine came back wrapped in her furs and this time, instead of going through the garden, they went out into the Close, to look at the wonder of the lime avenue under snow. The sun shone now in a cloudless blue sky and the splendour of the white world awed even Elaine. All over the city the bells were ringing and the shining silence of the white snow seemed to answer them. They walked slowly towards the south door along a path swept clear of snow. On either side it was piled in miniature snow mountains, silver-crested and pooled with azure. "We used to have white Christmases like this when I was a boy," said the Dean with satisfaction.

"How do you feel to-day, Adam?" asked Elaine. She was already beginning to dread his sermon and there was genuine anxiety in her voice.

21

"I feel very well," he answered. "Do you remember our walking through the garden together yesterday evening? You gave me strength, my dear, when you put your hand in mine. It is so, through every touch of love, that God strengthens us."

They had reached the south door and Hochicorn was beaming and bowing beside his brazier. The Dean stopped to speak to him and Elaine went on into the Cathedral. Although she was looking superbly beautiful in her sables and holly-green velvet her progress to her seat lacked something of its usual dramatic perfection. It was graceful but unstudied and Mary Montague, in her usual place in her bath-chair, noticed it. "Did she feel the Dean's illness at all?" she wondered. "Can the wells have broken? No, not yet, but the wind has changed."

The congregation in the Cathedral on Christmas morning at matins was not the large one of Christmas Eve, when the carol service was the only one in the city. It was the usual Sunday congregation, but larger than was customary because it was Christmas Day. It was a distinguished congregation, containing all the élite of the city. As the Dean walked in procession to his stall past the long rows of well-dressed, well-fed people, his nose was assailed by delicate perfumes, the scent of rich furs and shoe polish, and in spite of his happiness panic rose in him again, and this time he could not subdue it. How could he have imagined that he could preach a simple extempore sermon to people such as these? They would be outraged. He would bring shame upon the Bishop and his learned brethren of the chapter, upon the Cathedral and upon Elaine. He did not know how to preach extempore. Nervous and anxious as he always was when he had to speak in public he had never attempted such a thing. He was so dismayed that by the time he reached the choir his hands were clammy and trembling. Then, as he settled into the Dean's stall like a statue into its niche, reassurance came to him from the great joyous Cathedral. He was as much a humble part of it as the shepherd under the miserere seat, as the knights on their tombs and the saints and angels in the windows, as the very stones and beams of its structure. They all had their function to perform in its Christmas adoration and not the humblest or the least would be allowed to fall.

As the Te Deum soared to the roof, to the sky, and took wings to the four corners of the earth, he felt himself built into the fabric of the singing stones and the shouting exulting figures all about

22

him. The stamping of the unicorns, the roaring of the lions and the noise the angels made with their trumpets and cymbals almost drowned the thunder of the organ. The knights sang on their tombs and the saints in their windows, and the homely men and boys and birds were singing under the miserere seats. Adam Ayscough was not surprised. He had had a similar experience long ago as a child, although until this moment he had forgotten it. The human brain was an organ of limitation. It restricted a grown man's consciousness of the exterior world to what was practically useful to him. It was like prison walls. Without them possibly he could not have concentrated sufficiently upon the task he had to do. But in childhood and old age the prison walls were of cloudy stuff and there were occasional rents in them.

The tremendous music sang on in him after the Te Deum had ended but it did not prevent him from doing efficiently all that he had to do. He made the right responses, he walked to the lectern to read the second lesson and returned to his stall again, and during the hymn before the sermon he knelt in his stall to pray as he always did. But to-day he did not pray for strength to mount the huge pulpit under the sounding board, for he hardly remembered it. He prayed for the city.

Yet when he was in the pulpit he instinctively steeled himself against that wave of boredom and resignation that always rose and broke over him when he stood above the distant congregation like Punch on his stage. It did not come. There was no distance. They were all as close to him as his own body. His sight was better to-day and he looked down at them for a moment; at Elaine in her pew, her head bent and her hands in her muff, at Mary Montague in her bath-chair, at Mr. Penny over to his right, quite close to him. The knot in Mr. Penny's handkerchief had done all that was asked of it and Mr. Penny sat in the midst of his flock, Miss Peabody on his right and Job and Polly on his left. He was looking up at the Dean in a state of rapture and bland attention. He had not had to preach himself this morning. It was years since he had had the pleasure of listening to another man's sermon and he was enjoying himself. The Dean forgot all about the well-dressed critical men and women who had so alarmed him while he walked past them. He suddenly remembered Letitia and it was to this old shepherd that he preached his last Christmas sermon.

He took his text from Dean Rollard's psalm, the sixty-eighth,

"God is the Lord by whom we escape death." He spoke of love, and a child could have understood him. He said that only in the manger and upon the cross is love seen in its maturity, for upon earth the mighty strength of love has been unveiled once only. On earth, among men, it is seldom more than a seed in the hearts of those who choose it. If it grows at all it is no more than a stunted and sometimes harmful thing, for its true growth and purging are beyond death. There it learns to pour itself out until it has no self left to pour. Then, in the hollow of God's hand into which it has emptied itself, it is his own to all eternity. If there were no life beyond death, argued the Dean, there could be no perfecting of love, and no God, since he is himself that life and love. It is by love alone that we escape death, and love alone is our surety for eternal life. If there were no springtime there would be no seeds. The small brown shell, the seed of an apple tree in bloom, is evidence for the sunshine and the singing of the birds.

He came down from the pulpit and walked back to his stall and fitted comfortably into his niche in the fabric. Presently, when the last hymn had been sung, he went up to the altar and blessed the people.

4

All over the city men and women and children poured out of the chapels and churches exclaiming at the beauty of the day. It all looked as pretty as a picture, they said. The frost kept the sparkling snow from slipping away from roofs and chimney pots, but it was not too cold to spoil the sunshine. There was no wind. On their way home, whenever a distant view opened out, they could pause and enjoy it without having to shiver. The stretch of the snow-covered fen almost took their breath away, it was so beautiful under the blue arc of the sky. It was like the sea when it turns to silver under the dazzle of the sun. When they turned and looked up at the Cathedral its snow-covered towers seemed to rise to an immeasurable height. Then a wonderful fragrance assailed their nostrils. In steam-filled kitchens the windows had been opened now that the day was warming up. The turkeys and baked potatoes and plum puddings were also warming up and in another forty

minutes would have reached the peak of their perfection. Abruptly
Christmas Day swung over like a tossed coin. The silver and
blue of bells and hymns and angels went down with a bang and
was replaced by the red and gold of flaming plum puddings
and candled trees. Everyone hurried home as quickly as they
could.

Christmas Day at the Deancry was one of the busiest of the year.
When the morning services were over there was the ritual of the
Christmas dinner, to which the Dean insisted that Elaine invite all
the lonely people connected with the Close, such as bachelor minor
canons and widows of defunct Cathedral dignitaries. This was
usually something of an ordeal for all concerned but to-day not
even the sight of the vast dead turkey could depress the Dean, and
old Mrs. Ramsey, whose terrifying privilege it was to sit upon his
right, found him almost a genial host. When the guests had gone
Elaine dissolved upon the sofa, but the Dean went out to visit the
old men at the almshouses until it was time for evensong. Then
there was a late tea, followed by the ceremony of the servants'
Christmas-tree. The difficult occasion had never seemed so happy.
The servants almost forgot their shyness in their pleasure at seeing
the Dean looking so much better. Elaine had never been so suc-
cessful in disguising her boredom or the Dean in overcoming his
trepidation, and Garland was so happy that he unbent sufficiently
to utter a few mild jokes as he cut the presents from the tree. Yet
he did not hold with the Dean going round to the choir school
Christmas-tree as soon as he had finished with the servants'. It
was his custom on Christmas Day, and boys were his delight, but
Garland considered that Cook was in the right of it when she remarked that the boys should have made do with the Archdeacon
this year. They'd scarcely have noticed the difference; not with
their stomachs full.

Elaine went to bed directly after supper, her husband carrying
her candle for her to her room.

"Are you very tired, my dear?" he asked her. "It has been a
long day for you."

"Not so tired as usual," she said, pulling off her rings and dropping them on her dressing-table, and she added softly, looking
away from him, "It has been a happy Christmas Day. I liked
your sermon, Adam."

She had never said that before and his heart seemed to make a physical movement of joy. "It is true, Elaine," he said. "All I said so haltingly is true. I'm glad you liked it. Good-night, my dear. Sleep well."

She lifted her face and as he kissed her smooth cool cheek he felt suddenly that he could not leave her. He wanted to ask if he might sit in her arm-chair for a little while, in her warm scented room, and watch her brush her hair. It was years since he had seen her glorious hair down on her shoulders. But her eyes were drowning in sleep and he feared to weary her. He tiptoed from her room and closed the door softly behind him.

He went into his study, where Garland had lighted the lamp for him. He was deeply grateful that the labour of the last two days was now accomplished, and most thankful to find himself so well. He was abysmally tired, but he did not feel ill. He would work for a little longer before he went to bed.

He opened a deep drawer in his table and took out two piles of papers. One was the manuscript of his book and the other the architectural plans. The unfinished book cried out to him in its plight but he put it to one side. It was himself and so must be denied. For the hundredth time he unfolded all the plans and opened them before him. They were dog-eared now, and stained in several places, for they had been through so many hands and had been argued over so hotly for so long. And now it was all to do again. Tomorrow he would start the fight once more. He thought of it with dread, but that cancer could not be left in the body of the city. He remembered Dean Rollard singing the sixty-eighth psalm. "This is God's hill, in the which it pleaseth him to dwell." With what grief must God look upon the North Gate slums, and the rotting human bodies there. The Dean pulled a piece of paper towards him and wrote out the words in his fine handwriting, laying it upon the plan of the city. Then upon another piece of paper he began to calculate the cost of demolition and rebuilding all over again. If he could only get expenditure down a little he might meet less opposition. But he feared he had many enemies. In past years, stung nearly to madness by the sufferings of the poor, he had forced through reforms with too much anger and too much contempt for the oppressors. He was a gentler man now, but it was too late. Yet for an hour he went on working until the figures blurred and his gold pencil slipped from his hand.

"I must go to bed," he thought, and tried to get up from his

26

chair. Then it came again, the rising panic in his blood, the constriction of his throat, as though a rope were being drawn tighter and tighter about it, a roaring in the ears and the agonizing struggle for breath. He did not feel the joy this time, for it was too bad, but a great voice cried out in the crashing blackness of his mind, "Blessed be God."

Christmas on the Moor

1

EVER since the mist had come down Martin had kept a careful silence. His mind was bursting with the things he wanted to say to Maria, things about the superiority of a man's judgement, and obeying husbands and so on, but they had only been married for ten months and he still tried not to say the things. Nevertheless, since the whole adventure was her fault entirely, he could not help thinking them.

Maria was not country-bred and when he had brought her home to the old farmhouse under the shoulder of the moor, that had been his father's and his grandfather's and was now his, she had not found it easy to adjust herself. She had missed the parties she had been used to, and her sisters and their fun. She and Martin had no carriage, only the gig and a couple of riding horses, which was all a young gentleman farmer could expect to have in the 1800s. At first she was happy enough for the beauty of the country took her wild heart by storm and she loved exploring it on horseback, but the baby started to come and Martin got nervous and would not let her ride any more. And then the autumn closed down, with rain and gales from the sea, and gay and pleasure loving as she was she got depressed and restless. She must go home for Christmas, she said, and Martin must come too, for she would not go without him when it was the first Christmas of their married life. He said he couldn't leave the farm. She said he could. They had one of their flaming rows, for they were both high-spirited, and then one of their glorious reconciliations, for they were still deeply in love, and Maria won, because though she was five years younger than Martin, twenty to his twenty-five, she was just that much more determined on her own way than he was; though he was determined too, and he kept to it that they leave home on Christmas Eve and return on December twenty-eighth. Three full days at her papa's, but no more. He would not trust the farm hands with his precious beasts a moment longer than that. She knew that particular set of his firm lips and conceded the minor point, having won the major one, and honour being now more or less equally satisfied they became as excited as children as they made their preparations.

It wasn't far to go to the country town where Maria had been born, ten miles over the moor or eighteen miles round by the turnpike road. They would go the long way round, Martin decided. It was safer, with the weather uncertain and the baby due in a month. Maria arched her eyebrows and shot him a wicked sparkling look at the word "safer", which was to her what a red rag is to a bull. If anyone told her to go through the gap in the hedge rather than over the gate she set her horse instantly at the gate. A suggestion that it would be safer to close the window in a thunderstorm made her immediately open it as wide as possible. But Martin had not been married to Maria quite long enough yet to bear this fact continually in mind, and anyway he was lighting his pipe at the time and scarcely noticed her look. He was to remember it later.

Christmas Eve dawned sunlit and sparkling, and almost as warm as spring. They put the small corded trunk packed with their best clothes and the presents for the family under the seat of the gig and settled themselves happily together beneath the plaid rug. Maria looked enchanting in her crimson fur-trimmed pelisse and velvet bonnet. She was not beautiful, for her nose was too large and her cleft chin too resolute, but her brilliant laughing eyes made her seem so. She was a brown girl, her dusky hair springing wirily from her broad forehead and her golden skin clear and rose-tinted with her perfect health. Her pregnancy had not sapped her vitality in the least. She was looking forward to going home again in a month's time and having the baby with Mamma and Dr. Fothergill in devoted attendance. She loved the old doctor, brusque and outspoken though he was. It would be impossible to have a baby without him.

They bowled along through the village and swept out into the turnpike in fine style, for the grey horse Beauty was as high-spirited as his owners. The gig, new at the time of their marriage, had yellow wheels that flashed as though the sun were tangled up in them. Martin's holly-green greatcoat and curly beaver hat set at a jaunty angle were becoming to his flaming red head and freckled, sun-tanned handsomeness. He kept his back straight and drove with dash and skill. Maria adored driving with him and never loved him so much as when they bowled along together like this with the wind whistling past them and their glowing bodies warm together under the rug.

To the right the moor lifted in fold upon fold towards the sky, the tawny, dead bracken gold where the sun touched it, the withered heather wine-dark under the dry-stone walls. Those who lived beneath it could never forget the moor. It was always subtly present to their thoughts and dreams and they glanced towards it constantly, sometimes with a slight uneasiness, as men eye a mounting storm on the horizon. To the left was the good and gentle land, with its round green hills and fields where the sheep were feeding, its deep woods and ferny lanes.

A cock crowed loudly behind them, where a farmhouse stood crookedly among orchard trees, and they were startled, for they were looking towards the moor. "The cock, that is the trumpet to the morn," quoted Maria, who had been well educated and knew poetry by heart.

"It's afternoon," said Martin, who was literal-minded and impervious to Shakespeare. "We've started late, you know. All because you couldn't find your fan and wouldn't pack till the last moment. Women!"

But he was still good-humoured and looked down at her with his grey-green eyes screwed up in amusement and his wide mouth curling up at the corners. Maria laughed back at him and went on airing her Shakespearian knowledge, just to provoke him.

> "*Some say that ever 'gainst that season comes*
> *Wherein our Saviour's birth is celebrated,*
> *The bird of dawning singeth all night long;*
> *And then, they say, no spirit can walk abroad;*
> *The nights are wholesome; then no planets strike,*
> *No fairy takes, nor witch hath power to charm,*
> *So hallow'd and so gracious is the time.*"

To please her he was duly provoked. "Moonshine," he scoffed. "If you want to gabble by rote like a parrot why not get a few recipes by heart? Squab pie and dumplings. Dinner wouldn't be so late if you didn't waste so much time with your nose in a cook book. My mother made wonderful squab pie."

She let that pass, and went back to the subject of moonshine. "How do you know there are no fairies or witches? You don't know." She looked up at the great brooding presence of the moor.

"How do you know what lives up there? Whenever you've taken me there, though we've never been far, I've felt them. Haven't you?"

Martin looked down into her eager face, raised to his, and so full of laughter that he did not know if she was mocking or serious. That was one of the enchanting things about her; he never quite knew what she was really thinking. She was mysterious. He laughed without answering. Yet as a boy, birds'-nesting up there, he had felt them. Boys, he supposed, imagined things. "Good and bad," went on Maria. "But not bad ones to-day or to-morrow. Shakespeare meant the bad spirits. They've gone. They daren't be about at Christmas. But the good ones are about more than ever."

They drove on and came to the place where the narrow lane to the moors forked away from the turnpike. "Turn right, Martin," she said imperiously.

He should have known better than to pull up. He should have driven straight on as fast as he could. He knew quite well that if he gave ground at the start he was likely to lose the whole sparring match. He lost it now, though it was hotly contested. She said it was madness to go the long way round when it was miles shorter over the moor. He reminded her of the hazards of the moor, and could have reminded her of nothing more likely to harden her determination. She spoke of the beauty of the day and its extraordinary clarity, and looking up at the splendour above her was suddenly wild to be in it and of it. He'd always promised to take her right up over the moor and he never had. He would one day, he said. But what she wanted was never any good to Maria in the form of a distant promise. She wanted it now or not at all. What could happen? Was he afraid? She hated cowards. Hadn't he told her he knew the moor like the palm of his hand? This was a boast that he had made when he was courting her. He had boasted of much in those days, he had been so wild to win her, and not all his boasts had been strictly true. Afraid? He flicked his whip over Beauty's back and set him at a canter up the lane.

They drove up and up, the deep banks changing to dry-stone walls, and all about them the great views widened out. Down below the gentle land looked flat as a child's counterpane, sinking to unreality. This, now, was what was real, this world that was lifted up, the stark hills and the hidden valleys musical with streams, the

34

clear cold air and the silence. They seemed the only living creatures in this world but they could not feel that it belonged to them,
as a deserted meadow down below would have seemed their own.
They might presently belong to it, but not yet. It held them in the
hollow of its hand, watching them, but the hand had not yet closed
upon them.

But they were enjoying themselves. They spoke little but they
looked at each other often and smiled. Down below the surface
eddies their love for each other was already beginning to cut a
steady channel for itself and to flow strong and deep. Up here
they were aware that their quarrels, which had secretly worried
them both, did not matter. They would subside in time. What
each wanted of the other was secretly already in being. They drove
steadily uphill, into the woods and out of them, over the old stone
bridges and along the banks of the racing streams, and were too
absorbed in each other to notice that the sun had gone in and the
sky was veiled. When the mist finally came down it took them by
surprise. But Martin was quite sure he knew the way and repeated
the boast about the palm of his hand.

But as they went on he grew silent, and angry with Maria because he had not had the strength of mind to keep on along the
turnpike. He was getting very anxious about her and the more uneasy he was the more annoyed with her he became. He did not
look at her but now and then she looked at him, at his strong sullen
mouth and fine hands on the reins, and now and then she laughed
inside herself. They were lost, of course, but it was fun to be lost
with Martin. Presently he would stop being annoyed and then
they would be able to enjoy it together.

They jolted over a stone in the road and a wheel came off. It was
the most extraordinary thing to happen and was beyond Martin's
comprehension. They had been going very slowly and Maria
clung to the side and was not hurt at all, and laughed at Martin's
grave face as he helped her down and held her for a minute or two
in his arms. "One of the bad ones must have done it," she said.
"The last thing it did before it went into hiding over Christmas.
Don't worry, Martin. Take Beauty out of the gig and I'll ride
him, and you can walk beside me. We'll soon be there."

"We won't," said Martin. "We're lost, you know."

"Yes, I know, but we're on some sort of a road and it must lead
somewhere. To a farm or village. We've only got to follow it."

35

He did not tell her for how many miles one could follow these tracks over the moor and not get anywhere. He lifted her on Beauty and wrapped the rug about her, and took one of the lanterns from the gig, and now they were no longer silent but laughed and talked together in case the other should be feeling low-spirited. Then they fell silent again, for it was growing dark and late, the mist was thicker than ever and instead of the track going downhill towards the good and gentle land it was going up and up. Martin stopped and lit the lantern and Maria bent down and tried to see his face. "Martin," she said. "I'm sorry. It was my fault."

He looked up and smiled at her. "My fault too. We've been a couple of fools together."

"But together," she said. "Are you very tired."

"No, love. Are you?"

"Of course not," she said indignantly, but looking up at her in the lantern light he saw that there were dark shadows under her eyes and his heart seemed to turn over. Ten minutes later she gave a sudden glad cry. "Look, Martin! A garden wall!"

He stopped with an exclamation of astonishment and held up the lantern. The wall was old, buttressed and strong. Inside was perhaps one of those moor gardens, sheltered from the wind, where magnolia trees grew against the south wall, and in summer herbs and flowers were all knotted together to make a paradise for bees. But it was odd that he had not seen it before, and odd that they should have apparently left the track without noticing it, for under the wall and beneath their feet was only the mist-drenched grass. "We'll follow along, Maria," he said joyously. "There must be something here."

They moved on and came to a splendid old archway in the wall. It had iron gates in it and they were hospitably open; yet the steep carriage-way beyond was almost lost among the brambles and rhododendrons that had grown across it. Holding the lantern high, Martin led Beauty through its tunnel-like windings. He could not see the trees that arched above them but he knew they must be there because of the soft drip from overhead.

The way widened out suddenly and the glimmer of a white shape startled them, but it was only the stone figure of a boy with a dolphin standing in the midst of a stone basin where once there had been a fountain. Beyond it broken steps led up to a terrace and they could just see a shuttered house and a front door with pillars on either side and a fanlight over it. No light came from the door but it was open.

It seemed quite natural to them both that Martin should help Maria down and tether Beauty to a vast japonica tree that grew beside the fountain. Then hand in hand they mounted the steps and went inside the house. It seemed empty and dark but the lantern light gleamed on the panelling and the gracious sweep of the staircase beyond. Several doors opened out of the hall but only one was ajar. They pushed it and went in. Inside was a small parlour and it was partly furnished. There were branched candle-sticks on the mantelpiece, with candles in them festooned with cobwebs, and an old cracked French mirror between them. A bro-cade sofa, torn now but once rose-coloured and lovely, was drawn to the empty basket grate. Maria dropped down upon it and Mar-tin covered her with the rug. Then he lit the candles. It was a beautiful room, its panelling painted pale apple-green. The paint was peeling off in places and there were damp stains on the ceiling, but still it was beautiful.

"You need a fire, Maria," said Martin, for she was shivering violently beneath the rug. "I'll go round to the back and see if I can find some dry wood."

"There's Beauty," said Maria.

"I'll take him with me. There may be a stable there."

He found a stable at the back, and the door was open. In one of the loose boxes there was hay in the manger and a bucket of water. Martin was somehow not surprised and Beauty was well content. In a corner of the stable there was a pile of dry logs, oak and beech, and fircones and a couple of sacks. He filled both and went round to the front door again, bent almost double beneath his load. "Soon have a fire, sweetheart," he said gaily as he lowered the sacks beside the hearth, and he kindled one easily with flint and tinder. It was surprising how quickly the flame leaped up the chimney, orange and blue and sea-green, and when the warmth stole out into the room it brought a fragrance with it. Yet it struck him that Maria was being oddly silent. He had expected admira-tion and congratulation. He looked round over his shoulder and saw her with enormous dark eyes in a blanched face. She had taken off her bonnet and her dark hair was in a tangle on her shoulders. Yet when he smiled at her she gave him an impish grin.

37

He dropped on his knees beside her and took her hands and his face was as white as hers. He looked so like a terrified schoolboy who has seen a ghost that she laughed, though the laugh had a crack in the middle. "It must have been jolting over the stone, when the wheel came off," she said. "Don't look so scared, Martin. There must be a village or this house would not be here. Take the lantern and go and find it, love. There are always midwives in villages."

"But I can't leave you alone," he said.

"But you must, you silly. Nothing can happen to me. A first baby takes hours. Go on, love. What else can we do?"

He crushed her hands nearly to pulp in his, then released them and got up. Then he took the lantern and went. She was right. There was nothing else to do.

He followed a grass-grown road down through the dripping woods until it forked. Then he stopped and he felt nearly crazed, for there was no signpost, no glimmer of light either way to tell him where the village was. Yet the mist was thinning slightly and he thought he saw a slight movement to the left. "Hi, you there!" he shouted, and strode forward with his lantern. Yes, it was a man, a tall old Negro with white hair. For just a moment he was vividly aware of dark eyes, incredibly gentle, the flash of a compassionate smile and the gesture of a hand, and then he was following the old man down through the woods. They did not speak, for the other was always just ahead of him, not clearly seen through the mist but never difficult to follow. Yet the way through the woods he could not have followed had he not been led, for it twisted and turned and at times was almost lost beneath the undergrowth. It seemed hours to him before the trees thinned and he heard a cock crowing, and then they came out into a deep lane and there were the lights of the village down below. After that he ran and soon he was thundering on a cottage door. It opened in a moment and he was pouring out his story to the kindly woman who stood there with such comfortable stolidity. He had forgotten the old Negro.

38

2

When she was alone Maria tried her best not to be terrified. She had thought she did not know what it was to be afraid but then she had never had a baby before. Toothache had been the worst she had known. Never anything like this, rhythmic pain roaring up at her and dragging back like waves breaking, and in the dark curve of each wave as it broke over her there was this fear. She would not have been so terrified if she had not been alone. If Mamma and Dr. Fothergill had been with her she would not have minded. Or if Martin had been able to stay with her they could have held hands and it would not have been so bad. But Martin was out in the night and he might never find the village. He might fall and hurt himself and not come back. Then she and the baby would die here. They would die without Dr. Fothergill. It was the old doctor she wanted so badly, more than Mamma or Martin. Once she thought she heard his step in the hall and she called out to him, "Doctor Fothergill! The baby's coming. Please come quickly!" But he did not come and she remembered that he could not possibly come. He was miles away. She and the baby were alone in this empty house and they would die. She knew she was making no sound but inside herself she heard her voice crying out in panic. "No! No! No!" she was crying. "I won't die. I won't."

She sat up on the sofa and pushed the heavy hair back from her forehead. "No," she said aloud. "I won't. And I won't scream. It's Christmas Eve. Martin will come back."

She lay down again and found she had controlled the terror. Or else something outside herself had conquered it. Was it the room? Shabby and cobwebbed though it was it had a safe and friendly look. The candles were not burnt out yet and the small flames swaying in the draught and then righting themselves were like flowers blown in the wind. The reflected firelight glowed warmly in the panelling. The last great wave, the one that had brought her terror nearly to screaming pitch, had dragged back and another had not come upon her. Nature was resting and she was at peace. She began to feel sleepy in the warmth of the fire, and she did not feel alone. She was not alone. She slipped her hand under her cheek and shut her eyes and murmured drowsily, "I am not alone."

In her dream the fire was still warm and glowing and the candles burning, but they were not swaying in the draught because long rose-coloured curtains hung over the shutters. There were no cobwebs and the pale leaf-green walls were fresh and clean. Beau-pots of flowers stood against them, and chairs with slender gold legs. Miniatures hung on the walls, and garlanded shepherds and shepherdesses stood on the mantelpiece. There was a harpsichord between the two tall windows and a woman sat before it, her fingers running up and down over the keys. She was enjoying herself, for her lips were parted in a smile and she swayed very slightly to her music, her head bent, absorbed in it. The skirt of her deep blue silk dress, the colour of bluebells when they are still in bud, was so full that it swirled all round her on the floor and hid her feet. There was white lace at her throat and white hair was piled up on her head, though she was not old. But she was not young either, not like Maria. Her smiling mouth was not a girl's mouth, and no girl could have played the harpsichord as she was doing. The gay lambent music was like a shower of spring rain when the sun is out, or like a family of young robins singing together. It was like a candled Christmas-tree or a child laughing. Maria laughed as she listened to it and she thought it was her child laughing, her child safely born and grown and clapping his hands at the candled tree. "See how pretty he is," she cried to the woman. "Look how he laughs at the tree!" But the room was growing darker and the music silent. Instead of the rippling notes she heard only the frou-frou of a woman's skirts as she came swiftly across the pol-ished floor. "Don't let me wake till I see you," Maria said to her. "Don't let me wake till I see your face."

But she could not hold the dream and when she woke the cob-webbed room was as before and there was no one there. Yet still she felt she was not alone. She lay quietly relaxed, still hearing the laughter of the child. Far away in the distance she heard a cock crow, and she smiled.

3

Everyone had a greeting for Dr. Fothergill as he drove down the street in his battered old gig; and for everyone he had a cheery smile, a wave of the hand or a facetious remark. He was a character. No one could visualize the little town without him and no one wanted to or ever tried to. He seemed as much a permanent feature of the place as the weathercock on top of the church tower. He was old, people supposed, though they did not know how old. His hair was grey and his rosy weather-beaten face deeply seamed, but he was stout and robust and his hearty laugh could be heard almost from one end of the town to the other. He held himself so well that it was generally supposed that he wore corsets, and possibly he did, for he was a dressy man. He affected an eyeglass, the latest in cravats and waistcoats and curly-brimmed hats, and even on his country rounds he wore his jewellery; his gold watch with its dangling seals and a couple of fine rings. And he always seemed to carry a good deal of loose money in his pockets. Whenever he was considering a case he would stand in front of the fireplace with his legs apart and his hands in his pockets and jingle the coins. Patients knew just how ill they were by the amount of jingling that went on. He was an excellent doctor. Each patient was as important to him as though he had no other and neither weather nor distance nor any trouble of his own had ever caused him to refuse a call for help.

Nevertheless he was glad to be on his way home now to his warm fireside and his good stout wife Jemima, and he hoped in heaven's name that he would not be called out over Christmas. There were no babies due just now, for that young hussy Maria was not expecting hers for some weeks yet, and he had done his best to put all his old folks into pickle for a day or two. With any luck they should last. His thoughts turned fondly to roast goose and plum pudding, his pipe and a locked surgery door.

"Doctor! Doctor!"

It was the high cry of distress that he knew only too well. The ragged little boy came running across the road to him, dodging under the very noses of the horses, and cursing profusely he reined his own horse in beside the curb.

41

"What the hell do you want, boy?" he demanded angrily, as the urchin leaped up on the step and hung there clinging to the side of the gig.

"Farmer Mudge, sir, up at Longbarton Farm, took terrible bad."

Longbarton Farm was up on the moor, an isolated place and a lonely ride to get there. "Damn Mudge!" said Dr. Fothergill. "What's the matter with him?"

"Dunno, doctor. But I was to say he's terrible bad."

"Damn and blast him," said Dr. Fothergill, and then sticking in his eyeglass he had a good look at the small boy clinging to the side of the gig. "Who are you, boy? Never set eyes on you before. Who sent you?"

The boy's dark eyes stared up at him out of a blanched and peaky face. "He's terrible bad, doctor," he pleaded huskily. Then he jumped down and dodged away through the traffic, dived down a side street and was lost to sight. "Must be one of the Mudge brood," thought Dr. Fothergill, as he whipped up his horse and drove on. Yet the Mudge brood were a healthy lot, with full stomachs and brown faces, and if the boy had been one of them he would have asked for a lift home. It was damned odd. He wouldn't go. Damned if he'd go. It was Christmas Eve.

Yet at home, when he had clattered into his stable yard in a tearing rage, he flung the reins to his groom and shouted at him to saddle the strong cob he kept for his country rounds. Indoors he leaped upstairs two at a time and while he changed into his riding clothes he roared at Jemima, in the kitchen stuffing the goose, to bring him a hunk of bread and cheese and a glass of ale to the surgery. While he ate and drank she packed his saddle bags, as she had done so many times before, pausing every now and then to wipe her eyes, for though she had been a doctor's wife for forty years, and should have learnt resignation by this time, she had been looking forward to this Christmas. "Don't be a fool, Jemima," he growled at her. "I'll be back before morning."

"You'd better be," she sobbed. "It's a beautiful goose. John, if I've told you once I've told you a hundred times not to wear your gold watch and rings with your riding clothes. It's not suitable."

"Always have worn 'em and always shall," said Dr. Fothergill. He put his arm round her waist, gave her a smacking kiss and was gone. She heard him clatter out of the stable yard, burst into tears and went back to the goose. Luckily she was too absorbed in it to notice that the sunlight had gone and the sky was veiled.

Dr. Fothergill noticed it as he rode up into the hills. He would be mist-bound quite soon and he urged his horse forward. Noah was a good horse, and used to the moors, and they went at a good speed, but Dr. Fothergill still swore under his breath and vowed that if it turned out to be nothing but the colic he'd have something to say to Mudge.

An hour later he very nearly missed the farmhouse altogether. If Noah had not swerved to avoid the mounting block by the gate he would have missed it. He was thankful when at his knock the door opened and the warmth and light flowed out to him, but astonished beyond measure to have it opened by Farmer Mudge himself, stout and hearty as ever.

"Doctor!" ejaculated Farmer Mudge. "Whatever brings you here at this time of night?"

"Your severe illness," said Dr. Fothergill grimly. "I shall be obliged to you, Mudge, for an explanation." And he stepped forward into the warm kitchen, where a brood of happy children and a smiling mother were absorbing rabbit soup.

There was no explanation. Farmer Mudge had sent no message. He did not know the boy. Obviously some other farm had been meant. There was a muddle somewhere. One thing however Farmer Mudge did know and that was that the doctor must spend the night with them. Only a moor man would be able to find his way home in this mist.

"Only a moor man?" ejaculated Dr. Fothergill indignantly. "I'll have you know, Mudge, that I could find my way blindfold over the moor before you were born. Thank you, ma'am, I'll take a sup of that soup and then be off home to my wife. Christmas Eve, you know. She wants me at home."

The farmer tried again to dissuade him, for there was a fear at the back of his mind that he could not mention aloud. Failing, he offered to come with him, but this suggestion got Dr. Fothergill's back up to an alarming extent. "I know the moor like the palm of my hand," he exploded. "I've only to follow the road straight down. Well, a happy Christmas to you all and I never tasted better rabbit soup."

He fished up a handful of loose money from his pockets, gave

43

the children sixpence all round, slapped his hat on his head and stumped away. The farmer saw him go with anxiety. But for his wife's grip on his coat tails he would have run to the stable for his own horse and followed after.

Half an hour later, after a somewhat anxious period of not admitting even to himself that he was not quite sure where he was, Dr. Fothergill ejaculated "Aha!" with pleasure and self-congratulation, for through the mist he could recognize a landmark that he knew, a parting of the ways where one path led down off the moor and the other branched uphill again to the right, and in spite of his boast that he knew the moor like the palm of his hand it was a way that he had never followed. His pleasure seemed to have communicated itself to Noah for the horse suddenly gave a sharp whinny of pleasure, almost as though he had seen another horse, trotted forward and swung round uphill to the right.

"You're wrong, Noah," said Dr. Fothergill, and tried to force the cob round again into the right path. But Noah would not go. He reared up when his master used the whip but he would not turn round. He stood with his legs splayed out, sweating with distress, his nostrils dilated, but he would not take the other path. Dr. Fothergill took off his hat and wiped his forehead. Had he made a mistake? Was he right off his proper track and was this branching of the ways not the one he knew but another? Suddenly he decided to trust Noah. He knew the wisdom of horses and of Noah in particular. "Have your own way then, lad," he said, and let the reins go slack.

Noah instantly started off uphill to the right, and though the mist was still thick and darkness was closing in he climbed at a good pace, as though sure of his way, and now and then he turned his head to the left and whinnied happily. He kept always to the right of the path. Several times Dr. Fothergill tried to coax him to the centre, where it was easier going, but he would not respond to the pressure on the bridle. He kept to the right.

It was the strangest ride Dr. Fothergill had ever taken. The mist decreased slightly, but the darkness increased. Sometimes they rode under the dripping darkness of trees, sometimes out in the open. Twice they came to a gate and Dr. Fothergill had to dismount and open it. Each time Noah moved confidently through, keeping to the right. Once he thought a village must be near, for he thought he heard a cock crowing. Then the path

44

moved into a thick wood and went steeply uphill in darkness. But Noah had no difficulty in keeping to the path, and Dr. Fothergill himself, though he had not the faintest notion where he was, felt oddly secure and happy, as he had felt ever since he had yielded his will to Noah's. The wood ended and they rode under an archway in a stone wall, and up a carriage-drive, and at the foot of some steps, in front of a house where light showed through the chinks of the shutters of a downstairs room, Noah stopped abruptly. Dr. Fothergill dismounted, walked up the steps and across the terrace and knocked at the door. It was opened by Martin, holding a lantern in his hand. He looked haggard and distraught, his red hair rumpled and his eyes sunken in pits of shadow.

"I'm the doctor," said Dr. Fothergill calmly.

"The doctor!" Martin lowered the lantern and peered in the other man's face. "My God! Doctor Fothergill!" His hand shot out and gripped the doctor's shoulder. "How did you know? It's Maria. She's having the baby and it's going badly. Go in quickly. I'll take your horse." He ran across the terrace, unfastened Dr. Fothergill's saddle bags and brought them to him. "Hurry, doctor," he said. "The room to the left. Hurry, for God's sake!"

"Keep calm, young man," said Dr. Fothergill. "I very much doubt if it is going badly. Look after my horse. He's a good horse." As he passed into the house he heard a church clock striking in the distance. Midnight. It was no longer Christmas Eve. It was Christmas Day.

4

At the first cockcrow, that moment of mystery when all living creatures are said to wake and stir, and turn again to their rest, but only the cocks give utterance, the boy was born. He was small but quite sturdy, for all he had been in such a hurry to be a Christmas baby. When he and his mother were sleeping, with Martin to watch over them, Dr. Fothergill went to the kitchen to wash his hands and spruce himself up before riding home to bring the good news of a grandson to Maria's parents. Mrs. Appledore, the midwife whom Martin had brought back from the village, came with him that they might discuss together the excellent termination of what at one point had very nearly been a difficult confinement.

45

"You came just in time, sir, I do believe," said Mrs. Appledore.

"You would have done it alone, my dear," said Dr. Fothergill.

"I'm not sure, sir. The young gentleman, poor lad, was no help to me. The young lady, she helped herself. She seemed never afraid."

"She's a plucky girl, though devilish headstrong," said Dr. Fothergill. "Who owns this house? Nothing in it but a few rags and sticks of furniture, yet it feels lived in."

"The owner is in foreign parts, sir," said Mrs. Appledore. "He's a queer gentleman. When his brother died and the house came to him he sold all the valuable furniture, and left the rest. He let the stables to a farmer nearby but he's never let the house. Means to live here one day, I'm told."

They moved out into the hall. There was a window beside the front door and through it came flooding the first light of Christmas Day. A west wind from the sea had carried the mist away and one great planet still burned in a clear green sky. Beneath the window the wooded ground fell sharply away to the glory of the moor. For a moment Dr. Fothergill stood at the window for though he knew the moor so well he could never see it unexpectedly like this without profound awe. As he turned back from the window again he saw a portrait hanging on the panelling close to the window. It was of a middle-aged man with powdered hair tied back in a queue. He had straight shoulders and a face of great integrity. Dr. Fothergill looked at it for some time, much moved by it. "Who's that?" he asked. "The owner?"

"Not the present owner, sir. His brother who died."

"How long ago did he die?"

"Ten years ago, sir." Suddenly Mrs. Appledore became garrulous. "He and his lady lived here for many years. They loved the place. They lived here with an old Negro servant. Very attached to them, he was. They had no children and it was a grief to them. Then suddenly my lady she found she was to have a child. She was so happy, and her husband and the old servant too. They were like children, they were so happy. But she died, sir, and the child as well. Her husband and the old servant were heartbroken. They shut up the house and went to foreign parts but after a few months they both caught a fever and died there. I was glad when I heard it. No one couldn't have wanted them to live without my lady."

46

It seemed a sad story but it was not a sad house. Dr. Fothergill thought he had seldom been in a happier. He opened the parlour door softly to have a last look at his patient, then beckoned to Mrs. Appledore to come and see.

She had brought blankets up from the village with her and Maria lay on a pile of them before the fire. She was asleep, her baby cuddled against her. Martin had stretched himself out on the floor beside her and he, too, was asleep. Utterly relaxed in the deep dreamless sleep of relief and exhaustion they looked much younger than their years. They looked a boy and girl. They had turned a little towards each other in their sleep, the child between them, and Martin had one arm stretched out protectingly over his wife and son.

The two elderly people tiptoed away again and out into the hall. With the door shut Dr. Fothergill blew his nose loudly. He could never get used to it. He had long ago lost count of the number of babies he had brought into the world, yet still the miracle of it seemed new and fresh. He went out and stood on the terrace, and it was the second cockcrow. In the still crystal-clear air he could hear the small trumpets sounding in all directions. Then the fanfare was silent, there was a moment's pause, and the Christmas bells began to ring. A child was born.

5

A month later Dr. Fothergill was called to the bedside of a sick man. He was a scoundrel whom authority had been after for some while and he had been caught at last red-handed; robbery with violence, and Dr. Fothergill was to patch him up to be hanged after the next session. But to his relief he found the man dying. It would be a matter of an hour or less and there was nothing he could do but keep the poor fellow company. He was a hard-bitten criminal type but he was a man, and the mystery of death had always stirred Dr. Fothergill's deep compassion only a little less than the miracle of birth. He sat with his hand lightly on the man's wrist, and he asked him his name and was told it was Tom Badger. He repeated the name quietly, with emphasis, as though he liked it. He believed it gave the dying a sense of their own value, a sense of being cared for as an individual, to say the name like that. Especially a fellow like this scoundrel, for whom probably no one had ever cared at all.

The man was silent for a while and then he said, "You're lucky, doctor."

"Lucky?" asked Dr. Fothergill.

"You nearly had my knife in your back on Christmas Eve."

Dr. Fothergill answered pleasantly, "How was that, Tom?"

"Do you call to mind the boy who brought you a message from Longbarton Farm? I bribed him to give it. I was after your watch and rings, and the money in your pockets. I was desperate that night." His voice died away and Dr. Fothergill waited. Presently he went on, as though he were anxious to get his story told with the last strength that he had. "I missed you going up, the mist was that thick. Coming down I thought I couldn't fail. I was in the bushes just below where the way forks. I was almost as near to you as I am now. I'd have let you pass me and then sprung at you."

"What stopped you, Tom?"

"You turned off right and I was afraid to come after you. I daren't do it. Not with the two of you."

Dr. Fothergill said, "I was alone, Tom."

"No, sir. There was another horseman wheeled in alongside of you."

Dr. Fothergill remained sitting quietly relaxed in his chair but for just a moment the wretched little room seemed to sway about him. Then it steadied and he said, "What did he look like, Tom?"

"A straight back, he had. Grey hair tied with a ribbon. I see his face as clear as though the moon shone on it; though that's queer when you call to mind how thick the mist was. But I see his face clear and I was afeared of him."

Dr. Fothergill had to bend over to catch the last words, and the man seemed to be going, but a few minutes later he opened his eyes again and said clearly, "So you'd best leave me, doctor. You'd have had my knife in your back if I hadn't been afeared."

Dr. Fothergill understood his meaning. He did not wish in his dying moments to claim a sympathy to which he had no right. Deep in his soul, at the last, there had come a moment of truth.

The doctor's hand tightened a little on his wrist. "I'll not leave you, Tom," he said.

48

Christmas on the
Island

D

1

A cow was sick and André was late in the stable that night. When he came out, leaving, according to the Island custom on Christmas Eve, fresh hay in the stalls and everything clean and sweet, he forbore to lock the door and left it just un-latched. This was so that Maximilian, when midnight struck and Christmas Day was born, could find his way in and kneel with the other animals. André laughed at himself as he pocketed the un-used key, and wondered what on earth Ranulph would think of him if he knew. But he was not ashamed. He loved the Island legends; his mother had taught them to him, and whenever he could he reverenced and followed them. On his way to the house he noticed that Sophie had left Maximilian unchained in his ken-nel, and also that Maximilian was awake and waiting. His eyes in the darkness were like two bright stars. André patted him as he passed and Maximilian's tongue shot out like a long pink snake, and coiled itself for a moment damply and lovingly round André's finger. Marmalade was also awake and in the yard, but she was not waiting for anything. She was curvetting about, her green eyes like the lights of the "faeu Bellengier" and her tail twitching. Sometimes she would crouch on the ground watching something invisible, then she would leap at it, swerve aside from it, spit at it, and then tear round the yard as though chasing it. But whatever it was she liked it. There was an unholy glee in her face and the lights in her eyes were the wicked lights such as witches tie on the ends of their broomsticks. Whatever it was she was chasing André was quite sure it had no business in his yard on Christmas Eve. Had it not been that Maximilian was absorbed in the stable door, André would hardly have liked to leave him alone with Marma-lade and the thing she was playing with. But so engrossed was Maximilian with holy things that he seemed safe from the unholy . . . André let himself into the house and went upstairs to Rachell.

Ranulph's little room over the stable had a window that com-manded both the stable door and Maximilian's kennel. Ranulph, sleepless, was sitting and smoking at it as the night crept on. A

51

little fire of vraic was burning in his grate but there was no other light. Only the moonbeams slid from wall to ceiling and mingled their silver with the golden glow of the vraic. It was Ranulph's first Christmas Eve in the Island since his young manhood, and he should have been thinking solemn thoughts. The past should have passed before him like a depressing pageant, and remorse and regret for a mis-spent life should have been with him in the room. But in reality he was trying to think of nothing at all except the peace and warmth of the room and his own sense of well-being. He preferred not to inquire into the cause of his satisfaction. He had no wish to admit to himself that he had utterly capitulated at last. All his life he had pursued complete independence as the highest good and now he had abruptly given up the chase and allowed himself to become hopelessly involved in place and person once again. He had no wish to look himself in the face and own up to his weakness. Sufficient that his captive state had brought him to this warm and peaceful room and to this dreamy pleasure and—freedom? Was it true that he felt, as he sat there, a free man? That corroding bitterness that his failure to find freedom had produced in him was now, to a large extent, gone. He was almost free of it and with it of his past life and all its horror. Was the paradox he had spoken of to Colin present in his own life? Had the acceptance of fetters unlocked the prison house? That eternal paradox! But he would not think and abruptly, as thoughts came, he turned from them to stir the fire or knock out his pipe. Thought was too confusing. He wanted only to enjoy with simplicity—a thing he had not done since his childhood's days. He began to think of his childhood and of the many Christmas Eves he had known in the old house in Le Paradis. While his mother lived Christmas had been Christmas, in spite of his father, whose tyranny brooded even over such things as Christmas-trees and cakes and threatened to take the heart out of all rejoicing. He marvelled now to think how his mother must have fought and toiled to keep a little spontaneity in their common life. When she had died spontaneity had died with her. He and André had had no choice but to fit into an iron groove or cast themselves adrift. The thought of past Christmases made him think of the Island legends his mother had told them as they sat around the fire on Christmas Eve roasting their chestnuts. In imagination he could see the drawing-room at the Le Paradis house lit by the leaping

52

flames of the fire and the starlight over the sea. His father was in the library, and they had dared to pull the curtains and open the window. His mother, her hand raised to keep the heat of the flames from her face, would sit on the floor by the fire, her dark maroon dress billowing out around her so that she looked like a dark rose flung down on the hearthrug, and tell the Christmas stories to him and baby André. It was so he liked best to remember her, for it was only when her husband was absent that she seemed truly herself – when he was there she was not allowed to sit on the floor and there seemed a constraint and heartbreaking sense of frustration about her. Watching the leaping flames of his own fire, seeing the stars through the window, he could hear her voice telling how at midnight on Christmas Eve the animals all knelt down to worship and the water was turned to wine . . . A faint sound crept through the quiet of the room, hardly louder than the stir of the flames and the whisper of the sea. The bells were ringing. Down in St. Pierre the steeple of the Town Church and the squat little tower of St. Raphael's must be rocking and trembling with a cascade of sound, but up here at Bon Repos the chiming was so faint that it seemed unearthly. Ranulph glanced at his watch. Twelve o'clock. He looked out of the window. There was a line of light under the stable door. André, the idiot, must have left his lamp there when he went to tend the sick cow. As Ranulph watched he saw a dark shadow slip across the yard, push open the stable door and disappear. It was Maximilian. Ranulph suddenly decided that it was his duty to go and put out that light in the stable – no point in wasting oil. He was half-way across the room when he remembered his mother had told him as a small boy that no human being must set foot in the stables at midnight on Christmas Eve. It was the animals' hour. The poor ill-treated donkey, kicked and cuffed through the centuries, yet permitted to carry a King to Jerusalem; the cow, slaughtered for man's food yet giving its own sweet hay for a babe to lie on; the horse and the dog who bear so patiently with the folly of human kind, these are safe from man and may worship alone and at peace. Ranulph decided to leave the light alone and sat down again. As he did so he laughed and wondered what on earth André would think of him if he knew.

Colette, being the youngest of the family, was naturally the first to wake up on Christmas morning. She wriggled up from the bottom of her bed and popped her head out. It was still dark, but a faint greying where the window was gave promise of dawn. It was very cold, and Colette, like a tortoise thinking better of it, withdrew her head and crept beneath her shell again. There in the warm darkness she remembered her stocking. Now that Jacqueline was growing up, Colette and Colin were the only ones of the family left to have stockings, for Rachell had decreed that those old enough to go to early Mass should lay aside such childish things as stockings. The sucking of pink sugar pigs in the early hours of Christmas morning was, so she said, for the consolation of those who had to be kept out of mischief until their elders returned from church. When she remembered her stocking Colette scrambled down to the bottom of the bed, dragged away the bedclothes, thrust her head out of the aperture and grabbed it. Then she retired under cover again, hugging its delicious hard bulkiness to her bosom. She did not want to wake Peronelle by demanding a light, so, having satisfied herself by pinching that the sugar pig was there, and the orange and the apple, and the boiled sweets, and the doll, she fell asleep again, clasping it to her as a mother her babe. When she awoke it was to find Peronelle removing layers of bedclothes off the top of her head.

"A merry Christmas, darling," cried Peronelle. "How it is you don't suffocate, I don't know. And you've lain on your stocking. The doll will be all over pig."

Collette got up and hugged Peronelle.

The candles were lighted, but day was faintly blue behind the curtains, and Peronelle was in her hat and coat ready to go to Mass.

Then began a frantic hubbub of Christmas hugs. Michelle and Jacqueline in their coats and hats came along to kiss and be kissed. Rachell in her best mantle, with her prayer book in her hand and every hair in place, sailed in to bless them. André, with his waistcoat inside out and his hair awry, rushed frantically everywhere looking for a lost stud. Colin in his white nightshirt playing leapfrog over the beds, and down below the back door clicked as Sophie came back from an incredibly early Mass to get the breakfast and keep an eye on the youngest children while the others went to church.

At last the hubbub subsided and Colin and Colette hung out of the window to watch the landau drive off to church in the dim frosty dawn. Over the sea a star shone faintly in a brightening sky but night still clouded the land, and the landau, driving off under the trees with its swinging lamps, disappeared in a mysterious darkness. Colin stayed at the window watching the lights disappear and listening as the sound of the wheels died away. He felt awed. The darkness that had swallowed his family held the mysteries of religion that were yet unknown to him but known to them. Out of the darkness he felt fingers stretch out and touch him, and something in him awoke and stirred a little.

Colette brought him back to reality by butting him in the back.

"Look," she said, pointing, "is that *the* star?"

Colin looked. The star over the sea was still there, though the deep blue of the sky behind it was slowly changing to a dove-grey with pale lemon and lavender.

"It might be," said Colin, "but I don't think it's fat enough. The star in the Christmas pictures is always fat, with spokes."

"Perhaps they've fallen off," suggested Colette, "if the star was new when Jesus was born it must be very nearly worn out by this time."

"Stars," said Colin, "don't wear out. They are like God. Always as good as new."

"My stocking!" squeaked Colette suddenly and trundled rapidly back to her bed.

Following a time-honoured custom in the du Frocq family they wrapped themselves in quilts and got into their parents' bed to open their stockings, drawing the curtains to form a sultan's tent, and sitting enthroned on the high pillows in great state. The stockings were all that could be desired. Each contained the essentials, the sugar pig, the orange, the apple, and the boiled sweets, and many delights besides, such as a doll and a miniature flat iron for Colette, a water pistol and a sailor's whistle for Colin. They had a lovely time. They ate all the boiled sweets except a few moist globules kept for the family, and all the pigs except the hind quarters, kept for Rachell. Colette's pig, as Peronelle had predicted, had stuck to the doll, but it didn't really matter, and

55

the paint from the doll's face that adhered to the flanks of the pig tasted quite nice. Colin filled his pistol with water and squirted at the picture of the Last Judgement, getting the angel with the trumpet full in the chest every time, and Colette, each time he hit the mark, blew the whistle. After an hour of this Sophie came up, took away the pistol and the whistle, mopped up the water and dressed them. Sophie seemed in an extremely good mood. She did not scold at all, even though the water was dripping down the Last Judgement and collecting in a pool on the floor, and she never smacked them once as she hustled them into their clothes. Her eyes were shining, her round red cheeks were redder than ever, and her stays creaked and popped like joyously tapping drums. Colette, quick to feel what others were feeling, sensed her joy.

"Have you had a sugar pig, Sophie?" she asked.

"Better than that," said Sophie, bursting to communicate her news, if only to children. "I've had the offer of a husband. Holy Virgin! On Christmas morning, too!"

"Is that all?" said Colin, disappointed.

"Walking back from Mass he popped the question, as they say in England," said Sophie, "and there was I looking in the fairy well only last night and never saw a thing but the stars and the sky – just shows you there's nothing in these tales."

Colette, pleased but uncomprehending, put her arms as far round Sophie's waist as they would reach and kissed her.

"Who popped the question?" asked Colin.

"Jacquemin Gossilin," chattered Sophie. "It was that blue coat and skirt did it. All yesterday afternoon his eyes were on it."

Colin politely said nothing, but he was dismayed. How are the mighty fallen! He could not believe that his friend Jacquemin Gossilin could be such an utter fool as to want to marry Sophie – he could not have seen Sophie with her hair curlers in.

But it was impossible to dwell long upon depressing topics on Christmas morning. Colin was soon racing round the garden pursuing Marmalade with the water pistol, while Colette trotted backwards and forwards from the scullery to the kitchen helping Sophie.

The breakfast was wonderful. Ham and boiled eggs and steaming coffee and jam and fresh rolls and, most marvellous of all, an Island speciality, the goche détremper, a milk cake always baked early on Christmas morning to appear on the breakfast table. Colette helped Sophie to open the oven door and take it out. Its exquisite milk-white freshness was faintly tinged with golden brown on top, and its lovely crisp smell filled the whole kitchen and floated out to greet the churchgoers as they drove into the courtyard, cold and famished.

Ranulph put in an appearance at breakfast time and ate more than his fair share of the goche détremper, which seemed hardly fair as he had done nothing either in the way of devotions or stocking-opening to warrant such an appetite.

No sooner was breakfast over than it was time for church again. André usually escaped from a second church-going on Christmas Day on the plea of the farm, but to-day Ranulph, with a malicious twinkle in his eye, declared himself perfectly able to do all that was necessary on the farm in order that André might enjoy the felicity of accompanying his family. Rachell was grateful and delighted, and André went miserably upstairs to find his top hat.

With the family at church, and Sophie shut in the kitchen with the turkey, Ranulph spent an extremely profitable morning. Quick and efficient as he was he had done all that was necessary on the farm in half the time that it would have taken André. His work ended, he went into the little room adjoining the stables, half office and half outhouse, to enter the number of eggs he had collected in the egg book. He had only been here once or twice before, and that in the company of André, when politeness had forbidden a too great inquisitiveness. Now, closing the door behind him, he looked round with interest. The little narrow slip of a room, known to the family as the "corn bin" because the hens' food was kept there, was André's private sanctum. No one but himself and the hens had any interest in it. From certain signs it was obvious to Ranulph that André withdrew to it, as Rachell to her bedroom and Michelle to Le Baie des Mouettes, to possess his soul. Ranulph went to the middle of the room, put his hands in his pockets and stared. He meant to go through this room thoroughly, as a thief the pockets of an unconscious man, and get to the bottom of André. He had no qualms of conscience about lifting the lid off another man's secrets. He had long ago dispensed with a conscience as a tiresome and hampering article, constantly interfering with desire.

There was nothing in this room at first sight to throw any light

57

upon André. On one side of the little room stood the corn bins, opposite them was an old roll-topped desk containing the farm account books and the egg book, with an almanac hanging over it, opposite the door was a window which looked out across a rough field towards a distant line of stunted trees and held to the left just a glimpse of the sea. Under this window was a table with a chair in front of it, and under the table was a roughly-made bookcase with a sacking curtain to protect the books. Now what books could André possibly want in the corn bin? The roll-topped desk already contained a dictionary, and various noble tomes on manure, cows, bee-keeping, hens and mangel-wurzels. What more could the man want? Ranulph dragged out the little bookcase, lifted the sacking curtain and looked. Plato, Shakespeare (Michelle had declared to him that there was apparently not a Shakespeare on the premises), Keats, Essays of Elia, Moby Dick, Molière, Euripides, Undine, the Arabian Nights (had André stolen these two from the children?), Dante, a book on pigs (this last evidently uneasy in its company), Goethe. An assorted lot. No wonder André was such a bad farmer. Obviously he withdrew to this sanctum to study pigs – the presence of the pigs between Dante and Goethe showed that an attempt on pigs was actually made – studied them for a couple of minutes and then turned to – what? To the cloudy splendours of Shakespeare – rainbow-tinted mists of poetry wreathing and coiling over the still black tarns of insight; to the gentle calmly flowing stream of the Essays; to the sparkling water-falls of French comedy. But did he only read? What was that table standing there? Ranulph turned abruptly from the books, went to the desk and began pulling out the drawers and ran-sacking their contents – but not to find the egg book – that he found at once and cast contemptuously aside. Account books and old bills and farm records and advertisements, these he cast from him like autumn leaves whirling before a north-easter – the desk was already so hopelessly untidy that André would never notice confusion had been worse confounded – until he found what he sought.

He lifted them out and carried them to the table – a handful of notebooks and school exercise books (filched from Colin?) filled with André's small neat writing. For André, so wildly untidy that his passage through a room was like the passing of a tornado, wrote neatly. These little books, filled apparently with poems and essays, were written with the loving care, neatness and beauty of

58

an etching engraved on copper. The form was perfect, what of the substance? Ranulph drew up the rickety chair to the table and read. He read for an hour without stirring. There was no sound in the room but the occasional turning of a page and the scurry of a mouse as it pattered across the wooden floor. Outside the window, over the gorse-starred fields, the sun rose to its glorious zenith and the line of the distant sea was molten gold. Then Ranulph closed the books. One, which had been at the bottom of the pile, he slipped into his pocket, the rest he carried reverently back to the drawer from which he had taken them, and closed it. He removed all traces of his presence, arranging the room exactly as he found it, and went out, closing the door with the quietness of a doctor leaving a sick room. For assuredly André was a sick man. If he could write like that in his fugitive leisure moments, and bind his life to a wheel of toil that he must hate and loathe, the conflict in him must have exhausted his body and dragged his soul nearly in two. His life must be a veritable crucifixion, the upward surge of the artist crossed out, bound down always by the arms of necessity and frustration.

Ranulph went to his own room over the stable and sat down by the window and marvelled. Hitherto he had thought of his brother as a weak fool. Weak in practical ability and driving power he might be but as an artist he was supreme. His were not the lesser gifts of a retentive memory garnering the thoughts of others and dishing them up with a fresh sauce, nor yet of a quick wit ready to note and seize the humour and piquancy of contrast, but the greater gifts of the creator, born to endure passing things with immortality. He had, too, the passionate observation of the true lover of beauty. No procession of clouds, no fall of a leaf or a flash of a bird's wing, had passed by him unseen, and out of these moments of fugitive beauty, caught and held, he had created an enduring beauty. With perfect simplicity, with thoughts that were his own, clothed in phrases coined by himself, he had built of captured moments an unchanging monument to changing nature. Those particular sunsets and storms and unfoldings of spring had passed and gone, but in André's poems they were alive for ever. Ranulph got up and walked about the room. What was to be done about it? André in his harried life had only had time to produce that handful of poems and essays, and they, as far as Ranulph could see, unless something were done about it, were doomed to be thrown in the dustbin with the egg accounts. He was an example of the greatest tragedy of all, a life denied its true vocation. Some words frequently quoted by Peronelle when in the midst of the Browning epidemic seemed to say themselves in the room.

> *"The honest instinct, pent and crossed through life,*
> *Let surge by death into a visible fire*
> *Of rapture; as the strangled thread of flame*
> *Painfully winds, annoying and annoyed,*
> *Malignant and maligned, thro' stone and ore,*
> *Till earth exclude the stranger: vented once*
> *It finds full play, is recognized atop*
> *Some mountain as no such abnormal birth,*
> *Fire for the mount, not streamlet for the vale!"*

Ranulph swore suddenly and loudly. No! André should not wait for death to fulfil himself in this only life he had to live upon the earth. He should do it now. Who knew if there was any after death? Browning, with the easy optimism of a man with private means, seemed to think so, but Ranulph himself thought not. He began to walk round and round the room. His mind, hitherto occupied over the problems of Michelle, Jacqueline and Colin, began to be busy over their father. He muttered as he walked. He would set André free before he died. The path was not clear to him yet, but he knew that he would do it. He, the failure, would keep his brother from following a like path.

André, Rachell, Michelle, Peronelle, Jacqueline, Colin, Colette. A rope of seven strands bound the advocate of independence, but he was so busy with his thoughts for them that morning that he had no time to notice how the touch of the rope had set him free from the fetters of his own obsession.

3

To dine with grandpapa on Christmas Day was more than any-one could bear, but since grandpapa could not possibly be expected to absorb turkey and plum pudding by himself at the festal season, there was nothing for it but to bring him back to Bon Repos after church.

Ranulph, meditating in his own room, heard the spanking clip-clop of grandpapa's trotting horses mingling with the thump-thump of the ambling Lupin. Ten minutes later the dinner-bell rang. Ranulph surveyed himself in the scrap of looking-glass that hung on his wall. His hair was rumpled and his coat buttoned crooked, but he decided to leave them as they were. It would annoy the old man. It was not in his power to revenge himself for the blows his father had dealt him in the past, but little pin-pricks of annoyance he could and would drive in. His untidiness would, unfortunately, annoy Rachell too, but never in this world can one aim a blow at another but some innocent victim catches the rebound. He strolled at his leisure into the kitchen. This also was intended as a pin-prick. They were all waiting for him, and grandpapa was fuming.

"Didn't you hear the bell, sir?" he demanded.

"Certainly, sir," replied Ranulph, "otherwise I should not have been here. You will eat the more that I have kept you waiting."

Grandpapa blew out his cheeks and humphed. Their glances caught and held, like magnet and steel. It had been so at their first meeting. Ranulph wondered uneasily if it were possible that his father could recognize him. He wrenched his eyes from the old man's compelling, troubled gaze, and looked at his brother. André, irritated by his rudeness, was looking at him, and was astonished beyond measure to see admiration, reverence, and even affection in the older man's regard. There had always been a veiled hostility between them, born of their mutual love for Rachell, and of André's jealousy, but now, for some reason unknown to André, it seemed gone. In spite of himself a movement of liking stirred in him and stretched out to meet Ranulph's affection. Rachell, intercepting their glances, blessed Yuletide the peacemaker.

The dinner was perfect and grandpapa, who had had the forethought to bring his own drinks with him, André, the fool, being a teetotaller, expressed himself as not too dissatisfied. The turkey, stuffed at one end with herbs, and at the other with chestnuts, according to the Island custom, was browned to a turn and held out gallantly against the inroads of everybody's second helpings. The plum pudding, when carried in by a purple-faced Sophie, was seen even under its covering of blue flame to be of the colour

61

of folded wallflower buds and stiff with fruit . . . After a quarter of an hour there was none left.

"You're all eating too much," announced grandpapa, passing up his plate for more. "What? What? You all eat too much. You always have." He became aware that Colette was eating plum pudding, and his eyes nearly popped out of his head. "To give that child plum pudding," he told Rachell, "is equivalent to digging her grave. And don't say I haven't told you."

"It's only a thimbleful," Rachell pleaded.

"I never remember such heavenly weather at Christmas," said André nervously, terrified that grandpapa might revert to the topic of the dead children.

"What?" said grandpapa. "Yes. Warm. Damned unseasonable. Well, as I was saying, if you overfill a child's stomach —"

Trouble was dawning in Rachell's face and Ranulph threw himself into the breach. Turning to grandpapa he began to talk as the du Frocqs had never heard him talk before. He talked as brilliantly as André wrote, and with the same creator's gift. Picking out the most gaily coloured of his memories he built for them, bit by bit, the story of his travels, building up with skilful words an edifice of colour and scents and adventure that took their breath away. André listened spellbound and the children, reaching mechanically for nuts and oranges, never took their eyes off him. Rachell, her eyes slipping lovingly from face to face, was perhaps more interested in their pleasure than in the story, but she gave Ranulph his due as a narrator. Even grandpapa seemed curiously interested in the tale, or perhaps, not so much by it as by the teller. He sat twisting his wine glass between his fingers and glancing every now and then quickly and sharply at Ranulph, at his eyes, at the shape of his head, his hands. But for the most part, he sat looking at the cloth and listening. Even so had he once sat in his library and listened while Jean his son, outside in the garden and unaware of him, had told some tale or other to the infant André. He had marvelled then at the boy's power of telling a story and he marvelled now at this man's power. They had told a tale in just the same way, with the same varied inflection of voice, stressing the lights and shadows of the story, the same power of painting pictures in the minds of their listeners, the same power of making a dead past live. Once more he raised his eyes sharply to Ranulph's face, and kept them there. Like the steel to the magnet, Ranulph's eyes slipped round to his, were held and gripped, and for the first time the story faltered. Grandpapa, strangely moved, got abruptly to his feet, spilling the dregs of his wine glass across the table.

"Are we to stay here all the afternoon stuffing ourselves?" he demanded fiercely and a little wildly. "Is it necessary because you live at a farm that you should ape the manners of the lower animals? Look at those children."

This was unfair, for though the children were eating nuts and the table was considerably littered with the débris, there was nothing in the least piglike in their methods. You could not hear them eat and they did not slobber.

"We will go into the other room," said Rachell with dignity, and, rising, she swept into the parlour, followed by grandpapa and André. To her great relief Ranulph took himself off. When he and grandpapa were together the air was positively oppressive with a surcharge of electricity. The children scampered off on their various occupations. Michelle and Peronelle to help Sophie, wash up, Jacqueline and Colin to mysterious private business. Only Colette trotted in the wake of her elders to the parlour.

Rachell sighed with relief as she established herself and her menfolk in chairs before the fire, with sleepy Colette on her lap. The sun-filled parlour, shut away from the clamour of dinner and washing up, was fragrant and peaceful as the inside of a flower. Part of the tronquet de Noel, the yule log, was burning in the grate and its blue and yellow flames, whispering sweetly, lit up with the sunlight the soft little gillyflowers and forget-me-nots on the curtains, the delicate fluted china, the Chinese dragons and the rose-wood table. Rachell looked round on all her treasures and was comforted. André, worn out, was soon asleep, and Colette, overcome by an excess of food and joy, leant her head against her mother and slept too. Only grandpapa, though he spread his handkerchief over his head and folded his hands across his stomach, seemed unable to pop off. He was restless. He snorted and sighed, and shuffled with his feet. Rachell, her chin resting on top of Colette's head, considered him. He seemed upset about something. She felt sorry for him. He looked old to-day, and lonely. If his loneliness was his own fault, it was none the less pitiful for that. He snorted again, gave up the chase of his forty winks, whipped the handkerchief from off his head and looked round the room. His eye travelled with disfavour over the soft pale colours of it, and he sniffed at the scent of pot-pourri and burning wood with obvious dislike.

"Draughty," he announced, "musty and washed-out looking. Damp. That's what it is, damp. I've always told you this house was damp."

Rachell smiled at him. Her pity this afternoon was stronger than her dislike.

"Don't you like my room?" she asked.

"High-falutin'," said grandpapa. "I suppose you call it artistic?"

"I think it is beautiful," admitted Rachell.

Grandpapa shifted his weight in his chair.

"Deuced uncomfortable furniture," he said. "Beauty be damned, I like comfort . . . No, you needn't 'ssh' me; the child's asleep."

He blew out his cheeks and his eyes travelled round the room again. They came to rest on the strips of Chinese embroideries sent home by a sailor du Frocq. He looked at them fixedly.

"Cousin Matthieu du Frocq gave them to me, you know," Rachell said, smiling at her blue butterflies and golden dragons dancing on the wall.

"He was a great traveller," grandpapa announced. "Wild fellow, too. Humph. Well. He's dead now. Sailors and travellers – there've been several of 'em in the family. There's a restless strain in us. That's what it is. Restless." He stared at the fire and Rachell wondered if he was thinking of his son Jean.

"Tell me about this fellow Mabier," he demanded suddenly. Rachell told him the little she could tell without betraying Ranulph's confidence.

"Humph," muttered grandpapa, "a queer fellow. Restless. A traveller. That's what it is, restless. . . . He told that story well; damn well."

"Yes," said Rachell.

"Story telling is a gift," grandpapa informed her. "My son Jean had it."

It was the first time he had ever mentioned his son to her and she started. She supposed Ranulph's story-telling had recalled Jean to his father. She looked up and found the old man's eyes fixed on her. They were desolate. She made a little gesture of compassion towards him with her hand, but he ignored it.

"Often wondered if the fellow's dead or alive," he said gruffly.

"I think he must be dead," said Rachell gently. "If he had lived surely he would have come home again."

"Never expected him to do that," said grandpapa. "Hated me. Thought I'd killed his mother or some such damn nonsense. Bitter against me because I wouldn't let him be a sailor. Young fool! The young don't know what's good for them."

Abruptly he put his handkerchief over his head again and folded his hands across his stomach. Rachell dared say no more. The clock ticked on and there was perfect silence in the room. Grandpapa was quite still, but Rachell knew he was not asleep. His mind was voyaging savagely over the past, justifying all his actions for the thousandth time.

Rachell wished she could sleep a little before tea. There was a long evening of festivity to be got through first and she was very tired, but her arms and back were aching with Colette's weight and the pain kept her awake. She felt depressed. She distrusted for the hundredth time that "seeing" that had made her bring Ranulph to Bon Repos. She owed Jacqueline's happiness at the Convent to him, but except for that she could not see what good he had brought them. They were no nearer financial salvation. Faithful to their six months' compact, André had not so much as mentioned the word "money" to her, but she knew it was the five letters of that abominable word that were robbing him of his sleep and making him thinner and more bowed than ever. She looked at him as he sat in his chair. He looked ten years older than he was. Why, oh why, had she added to his burdens the continual friction of Ranulph's presence in his home? . . . She was weighed down by many things as she sat in her chair that afternoon, but the heaviest was the as yet unacknowledged fact that Ranulph loved her . . . What would be the end of it all? She saw all their lives as a lot of strands hopelessly knotted and could see no way to unravel them. She looked round her pretty room for comfort. She looked at her French carpet, its pinks and blues faded to the colour of a dove's breast, at the miniatures over the mantelpiece and the French gilt mirror, at her tea-set patterned in blue and scarlet and gold, and at the stiff-backed chairs that her grandfather had given her grandmother, and all these things stretched out fingers and touched her, whispering "wait". She was comforted. In spite of her aching arms she began to nod a little. The blue butterflies and the scarlet dragons, and the blue and yellow flames of the tronquet de Noel closed round her and began to pull her gently down and down, through depths of tranquil light that grew cooler and sweeter the farther she sank, until she found herself resting serenely against something, drawing in strength and peace through every fibre of her being.

<h1 style="text-align:center">4</h1>

She was awakened by Peronelle, vibrating with excitement, rushing in to announce that tea was ready in the kitchen. Sophie had gone out to spend a blissful afternoon and evening with Jacquemin Gossilin and the refreshment of the inner man was now in the hands of Peronelle and Michelle. They had prepared a tea of a sumptuousness passing description. It was a proper Island tea, such as they indulged in on festival days, served at twilight and combining tea and supper, and the food of both. There were tea and coffee, ham and eggs, jams and jellies, and bread and biscuits, and in the middle of the table the stupendous, mountainous, snow-white Christmas cake.

The major part of the tronquet de Noel blazed in the grate, and all the holly berries were awink, and the lamps were lighted. In front of the dresser stood the Christmas-tree, glimmering with candles and golden and scarlet balls, and round its feet were piled the presents. The windows were uncurtained so that as night deepened they would be able to see the stars.

Tea till bedtime was to the children the best part of Christmas Day, and to grandpapa, Ranulph, Rachell, and André, vicariously young again, the hours passed with a chiming of bells that drowned the mutter of life surging past and towards them. Tea and presents and carol singing and games filled their evening brimful of delight. The sparkling kitchen shone like a glow-worm in the darkness of the world all round them. Out through the windows poured the laughter, and the singing, and the light, conquering a little and no more of the silence and the blackness.

Now and again, as the hours passed, there would come a knocking at the hall door and André would open it and find a little group of peasants standing outside, their figures grimly black against the stars. "Monsieur, alms in the name of Noel." Sometimes they asked it in halting English, sometimes in patois that sighed in the night like music. And André, though he had little to give, and had no business to give that little, never refused them.

This house-to-house begging was an old and reverenced custom, and he was glad too, this night of all nights, that the Bon Repos hospitality should shine far . . . For it might be the last time.

As he bade God speed to one little group he stood for a moment in the darkness outside listening to the laughter and singing, and watching the long beam of light from the kitchen window stretching a caressing finger out across the courtyard, over the winter-bound garden, across the cliff almost to the cliff's edge. It seemed like a living thing, the radiance of something that he and Rachell had brought to life at Bon Repos. He turned abruptly on his heel and walked in . . . The thought of that light quenched was intolerable.

5

Grandpapa had gone. The clip-clop of his horses' hooves had died away in the frosty night. Ranulph had gone. The children were in bed and asleep. The little lights on the Christmas-tree had died with Christmas Day, and the lamps were turned low. Only the tronquet de Noel sent out a warm crimson glow from its falling ash. Rachell and André, moving with the slowness of exhaustion, were trying to bring a little order into the untidy room before they went to bed. Now that the children had gone they could hear again the mutter of life surging past and towards them, and the mutter was ominous. Where would they be next Christmas? They neither of them spoke, but the question was there in the room with them, pressing upon them intolerably. They finished their tidying, put out the lamps and crossed the room arm in arm, wearily. At the door Rachel paused. Through the window she could see the light still shining in Ranulph's room, and at the sight of it her heart felt unaccountably lightened. She glanced round the room. The willow pattern china and the warming-pans, those incurable optimists, had each of them a little twinkling reflection of the tronquet de Noel. To Rachell's lightened heart each little friendly gleam seemed a promise of yet another Christmas to come, yet another Christmas at Bon Repos. In the doorway, under the mistletoe so thoughtfully placed there by Ranulph for the purpose, she turned and flung her arms round André.

"It will be all right, darling," she whispered, "it will be all right."

André, too, felt his heart lightened by what he considered her quite unreasonable optimism. They went upstairs hand in hand, undressed in their candle-lit bedroom under the picture of the Last Judgement, climbed into their big four-poster, and drew the crimson curtains. The last sound they heard as they fell asleep was the murmur of the sea.

Christmas at the Inn

1

EVERY grown-up at the Herb of Grace and at Damerosehay was determined that this should be the children's Christmas – such a Christmas as they had not known before in their unsettled young lives. They themselves looked forward to it with a certain amount of dread . . . The state of the world and their own fatigue combined to make them feel that a condition of mind humble and prayerful, meals requiring the minimum of preparation, and recreation consisting of nothing more strenuous than dozing in an arm-chair with a detective story, were their idea of a suitable Christmas in the circumstances . . . But that would not do for the children, and they girded themselves with heroism for the fray. And, as it turned out, not in vain, for when the time came it was for all of them – the grown-ups as well as the children – a day of sheer delight, one of those magical times that are not forgotten while life lasts, when it seems as though nothing can go wrong; as though human imperfection were aided and sustained by something outside itself, and just for once allowed to bring to perfection everything that it attempted. John Adair, looking back afterwards, remembered that from the very beginning he had been aware of the pulse of creative joy beating in the house. So great was its strength that he should not have been taken by surprise when it broke right through the crust of things and took them all in charge.

Yet he was surprised, for during the week before Christmas, in common with the rest of the grown-ups, his emotional state had been one chiefly of profound exasperation. As if the preparation of festival meals with not enough sugar, less butter, and no suet at all, the decoration of a large Christmas-tree when you couldn't buy so much as a silver star or a strip of tinsel, the purchasing of Christmas presents when you hadn't a single coupon left and all the books you ordered were out of print, were not enough to try the temper, Ben had decreed that there must be a dramatic entertainment; and not only an entertainment, but a carol service in the Chapel to inaugurate it properly as a chapel, and not a store-room.

"Must we have both?" Nadine had asked patiently, trying hard to keep the weariness out of her voice, as she and George, David, Sally and Ben sat round the fire at tea one day, a few days before the twins' visit to the Buckpen. "Wouldn't the carols be enough without the entertainment?"

"But we said when we first came that we'd have a play at Christmas," Ben reminded her. "Don't you remember? They always did in the old inns. The actors used the gallery, and the audience sat in the yard below."

"If you want to sit us all out in the stable yard in mid-winter, and prance about on that outdoor gallery of Malony's, just say the word, old boy, and I'll order a large hearse for the lot of us and have done with it," said George resignedly.

"No, we'll do that in the summer," said Ben. "This time we'll act in here, in the hall. We'll have the stage at the foot of the stairs, and use the stairs for exits and entrances. Part of the show we'll stage actually on the stairs, where they branch in front of the alcove. It'll be awfully effective. You and Father needn't have anything to do with it, Mother. Tommy and I and Caroline and the twins will do it all. At least, Sally will coach us in the carols; won't you, Sally? You're awfully musical. And of course David must do something spectacular. And you, Sir," he said shyly, and sweetly to John Adair, "you'll help me make the costumes, won't you?"

Only Sally showed enthusiasm for the task assigned. John Adair growled tragically, yet with a gleam of interest in his eye, for, exasperating though it would be to have to set aside his work for a week and play the fool with bits of coloured paper and what not, yet it would interest him to see what ideas his pupil Ben had on the subject of costume design. But David groaned with no gleam in the eye, for he had to the full the professional actor's hatred of getting mixed up in amateur efforts.

"What were you thinking of doing, old boy?" he asked gloomily. "It will be darned awkward getting about on those stairs. There's no space."

"We can do the getting about parts on the stage below. First we'll have a dramatization of 'The Wind in the Willows' that I've planned out. Rat and Mole and so on. That'll be just us five, so you needn't bother with it. And after that you and Sally can do the balcony scene from *Romeo and Juliet* —"

"*What?*" interrupted David in horror.

72

Sally, who had glowed with delight at the thought of the carols, now went pale with dismay.

"Oh, I couldn't, Ben; I just couldn't!"

"Why ever not?" demanded Ben.

"The size of me!" cried Sally. "And I can't act, either. And with David —"

"Won't you like acting with David?" asked Ben in surprise. "You're engaged to him, aren't you?"

"That's why!" groaned poor Sally.

"Leaning over a balcony, no one will notice your size," said Ben inexorably. "We'll rig up the balcony across the stairs, in front of the alcove, with a lamp burning behind your head in the alcove, making your hair all golden. It'll look grand. I've thought it all out."

John Adair was chuckling into his beard.

"It just can't be done, old chap," said David firmly. "I'm having a rest cure."

"You've had it," said Ben heartlessly. "And by this time you ought to be able to play Romeo in your sleep."

"No hope, you two," said John Adair. "Haven't you discovered, yet, that what Ben ordains sooner or later comes to pass? Always, throughout life, Ben will get his own way. It's not selfishness, mind you, but his perfectly accurate conviction that his way is the right way. In this respect his Grandmother lives again in him. When a man has a strong will, backed by the conviction that he is right, he turns into just a common dictator, but when his will and his conviction are backed by the fact that owing to some felicity of vision he *is* right, the chances are that he may become a great man. Time will show whether Ben —"

But Ben was not attending.

"Mother, you know that old fur coat of yours – the stripy one – it would do nicely for Badger, wouldn't it? And Grandmother has an old sealskin coat that would do for Rat. You'll help with the costumes, too, won't you, Mother? You're so awfully good at dressmaking." Nadine, who had been clinging as to a lifeline to Ben's statement that she and George need have nothing to do with this affair, let go of the lifeline. "And Father will manage the lighting, won't you, Father?"

"Malony's better at that kind of thing than I am," suggested George weakly.

"I know, but Malony and Annie-Laurie will be taking part in the show."

"Good heavens!" ejaculated David. "What are they going to do?"

"Some sort of turn on their own. They've just got to be in it. They're troubadours."

"You've asked them?"

"No. I thought you could."

"Not on your life!" said David violently.

"Then Sally will," said Ben placidly. "They won't like to refuse Sally when she's just got engaged."

"No, Ben!" implored Sally.

Ben waved this refusal aside for the moment and returned to the subject of her clothes.

"You'll wear the Botticelli thing, won't you? You know, the blue-green thing —"

"Oh, Ben —" pleaded poor Sally.

David stretched a hand under the tea-table and gripped hers. He loved in her this sensitive shrinking from making a show of her love. During these last days, since they had taken the plunge, each response of hers to all the new situations created by their coming together had seemed to him lovely and right. Always she rang true. With each new day he fell more deeply in love, and became not only more sure of her, but more sure of himself. He would be able to make her happy. Grandmother had been quite right.

"'But lo, a light in yonder window breaks. It is the east and Juliet is the sun,'" he declaimed, smiling at Ben in capitulation, his hand gripping Sally's tighter.

His meaning came to her. Because of her, there was a new morning, a re-birth in his life. She was so happy she hardly knew how to bear it. She smiled at Ben, too.

"All right, Ben."

Nadine did not miss the tone in David's voice, the light in Sally's face. But she had taken the plunge, too, and she smiled at them, and because of them, with all her heart. And dear old George was looking at her with profound and loving commiseration, because of this darned entertainment. And John Adair with profound and loving admiration; because she had smiled. The love of these two older men was suddenly very precious to her.

"If we're all in this, even your poor old parents, it beats me where the audience is coming from," said George to Ben.

74

"Grandmother, Aunt Margaret, Uncle Hilary, Jill, Auntie Rose, and all the people round here who have been nice to us," said Ben. "What are you all groaning about? This is an inn, isn't it? If we aren't hospitable this first Christmas, then we don't deserve to live here."

"But they'll expect to be fed!" gasped Nadine in horror.

"Oh, not much, Mother. Just a few sandwiches and drinks and things. It's wonderful what Auntie Rose can rake out from under her nephew's counter if Tommy wheedles her."

And so it went on, like a snowball rolling. The exhausted elders would have died of the orgy of preparation had they not been sustained by the laughter of Tommy and Ben, Caroline, Jerry and José, ringing through the house from dawn to dusk.

2

One evening, after tea, Sally took a box tied with scarlet ribbon out of her drawer, slipped on her fur coat and went across the stable yard and up the steps to the flat above. She had chosen a moment when she knew that Annie-Laurie was alone there. She knocked at the door, and then stood waiting, decidedly scared. She understood Annie-Laurie better now, for David had told her something of her history; but she had no idea how Annie-Laurie would take this intrusion. She had no idea what she was going to say or do. She was just obeying Hilary and Ben – those two gentle Eliots whose gentleness did not seem to prevent them getting their own way with typical Eliot success.

The door opened, and Annie-Laurie and the cat Smith stood upon the threshold, with behind them the pretty lamp-lit room, a fire burning on the hearth. Annie-Laurie wore a flowered overall, and the smell of ironing made Sally wrinkle her nose appreciatively.

"Could I come in a moment, Annie-Laurie?" she asked shyly. "Or are you too busy?"

From force of habit Annie-Laurie had stiffened defensively at the sight of an uninvited visitor violating the sanctuary of her home, then she relaxed and smiled.

"Please come in," she said. "I've just finished. Won't you take your coat off?"

Sally hated herself for putting on her fur coat, as she saw Annie-Laurie's hand unconsciously caressing the lovely fur as she laid it over a chair. It had been lying in the hall, and she had just picked it up as the first wrap that came to hand. But it looked like flaunting her detestable opulence in front of Annie-Laurie. She felt, with shrinking, the firelight flashing on her emerald ring, lighting up her vulgarly bright hair, stressing those so commonly robust curves of her strong and healthy body. Beside Annie-Laurie's fragility she felt like an overblown dahlia towering over a snow-drop. She had everything. Even David now. There was not a single thing, now, that she had not got. When Annie-Laurie turned round to her again, her cheeks were hot with shame and her eyes as beseeching as those of a child caught stealing jam from a cupboard. And she stood as a child stands, straight and shy, holding the white box between her hands, wanting to give it, but not knowing how. Annie-Laurie's painful jealousy was suddenly eased. Really, she'd never been as shy as this, not even in her greenest years. It was she, so she discovered, who must take charge of this interview and put her guest at her ease.

"Do you like my room?" she asked. "Mrs. Eliot gave me the lovely bits of old furniture, and I made the curtains and cushions."

Sally looked about her with admiration.

"It's lovely, Annie-Laurie. You've arranged it all so well. I'll never be the homemaker that you are."

"Yes, you will," laughed Annie-Laurie. "I haven't congratulated you, have I? I'm so glad for you."

The words came out with a little difficulty, yet, as she said them, she found to her intense relief that she meant them. A large part of her past mental misery had been caused by the intense bitterness that, against all her desire, had choked her natural friendliness. It was queer, she thought, how the thing that she had done, unknown to a soul, had seemed to lie in her like an ugly rock in the centre of a stream, gathering to itself all other sins and failings, so that they piled up around it, damming the natural flow of her being. Now, everything confessed to Nadine and Malony, the thing seemed to have gone, and her reactions were natural again – almost.

Sally sat down in one of the two chairs before the fire, the white box still held between her hands.

"I'm glad for myself," she said simply. "I didn't know one

76

could be so happy. Yet I'm scared of not being equal to it. Letting David down. You know what I mean. Though Damerosehay will be our real home, we'll have a flat in town for the working times, and I'll have to be a good hostess – and – that sort of thing."

"You'll manage," Annie-Laurie assured her, and, sitting now in the other chair, she leaned back and laughed softly, luxuriating in the glorious, unchecked friendliness that was flowing now between the two of them. Not for years had she sat like this with another girl in the firelight and talked over the dear trivialities that make up the warmth of life. She could feel them all there waiting to be talked about; furniture, saucepans, trousseaux and the rest. "You'll have a big wedding? A white one?"

"Oh no," cried Sally in horror. "As quiet as we can have it. In Uncle Hilary's church, with him to marry us. And not white. I'd look bigger than ever in white."

"Blue?" asked Annie-Laurie.

"David says golden-brown – lion colour. He says I look like a lion; a nice one. And Ben told me this morning that I reminded him of Mogwli's wolf. I don't think it's very flattering of them, do you?"

"I know what they mean," smiled Annie-Laurie. "You'll have to have a hat of some sort, of course – not just a handkerchief tied over your head, like you usually have."

The talk flowed on quietly and happily for a little while, about nothing at all, and Sally was not shy and ashamed any more; but she still seemed unable to approach the matter of the box in her lap. As always when she gave presents, she was seized by a host of misgivings: that she had chosen the wrong thing; that it wasn't as nice as she had thought it was; that there would be a break or a flaw somewhere; that perhaps its value would seem too little and her friend be hurt by her lack of generosity; that perhaps it would seem too much and make her look like that detestable thing, a patroness; that present-giving was really only a form of self-indulgence and perhaps it was best not to indulge in it at all. Annie-Laurie, seeing all this in Sally's naïvely revealing face (really, she thought, she was as transparent as a child, and David Eliot would have his work cut out defending her from exploitation), was obliged to come to the rescue.

"What's in that box?" she asked, with a touch of mischief that took Sally completely by surprise; and no wonder, for all the swift changes of mood, the lightness and the humour which had once made Annie-Laurie so fine an actress had been extinguished in her for a long time, and never seen by those who had known her only at the Herb of Grace.

The swift happy question was suddenly in keeping with the red ribbon round the box, the Arcadian lambs inside. With a sigh of relief Sally leaned forward and put the box on Annie-Laurie's lap.

"It's for you. For Christmas. It's two little Rockingham lambs. You see, Uncle Hilary told me that you used to look after the sheep in your mountains. And I worked with the sheep, too, in Cumberland, during the war."

Annie-Laurie, smiling and murmuring her thanks, was savouring the pleasure of undoing the red ribbons, lifting the lid of the box, carefully unwrapping the lambs from their cotton wool. She adored pretty things, but until this moment she had forgotten that she did. With a cry of delight she held the lambs in her hands. They were snow-white, and they had blue ribbons and bells round their necks, and they carried Annie-Laurie straight back to her happy childhood.

"Sally, they're perfect!" she cried. "Bells! I used to tie bells round the lambs' necks at home. It used to make the old shepherd furious. But he couldn't swear at me as he wanted to because he'd given me the bells. Very old Morris-dancers' bells." She looked up at the bright bunch hanging from the beam. "There they are."

"I thought of your bells when I saw the lambs," said Sally happily. "Are those the ones that you wore for your Christmas-tree dance that David told me about?"

"Yes, those are the ones."

"Annie-Laurie," cried Sally, with impulsive eagerness. "I wish you and Malony would come back on the stage again. It would be lovely to have you in London. We'd be friends and help each other."

Annie-Laurie had felt her reactions to be normal again . . . almost . . . not quite. Suddenly the old terror gripped her again – that fear of the shame, the whispering voices behind her back.

"No, Sally, I couldn't! Not possibly. I can never go back, Sally. Never!"

Sally's cheeks went crimson with shame at her blunder.

"I'm so sorry, Annie-Laurie. Please forgive me. I'm about the most blundering fool who ever lived."

78

Annie-Laurie mastered herself quickly, stood up and put the lambs on the mantelpiece.

"No, you're not. You say straight out what's in your mind, and I like that in you. I know I ought to go back, for Jim's sake – but I can't." She sat down again. "Tell me about Damerosehay. I've not been there."

They fought their way back to the warm trivialities, and were at ease again until the clock struck six.

"Those carols!" cried Sally. "We were to have a carol practice at six. You're coming? Without your voice we're just no good at all."

"We're no good with it," said Annie-Laurie gloomily. Then she brightened. "They always say depressing rehearsals make a good performance, you know. If things go too well in rehearsal you crash on the night."

"If only all these outside people were not coming!" sighed Sally, struggling into her fur coat. "Ben keeps thinking of more and more he'd like to come – and Juliet in the balcony scene gets worse and worse."

"Poor Juliet!" laughed Annie-Laurie. "How is the children's animal thing going?"

"Ben says it's dreadful," said Sally. "They're trying to do a telescoped version of 'The Wind in the Willows', and it won't telescope."

Annie-Laurie had moved to put out the lamp, and while she did it Sally looked up at the bunch of bells over her head, gathering her courage to obey Ben's command and ask for the help of the troubadours. She could not have done it but for her father's remark, "Ben's perfectly accurate conviction that his way is right."

"Annie-Laurie! Do your Christmas-tree dance for us, you and Malony! Just at the end. On the stage at the foot of the stairs. It would be lovely, and just right. If everything else is a mess, there will be that one perfect thing. Annie-Laurie, you must!"

She had put her arms impulsively round Annie-Laurie, and could not see her face, but she felt the stiffening of her body. But this time she did not apologize. Ben was always right, and her own instinct, too, told her to hold tight and go on.

"Yes, Annie-Laurie. Please. You owe it to the Herb of Grace."

As a rule Annie-Laurie disliked endearments, but there was no suggestion of an endearment about the embrace of Sally Adair. The strength of her arms, the whole-heartedness of her hug, were

79

more like some act of nature, like a great breath of spring wind that nearly takes you off your feet, or a sudden burst of sunshine through the clouds. Sally's embrace was given rarely, but when it was given it definitely altered things. Annie-Laurie felt warm and safe in her arms, even as she had felt when she first came to the Herb of Grace. "You owe it to the Herb of Grace." It was true. She did. She withdrew herself gently and reached for her coat hanging on the peg beside the door.

"Very well," she said. "I'll do it."

Together they went out into the moonlight and down the steps to the yard. Each of them knew now that they were necessary to each other, and would be friends until the end of their lives.

3

Ben's dramatization of "The Wind in the Willows" continued to be no good at all. His designs for the costumes were admirable, and they were superbly made by himself, Nadine and John Adair, and he was full of bright ideas. But they were too bright. His cast – Tommy, Caroline and the twins – were incapable of carrying them out. Tommy and Caroline could learn their parts, but they were without dramatic ability. Jerry and José had plenty of dramatic ability – too much, in fact – but were of too tender years to commit their lines to memory. Or else they wouldn't. Patiently Ben repeated the short, simple sentences to them; but when asked to say them after him, they merely replied with the two words, "Hot Sausage". No one knew what they meant, but the fact had to be faced that they had decided to be not only unco-operative, but definitely obstructive. Ben finally, just two days before Christmas, fell a victim to despair, and David was called upon in his professional capacity to give advice. John Adair came with him, and stood leaning against the mantelpiece in the hall, chuckling into his beard, intrigued to see how the famous actor would deal with the situation, and finding him, as he expected, nervous.

"Scrap it," was David's advice to Ben. "Much too difficult, old boy. You've aimed too high. Cut your losses and start again. Why not turn the speechlessness of these darned twins to good use and have mime?"

The drooping spirits of Ben, Tommy and Caroline rose a little. The twins, who were seals this morning, stopped slithering round and round the hall floor on their fronts and lay still to listen, with lazily flapping fins. David looked at them. Gently the fins rose and fell, now and then a tail waved, or a nose was lifted to sniff the air. They were lying in the ripples with the hot sun on their backs. For a queer flashing moment he saw the gleam of the water and felt the sun; it gave him quite a shock. Then he saw the light. No good trying to control genius with whip and rein. It must take its own way. He addressed them.

"Jerry and José!"

"Hot sausage," said Jerry.

"Hot sausage," said José.

"Stow that," he said sternly. "Life is real, life is earnest, especially in such a terrible crisis as has now arisen. If you don't want to do the nice play that Ben has written for you, what *do* you want to do?"

"Hot sausage," said Jerry.

"In the little house," said José.

"What little house?" asked David.

"In the Place Beyond," said Jerry. "The man gave them hot sausage."

"And bandaged them," said José.

Memory stirred in David.

"The Place Beyond. That's where you went that day in the autumn when Sally lost you and I drove you home in my car. It's in Knyghtwood, isn't it?"

"Yes," said Jerry. "But Beyond."

"Beyond what?" asked John Adair.

"Where the rest of you go."

"What was the man like?" demanded Ben.

"Big," said Jerry. His eyes went to John Adair and fastened on his beard. "A beaver. And he laughed. He had a dressing-gown on."

"How do you know it was hot sausage he gave them?" asked Tommy, always interested in food.

"It was good," said José. "They liked it."

"The term hot sausage is used symbolically?" suggested John Adair. "Another would perhaps have described the nourishment provided by this unknown personage as honey dew and the milk of

Paradise. It's all a question of digestion. Coleridge's was weak, I believe. He would have turned nauseated from the thought of hot sausage. It was the unsubstantiality of honey-dew (what is it, by the way?) that doubtless appealed to him. And milk of Paradise sounds pre-digested."

The children never listened very much to Old Beaver when he rambled on.

"Who were the blokes the man gave the sausage to?" asked Tommy.

"They weren't blokes," said Jerry.

"Animals?" asked Ben eagerly.

"Some of them," said José.

"And birds?" asked Caroline, with shining eyes.

"Yes," said Jerry.

"And he bandaged their hurt paws and mended their broken wings?" asked Ben.

"Yes."

"Was his beard brown, and had his dressing-gown a dark hood that he wore over his head?"

"Yes."

"Was he like the man in the picture I painted?"

"Yes."

Ben was almost panting with eagerness.

"The man who painted the Chapel walls and carved these posts and the little white deer in the alcove, and was Mine Host of the Herb of Grace? And you saw him out there in the wood?"

"Yes."

"Had he the white deer with him?"

"Yes. The Person with the Horns."

"They're saying yes like a parrot," said David. "You're getting them rattled."

"We never get them rattled," said Tommy. "It's they who get us rattled. They've made it all up, of course. They've got it from that yarn of Auntie Rose's."

"What yarn?" asked David.

"Oh, some yarn Auntie Rose's Fred's great-grannie told him when he was a boy. Ben will remember."

"A monk from the Abbey," said Ben, quickly and softly, "loved birds and beasts. He built a chapel in the woods and fed them there and looked after them when they were sick. That's a legend

82

that must have been handed down for generations. Fred's great-grannie, perhaps, heard it from her great-grannie. Auntie Rose told it to us. If she hadn't, perhaps it would have been lost."

"Well, we'll see that it isn't," said David. "We'll drive it home. Did Auntie Rose's Fred, by any chance, identify our chap here with the monk of the woods?"

"Yes. He told Auntie Rose that only a chap who loved birds and beasts could have carved those pillars and the white deer. Fred must have got to know the man from living in the house, like we have. Fred was keen on the creatures, too. Auntie Rose said he never shot anything."

"You don't either," said Caroline. "Not like Tommy."

"The dynasty goes on," said John Adair. "And a man's sons are not always those of his own flesh."

"What had better go on," said David, "is the rehearsal." But for a moment his eyes met those of John Adair; he had lost his own father in his boyhood, but in these last few weeks the loss had been made good. "I can see the thing shaping. We'll have a stage shaped like an L, taking in the stairs and the drawing-room door as entrances, with the Christmas-tree at the angle of it. Write out the legend, Ben – in blank verse, if you like – and then you can sit under the tree, as Badger, and read it. The stage will be Knyghtwood. The stairs will lead up to the Place Beyond, where the alcove is. Our monk will be there, with the white deer in the alcove behind him. The creatures will come in through the drawing-room door and go up the stairs, and he'll deal out hot sausage. The twins will show us how it should be done. Mr. Adair will be the monk."

"Not on your life," said John Adair.

And the twins agreed with him.

"His beard's all wrong!" they yelled in outrage.

"Thank heavens he's got a beard," said David, "and don't cavil as to its colour. Now we'll have to work like hell. Only two days. Where's Ben?"

Ben had already slipped away into the drawing-room to write out the legend in his best blank verse.

4

Through the blue dusk of a perfect Christmas Day the guests drove to the Herb of Grace. The gate had been left open for them, and the oak-trees seemed to bend over them in a friendly sort of way as they bumped their way along the lane. The headlights of their cars showed a few sparse flowers on the gorse-bushes – the English gorse that keeps a few golden blossoms all the winter through, even beneath a coverlet of snow. But there was no snow to-night, though it had turned frosty. The sky was cloudless, and the few stars that had appeared shone very brightly, giving promise of a blaze of glory to come. At the turn of the lane they heard the owl hooting in Knyghtwood, but the ghostly trees upon either side made no sound, for it was a windless night. The lanterns had been lit and placed upon the walls, and down at the bottom of the lane they could see the glint of them upon the water. Lights streamed from the Herb of Grace, from every window and from the open front door, and the very jubilation of that light had something to say of the utter happiness of the day that had been spent within. To most of the occupants of the cars the world seemed a dark enough place, but at the sight of that light their heavy hearts lifted a little. There were still children in the world, and while there were children, men and women would not abandon the struggle to make safe homes to put them in, and while they so struggled there was hope.

As they went up the steps to the green gate, and along the garden path to the front door, those men and women were typified for them by George and Nadine, standing at the door to welcome them, with their children behind them. And within were Lucilla, Hilary, Margaret, John Adair, Sally and David – men and women whose worth was a good thing to feel about one on Christmas Day. But it was the children who mattered. It was the children who were the point of it all.

As they were divested of their wraps they exclaimed in delight at the appearance of the wide old hall, with the yule log blazing on the hearth and the holly-wreathed lights burning in their candle-sconces all round the walls. Their seats had been arranged diagonally across the hall to face the L-shaped stage, with its exits to stairs and drawing-room. At its angle stood the glorious Christmas-tree, bright with lighted candles. In the end, as it represented Knyghtwood, it had been decided to give it no decoration except the candles that burned in the wood at sunset. And it needed no other, for the candles shone so gloriously that looking at them the Eliots almost forgot the awful job they had had getting them all fixed upright. The stage was covered in green cloth and Knyghtwood holly, and holly concealed the footlights. The old carved posts to the left of the front door were lightly wreathed with ivy, and looked like trees growing.

George and John Adair and David handed round cocktails (Sally and the children having mysteriously disappeared), and as they made them last as long as possible, the guests became conscious of a delightful jovial glow of hospitable warmth wrapping them round; which most of them put down to the potency of the admirably mixed cocktails, though just a few noticed the formation of the stairs, and were reminded of a great dark figure with arms held out in welcome. They all noticed the alcove where the stairs branched, and the strange little carved figure within it, so cleverly lit by a concealed light, so that it shone like a lamp. They became increasingly aware of that shining image. They did not know what it was, but it drew and held them.

Until their attention was captured by a thread of music reaching out to them, pulling at them. Somewhere in the depths of the old house young voices were singing the Adeste Fideles.

"Will you come this way?" said Nadine, and she led them through the hall to the kitchen, garlanded with greenery, and up the turret stairs to the Chapel.

They had heard of the discovery of the frescoes, and they caught their breath in amazement. The candles had been lighted in the branched candlesticks on the altar, and the pots filled with holly and fir, and above them rose the strange figure of the great white deer with the crucifix in his antlers, dominating the Chapel as the little carved figure below dominated the hall. They sat on the benches and looked about them with delight at the trees and flowers, the birds and beasts, and the young knight riding through the wood, while behind them Sally and Annie-Laurie, Malony, Jill and the children, standing in a row one on each side of the door, finished the Adeste Fideles and embarked upon the First Nowell with a perfection of tone and rhythm which they had not

85

dared to hope for during the preceding awful week. It was, as Annie-Laurie had prophesied, all right on the night, and the glorious conviction lent such wings to their voices that the tentative efforts of the guests were soon caught up and lifted into a volume of sound so satisfactory that Sally, followed by David, was able to leave them and slip away.

When she had gone, Annie-Laurie led the singing, her sweet clear voice rising in carol after carol. They were all so absorbed, singing in that lovely glowing place, that only Malony looked at Annie-Laurie. And he could not take his eyes from her face as she stood there singing, sword-straight, her hands behind her back, her eyes quiet and happy. Just so, with that perfection of simplicity, had she sung in the old days. His heart pounded with joy. She was coming round, his girl. At last she was coming round. This place, this blessed place, had healed her. He could no longer sing, so much too large had his throat become for his too-tight collar. He loosened it impatiently with his forefinger and croaked like a raven. Annie-Laurie heard him and looked round, her eyes lighting up with tender amusement. It was a sweet look that she gave him, over the heads of the twins – the kind of look she had given him when Midge was a little thing. That good old bloke the Reverend Hilary had been right. He had said it would all come out in the wash (or words to that effect), and it had. His eyes holding Annie-Laurie's, he suddenly found his voice again, and bellowed of the holly and the ivy as loudly as any of them. That was the last carol. When it was over Annie-Laurie opened the door, and they went downstairs to laugh and talk in the kitchen, and be told about the frescoes, and eat home-made fudge, until a bell rang and Nadine led them back into the hall.

5

What next, they wondered, settling into their seats while the lights round the walls were put out and the hidden footlights shone in their place. These Eliots were extraordinarily good at throwing a party? What next? There was a moment of thrilled expectation, and then the drawing-room door opened and Romeo in his silver-grey doublet and hose, a short orange cloak over one shoulder, the light gleaming on his silvery fair head, came through on to the stage. There was a gasp, and then silence. It was difficult to believe their good fortune. They were to see one of the most famous actors of their generation playing his most famous part, and they were not to pay a penny for the privilege. Just one whisper broke the silence. It came from an old gentleman in the front row.

"Fifteen shillings, at least, a seat in the stalls costs you nowadays," he whispered delightedly behind a horny hand to his daughter.

"Ssh!" said his daughter severely.

But he had expressed the feelings of them all.

> *"He jests at scars that never felt a wound.*
> *But soft! what light through yonder window breaks?*
> *It is the east and Juliet is the sun."*

The familiar words floated out into the room like music. The incomparable beauty of the golden voice, the silvery figure, gripped their hearts. All David's family, with the exception of Lucilla, as always when they saw him on the stage, suffered from sudden shock. Was this David, often so edgy, so difficult, often (though of course they loved him) such a sore trial to them? The perfect co-ordination of voice and movement, that complete absorption of the artist in his art that gave to it a depth that suggested stillness even while he spoke and moved, the grace and beauty so quietly and unself-consciously worn, the exciting sense of power held back – those marks of a great actor gave an illusion of perfection that lifted this figure above all human frailty. Impossible to reconcile this David with the other. Then, abruptly, they didn't try. This was Romeo, not David. The two had nothing to do with each other.

But Lucilla was the exception. She sat between Nadine and George in the back row to which the family had been relegated to keep the heat of the fire off the guests. Though she was unaware of it, she looked beautiful in her old but well-cut, full-skirted black velvet dress. Draughts were inimical to her, and because of them she had a black lace scarf draped over her white hair and round her shoulders. She sat very upright, her blue eyes fixed on the man on the stage, and her hands were folded quietly in her lap. She saw no discrepancy between David her grandson and David the actor,

87

because for her the transformation of the one into the other was not a sudden thing, beginning with David and ending with Romeo, but a process that began much farther back than that and stretched much farther on; it began in her own being, and reached on through the beings of unborn children for she could not know how long. Her body had only partly helped to make the body of the man on the stage, but she knew that it was her spirit alone which had created his genius. David's father had been her very special child, spiritually the child of great love and sacrifice. Because of her anguish of self-denial, Maurice had been born. David's beauty was Maurice's, but his genius was the flowering of her anguish and the resurrection of her death. She knew now, at the end of her life, that that was always the way of it. "Except a grain of wheat fall into the ground and die . . ." The genius would flower again, perhaps, in one of his children or grandchildren, and in that child's child, and so it would go on; but it would have been lit from the same spark. She felt no pride, only a humble thankfulness that she had died that death. There was no discrepancy anywhere. It was natural that the lamp should be a frail earthen thing in comparison to the light within, for it had not created it, and only held it for a short moment . . . As the alcove up there held the shining figure of the white deer, as this house held a spirit of whose strength she was deeply aware this Christmas night, and to whom she offered salutation.

"Romeo . . . take all myself."

With a sigh Lucilla relaxed and looked up to the balcony from which the warm, deep voice floated. Sally was doing well, dear child; but she was not hoodwinking her audience into forgetfulness of her personality. She was not Juliet, but merely Sally Adair playing Juliet to the best of her ability in the circumstances. But she looked very lovely. A piece of scarlet brocade stretched across the stairs was her balcony, the illumined alcove was her window. Her peacock-blue gown made a wonderful splash of colour, and the light behind her set her hair on fire. David had taught her to speak her part very prettily, and Lucilla could feel that all shrinking and fear had left her once she was well launched, leaving her utterly glad to be his foil.

"For stony limits cannot hold love out,
And what love can do that dares love attempt."

Is it well with the child? That eternal question that goes with the begetter of life through every moment of every day and every night was very alive in Lucilla this evening. All was well with her grandchildren, David and Sally. She thanked God for it, and remembered the son and daughter upon either side of her. She put out her hand impulsively and took George's. He turned and smiled at her, and she saw the new happiness in his eyes. All that he had to give he had given Nadine long ago, all that love could do to make her happy he had done. Had she let him in at last? For the first time since Romeo had stepped on the stage to make love to the young Juliet, she dared to look at the woman beside her. On and off through the evening she had been haunted by those earlier words of Romeo that had not been spoken to-night.

> *"Did my heart love till now? Foreswear it, sight!*
> *For I ne'er saw true beauty till this night."*

Nadine met her look with a steady, smiling glance. Her face looked worn in the light of the fire, but peaceful as Lucilla had never seen it, and Lucilla knew that on this Christmas Day she had, at long last, let George in. With these, too, also, all was well at last.

Hilary was beyond Nadine; he was a happy man. And Margaret on the other side of George looked tired but happy; and when they were settled in Lavender Cottage, Lucilla hoped she wouldn't even look tired. And her five younger grandchildren, George's children – she looked about for them, but could not see them: bless them, they must be getting ready for some little entertainment of their own – they were all right. She had never been so happy about her dear Ben as she was now. He had grown steadily stronger this winter, and he had lost that nervous hesitancy that had so troubled her. He had a new confidence, a new certainty, which she believed he owed to that good man (where was he, by the way?), John Adair, her Sally's father. Sally! She was a little afraid to examine too particularly the elements of her quite extraordinary love for Sally. She loved her for herself, of course, but there was also in her love an element of quite selfish gratitude. Damerosehay, her beloved home, and David her dearest and her best, had nevertheless become a bit too much for her just lately. She was glad now to keep just her deep love for them, but to transfer the responsibility to Sally. She was equal to it. Her voice came floating down to Lucilla, assuring her of that.

"And yet I wish but for the thing I have:
My bounty is as boundless as the sea,
My love as deep; the more I give to thee
The more I have, for both are infinite."

Lucilla shut her eyes in unspeakable thankfulness. It seemed to her that she hardly had a thing left to wish for. The lovely rhythm of voice answering voice flowed on like music, but the words singing in her mind came from another play of her beloved Shakespeare. "If it were now to die, 'twere now to be most happy; for my soul hath her content so absolute —"

It was nearly over. The girl's voice, and the man's answering, for the last time.

"Good-night, good-night! Parting is such sweet sorrow
That I shall say good-night till it be tomorrow . . .
Sleep dwell upon thine eyes, peace in thy breast!
Would I were sleep and peace, so sweet to rest!"

6

Ben had opened the drawing-room door noiselessly from within, and Romeo had stepped into the wedge of darkness. Juliet had gone away up the stairs, and the balcony was empty. There was a moment's sense of almost intolerable loss, and then the lights were lit and everyone was laughing and talking, and congratulating Lucilla upon the brilliance of her family, and the home-made fudge was going round again.

"Are you getting tired, Mother?" Nadine asked Lucilla.

"Only nicely tired," said Lucilla. "I doubt if I've ever felt so happy in my life." She reached out a hand and laid it on her daughter-in-law's knee. "Nadine, my darling, you have done everything I wanted you to do, and you are my very dear child."

"I'm glad you're pleased with me, Mother," said Nadine, meekly, but with a flash of slightly sarcastic humour.

George, concerned that Lucilla should be even nicely tired, was shoving an exceedingly hard velvet cushion down her back.

"It's the children's show now," he said, "and then it's the turn of the domestic staff, and then I think that's the lot."

"Mother!" cried Margaret in distress, "you haven't got your footstool, and the draught under the front door is wicked. Hilary! Did you leave Mother's footstool in the car?"

"Don't *fuss*, dear," implored Lucilla. "Stay where you are, Hilary. The lights are being put out again."

They went out, and Nadine adroitly removed the hard velvet cushion from behind Lucilla's back and slipped it beneath her feet.

"My very dear child," repeated Lucilla.

The drawing-room door opened again, and a slim young stripling in striped tights and a striped cloak came through, wearing a realistic badger's mask that hid his face. But his grace and lightness of movement, like David's, but without the assurance of David's training, proclaimed him Ben, even before he lifted the badger's snout back over his head like a hood and showed his brown face. He had his Pan-pipe in one hand, and a long white scroll in the other, and he bowed to them very courteously before he sat down at the foot of the Christmas-tree and began to read from his long scroll. Lucilla's heart swelled with pride. There was not a trace of nervousness about him, and his voice was clear and perfectly modulated as he began to read the Knyghtwood legend in simple lovely verse that she knew he had written himself. She glanced at her son and daughter-in-law. They had, she considered, never fully appreciated their first-born, never fully realized his quality, that was perhaps the flowering of his mother's first and only willing yielding to her husband's love. She noticed with satisfaction that Nadine's head was almost arrogantly lifted and there was a faint tender smile on her lips. That's all right, thought Lucilla; as the years go on she'll take in him the same sort of delight that once she took in David. George's mouth had fallen open, and he was passing one hand in a bewildered sort of way over his thick grey hair. (How much better he was looking, by the way. Upon him, as well as Ben, the Herb of Grace had seemed to work a miracle of healing.) It's jolted him, dear old boy, thought Lucilla; do him good. Hilary, she noted, was smiling at her with an echo of her own delight. He had taught Ben, once, and had always been aware of his quality.

Ben's story began with the founding of the great Abbey beyond the river by King John as an act of reparation for his sins, and told how for forty-five years the monks laboured at its building, until at last the glorious place was finished and they could take up their work of prayer and labour, carried on until Henry VIII of detested memory drove them away. But before that evil day came there lived at the monastery a lay-brother, a fine artist and craftsman, a man of jovial disposition, bountiful and warm-hearted and over-flowing with goodwill to all God's creatures. As was only fitting for a man of such gifts, he was appointed by the Father Abbot as host of the Pilgrim Inn, Maison Dieu, where pilgrims visiting the Abbey were lodged and entertained; this same inn where they were gathered now. A great host was this Brother, with a huge welcome for all who came, and safely and warmly did he lodge them here, and tender was his care of them. The fare was frugal, perhaps, for such was the Brother's love for all living things that he would permit no snaring of the wild creatures to satisfy the greed of man; but there would be bread in plenty, made from the corn that the monks grew in their wide fields, and wine from their vineyards, and milk and butter and cream from the dairies. The pallets would be hard, and the furniture of the simplest; but in cold weather there would be a roaring fire on the hearth of the great hall, and their eyes would feast upon beauty wherever they looked, for the frescoes and carvings of their artist-host were lovelier than any tapestries and silken hangings. And great was this man also in wisdom and counsel, and skilled in the care of sick bodies as well as sick minds and souls, and those who became members of his flock for only a short while under this roof would not forget him while they lived. But it was not enough for this Brother that he should spend himself upon human creatures only. The animals and birds also were God's sons, and for them also he built a Maison Dieu within the woods. Here in the cold winters he would feed them – the deer and the rabbits, the badgers, the foxes and the birds. Such was his power over them that they were always at peace with each other within the sanctuary that he had made for them, and they were so tame that when they had hurt themselves they would come to him that he might tend their injuries. There was one animal in particular who was his special friend – a great white deer who was always with him in the woods, and was of such incomparable beauty that there were those who thought him not quite a creature of this earth. Of the death of this man there was no record, nor of the death of the deer. The body of the one, perhaps, lay within the Abbey garth, and the body of the other, if he was really a creature of this earth, within the woods. But their

92

spirits lived on. Still, in this house, was welcome and safety and healing for mind and body. Still, in the woods, the creatures found sanctuary. Still, both here and there, came sometimes a half-seen vision of great beauty to gladden the mind of a man and the heart of a child.

No one quite knew at what point in the earlier part of Ben's narrative they became aware of the figure who stood at the branching of the stairs, a bearded burly figure clothed in the rough habit of a Cistercian monk. His arms were held wide in welcome, and his hooded head was thrown into relief by the illumined figure of the white deer in the alcove behind him. First one and then another saw him, and when their awed attention had been entirely captured, Ben paused for a moment in his reading, glanced at the front door, which mysteriously opened at this point, and then with his eyes followed the progress of unseen pilgrims across the hall and up the stairs to their host. It was so cleverly done that those pilgrims were as real to the audience as though they had been actors of flesh and blood. They could hear their footfall and their voices, and see how their feet trod eagerly the worn, bent bow of each stair. Then the door softly closed, and Ben began reading again of how the animals, too, had had their sanctuary, and the drawing-room door opened and two little animals ran through – a water-rat and a mole, soft and furry, with brown bright eyes peeping through the masks that covered their faces. They ran upon all fours, but Mole held up his left hind foot because he had hurt it, and Rat kept stopping and holding a paw pathetically to one eye, which seemed to have something in it. They ran up the stairs to the Brother, and he held out his arms to them, and bound up Mole's paw and removed the obstruction from Rat's eye. A magnificent but extremely wicked-looking fox was the next animal, whom one gathered from his size to be Tommy. Half-way across the stage he paused and groaned, holding a stomach obviously a good deal too full of stolen goose. Everyone was laughing now, and their amusement was echoed by the big man above. His laughter rolled down to meet poor Fox, who hung his head comically, and then lolloped up the stairs to lap a healing dose from a big brown bowl. He was followed by a sweet-faced rabbit with a torn ear, who must be Caroline, followed by Mary and the cat Smith. They were attached to the person of the rabbit by green ribbons, as a precautionary measure, but the spirit of the thing

93

seemed to have entered into them, for it was they who pulled Rabbit, not Rabbit them, up the stairs to the Brother. Their entrance was the sign for Ben to finish his narrative, pick up his pipe, play a sweet air, and begin to sing the song that Annie-Laurie had written for the occasion, the other animals joining in with their clear, high voices, to the rumbling accompaniment of the Brother's deep bass.

> "*Sing hey for the moon and the starry sky,*
>   *The river, the wood and the sea,*
> *For the fish and birds and animals all,*
>   *And the grass so green on the lea.*
> *But most of all for the fair Christmas rose*
>   *And the lights on the candled tree.*
>
> *Sing hey for the chimney and roof-tree wide,*
>   *Sing hey for the walls and the floor,*
> *For the warmth of fire on the glowing hearth*
>   *And the welcoming open door.*
> *But most of all for the peace and goodwill*
>   *And the joy at our deep heart's core.*
>
> *Sing hey for the men, the hosts of this house,*
>   *Sing hey for the first and the last.*
> *Sing hey for the guests who have gathered here,*
>   *Both to-night and in pages past.*
> *And sing hey for the love between host and guest*
>   *That will hold them for ever fast.*
>
> *Sing hey for the God who fashioned for us*
>   *This bountiful splendour of earth,*
> *Sing hey for courage and wisdom and love,*
>   *For beauty and healing and mirth.*
> *But most for the Child Who on Christmas Day*
>   *Took upon Him our human birth.*"

During the last verse a chiming of bells was heard, and the children came trooping down the stairs, singing the first verse again. When they reached the stage they divided, and a fairy-like figure in silver and green floated out from among them. It was Annie-Laurie in a wide ballet dress of frosted fir-dark green. Her bells were round her waist, and she had a wreath of Christmas roses on her hair. Malony as Father Christmas came through the drawing-room door at the same moment, while David unseen in the drawing-room played the air of their dance upon the piano, and the children, gathered round the real Christmas-tree, hummed it very softly. The genius of Annie-Laurie was, as David had said, unforgettable. The comic antics of Father Christmas, the children in the animal costumes, the brilliantly lighted tree, made a bizarre background against which her delicate loveliness drifted like thistledown against the bright colours of a summer day. And it was the thistledown that captured the attention and held it as though with a spell. Hilary, watching her with an intensity that missed nothing, thought that most touchingly in her dancing did Annie-Laurie express her own personality; her essential childlikeness, her truth and tenderness, even her fear. She was like a child in her unself-consciousness and absolute absorption in what she was doing, and her simple movements had a clean perfection that was like light. The softly chiming little bells, the half-smile on her lips, the arms held out now and then in welcome to the Christmas-tree, peopled the shadows with unseen children. And now and then she would pirouette lightly to one side, as though a puff of rough wind had caught the thistledown and scared it; and then she would hold out her hand to Father Christmas, and he would swing her back to the centre of the stage again. Like a flame aspiring, David had said. Hilary thought it a perfect simile. She was like one of the flames on the tree behind her, as light and delicate, as fragile, and with the same power of lifting one for the moment out of the mud. Hilary always found it impossible to look at a candle-flame and remain gloomy. The shape of it, like tapering hands held palm to palm in faithful prayer, the wavering yet hopeful fight against the darkness, its tiny, loving glow of warmth. It was no wonder that Mother Church, all down the ages, had had such a passion for lighting candles. Go on, Annie-Laurie! he cried out to her wordlessly. Don't stop! Don't stop! But she had stopped. With a final tinkling of fairy bells the thistledown had drifted down to rest. And now she was holding out her hands to the invisible fire and singing the bell song, the children accompanying her very softly. Then, singing still more softly, they trooped noiselessly away, led by Father Christmas, and only Annie-Laurie was left, singing the last verse alone, with the Brother still up there

95

on the stairs. To the music of her own bells she drifted once more round the stage and then up the stairs towards him, and bending towards her he gathered her in as though she were the spirit of all delight. Then the lamp that illumined the alcove went out, and only the Christmas-tree was still shining.

7

The stand-up supper in the kitchen that now followed was uproarious, by reason of relaxed tension . . . For Annie-Laurie's genius had swung them rather high, and they returned to earth with a bang . . . Also the supper – the result of a genius in Nadine and Auntie Rose no less of its kind, and the vigorous rakings of Auntie Rose beneath the counter of her nephew the grocer – was almost pre-war. The guests ate and drank, waited upon by the actors, still in their costumes, until some lingering sense of decency bade them forbear, and even then they were reluctant to go home. Not for years, they said, had they been to such a splendid party; and some of them added softly, and with perfect truth, that not for years had they felt so welcomed, so happy and so hopeful; or so safe. It was not only the family, it was the house. There was something about the house . . .

But they had to go home. Pilgrimages, these days, were unfortunately not the leisured affairs they had been in the old days; they were over tragically soon. One by one they said their reluctant good-byes, went out into the night and drove away slowly, looking back at the lights still streaming from door and windows.

The family and household were left to sit for a little round the fire, devouring the food and drink that was left, and congratulating themselves upon the glorious success of their evening.

"It was worth it," said Nadine, sitting with Mary on her lap, exhausted yet happy. "I'm glad we did it, George."

And she yawned and leaned shamelessly against him, one of her hands in his, the other resting on Ben's shoulder, where he sat on the floor leaning against her knees.

"Taking it by and large, I'm glad we came to the Herb of Grace," said Tommy thickly, through the very last sausage roll, that he was sharing with the cat Smith.

"Everything," murmured Caroline, divested now of her rabbit's mask and curled up sleepily against George's other shoulder, "has turned out just perfect."

"Yes, darling, it has," said Lucilla, her hand in Sally's. "And I'll take a glass of sherry before I go home."

"Mother!" expostulated Margaret, propped against Hilary. "That's your second to-night. You'll have indigestion."

"Since when has sherry given me indigestion?" demanded Lucilla indignantly. "Don't fuss, darling. Up to the top, David."

There was now exactly half an inch of sherry left in the decanter, and David bestowed it upon Annie-Laurie, where she and Malony sat together on the settle by the fire, his hand in hers, Jill and Auntie Rose on the other settle, each with a twin asleep in her arms. It was a queer thing, but an extraordinary lack of reserve seemed to have fallen upon them all. Looking round, he perceived that he, Tommy and the cat Smith, were the only ones who weren't propped against somebody, or holding somebody's hand; Tommy and Smith because of their absorption in food, and he because both sides of Sally had already been appropriated by her father and Lucilla. He sat down on the other side of Annie-Laurie and took her hand gently.

"What about it?" he murmured. "Didn't it come back?"

She looked at him enquiringly.

"The love of it," said David softly. "It came back to me. A little while ago I felt never wanted to be behind the footlights again. To-night I knew it was the only place where I ever really do want to be; apart from in my home with Sally. We belong there, you and I and Malony." He still held her hand, and the firm clasp of it, like the clasp of Sally's arms the other day, told her what a steady strength the friendship of these two would be if she liked to trust to it in the days to come. Beyond her David could feel Malony's passionate encouragement. "Shall we go back, the three of us?"

"Yes," said Annie-Laurie.

Malony let out a deep sigh of relief and helped himself to the last mincepie.

The clock struck a very late hour.

"Those children should be in bed," said Lucilla, regarding the twins. "And so should I. I've finished my sherry. My dears, this has been a very perfect Christmas Day. A sort of heavenly day.

A gift to us, I think. Whatever happens to us all we'll never forget it. Hilary, dear, where did you put my coat? Sally, darling, you're coming back for the night, aren't you? Nadine, my dear, good-night. This is a wonderful home, this Herb of Grace, and to be the mistress of it will be the crown and glory of your life, I shouldn't wonder. Good-night, George, my dear boy. It's very sweet of you, Margaret dear, to be winding me up in this nice scarf, but it's not mine. Good-night, my darling Ben. Good-night, Tommy. Good-night, Caroline. Jill, what a blessing you are! And you too, Auntie Rose. Annie-Laurie, I'm glad I've lived to see you dance . . . Good-night . . . Good-night . . ."

She talked on at random as the Damerosehay party got under way, trying to ease for them all the hard parting from this perfect day . . . Good-night, good-night, parting is such sweet sorrow . . . She kissed the flushed, happy faces of her younger grandchildren, and went out into the night with the two elder ones, David and Sally, one on each side of her to help her down the steps. Sighing with thankfulness, she was tucked up in the back of David's car, with her faithful Hilary and Margaret one on each side of her, and David and Sally in front, where she could gloat upon the sight of them there.

Yet as they drove away under the Christmas stars it was of the two old houses that she was thinking, Damerosehay and the Herb of Grace. Their village helper and her daughter were spending the evening at Damerosehay, to look after Pooh-Bah and the Bastard. When they got home they would find the drawing-room fire burning brightly and the lamps lit, with the two old dogs dozing on the hearth. The house would welcome them and gather them in, and when they had talked a little in front of the fire they would go to bed, and, the spell of this happy day still upon them, sleep deeply and happily, wrapped in its peace. And in the Herb of Grace, too, the lights would go out one by one in the windows, and the sleepers would be at rest. But the houses would not sleep. Lucilla fancied that they would greet each other across the quiet fields and through the night. Each had its long and living history, sap rising in the wood of the old tree to nourish the new branches. And to-morrow would be a new day, and a hard one. But the sap rose from inexhaustible depths, and the spring would come again.

Christmas with
the Elizabethans

Come to your heaven, you heavenly choirs!
Earth hath the heaven of your desires;
Remove your dwelling to your God,
A stall is now his best abode;
Sith men their homage do deny,
Come, angels, all their fault supply.

His chilling cold doth heat require,
Come, seraphins, in lieu of fire;
His little ark no cover hath,
Let cherubs' wings his body swathe;
Come, Raphael, this Babe must eat,
Provide our little Toby meat.

Let Gabriel be now his groom,
That first took up his earthly room;
Let Michael stand in his defence,
Whom love hath linked to feeble sense;
Let graces rock when he doth cry,
And angels sing his lullaby.

ROBERT SOUTHWELL

1

NOT every scholar could go home for Christmas. Rich men who could afford horses, or who had hospitable friends near at hand, could leave Oxford, but for poor men who lived a long way off, the journey over roads knee-deep in mire would have been interminable; they would no sooner have got there than they would have to come back again. And Nicolas, this year, was one of the unhappy ones, for his family went down with the smallpox and he was forbidden to go near them lest the beauty of the son and heir should be tarnished by the pock-marks . . . He was perfectly miserable . . . Giles was dead, Faithful was absorbed by the Leighs, and all his other friends, including Philip Sidney, were of the fortunate band who could go home. He had no one to shoot with, no one to gamble with and no one even to curse with, and not being one of those who find pleasure in solitude he wished he was dead.

And he did not know what to do about Joyeuce. It was no use appealing to her again, he felt, for though good as the angels in heaven, she was at the same time obstinate as the devil himself. She might be stretched upon the rack, as her father had been before her, but she would not change her convictions. Sometimes he thought that he would go straight to Canon Leigh and demand the hand of his daughter in marriage, but then he bethought him of the horror of his Greek and the outrage of his Latin and he suffered from qualms. He was no favourite with Canon Leigh, that he knew well, and he feared that he might be shown the door. Wisdom was required, he felt, and tact and inspiration, and just at the moment he could lay his hands upon none of them. The star that guided his destiny seemed at the moment to have turned its face away from him. He must wait with what patience he could until its gracious beams once more lit his path.

As the month drew on the thought of the stars was in everyone's minds, for Christmas was coming in in the traditional way, with frost and snow upon the ground and such a blaze of constellations in the night sky that it seemed the heavens were hanging low over the earth in most unusual friendliness.

And certainly the city of Oxford was good to look at at this time. By day, under a brilliant blue sky, the gabled roofs and tall chimneys, the towers and spires, took on an added brightness from the tracery of sparkling frost that clung to them; and down below them the narrow streets were bright with the bunchy little figures of snowballing children, happy girls and beaming mothers going shopping with baskets on their arms, dressed in their gaudiest because it was Christmas-time, and laughing men with sprigs of holly in their caps, their faces as rosy as apples from the potations they had partaken of at the taverns and inns in honour of the festive season. The bad smells of the town had been obliterated by the continual snow showers and the hard frost – it would be a different story when the thaw came, but sufficient unto the day is the evil thereof – and delicious festive scents floated out into the streets from open doors and windows; scents of baked meats and roasting apples, of ale and wine, of spices and perfumes and the fragrant wood-smoke from innumerable fires of apple-wood and beech-logs and resinous pine-branches. And at night the city seemed almost as brilliant as the starry sky above. From sheer goodwill doors were left ajar and windows uncurtained, so that bright beams of light lay aslant across the shadows, and the gay groups that thronged the streets carried lanterns that bobbed like fireflies over the trampled snow. The bells rang out continuously and the laughter and clear voices of the children made unceasing music ... And outside the city walls the fields and the low hills lay silent, shrouded in white. The murmur of the streams was hushed by the ice and the willow trees drooped above them without movement.

2

On Christmas Eve, after the sun had set, it all seemed a little intensified; the stars shone yet more brilliantly, the bells rang clearer and sweeter, the firelight seemed ruddier and the laughter and gaiety of the townspeople more contagious. Yet Nicolas, as he strolled idly across Carfax into Cornmarket, felt oddly apart from it all. Used as he was to being always at the centre of whatever excitement was afoot this unusual loneliness was a little frightening. It was because he was so unhappy, he thought, that he felt so lonely. It seemed that suffering of any sort made one feel lonely. He had not suffered before and so he had not discovered this before. He wondered why it should be so, for one was not alone in suffering; the whole world suffered. Perhaps this loneliness had some purpose in the scheme of things. Joyeuce would know. He would like to talk about it to Joyeuce.

With his thoughts so full of her it did not surprise him that he should find himself outside Saint Michael's at the North Gate. He thought that if left to themselves his feet would always now take him either to where she was, or to some place connected with her, for where she was would now always be home, and it was with a sense of homecoming that he turned into the old porch and sat down on the wooden bench.

But it was a rather desolate home-coming. On Midsummer Eve it had been warm and balmy, with the scent of flowers coming on the wind, and Joyeuce had been in his arms, and now it was midwinter and dark and he sat alone on the bench, huddled in his cloak

103

against the cold. Why was one lonely? Where do the feet of the lonely take them? As the body turns always homewards at evening when the crowds are gone, so perhaps there is a country of the spirit to which the spirit turns in desolation. Perhaps one needed to be desolate to find that country, for if one were always happy one would not bother to look for it. Sitting with his eyes shut he remembered that Joyeuce had said something like that when they were together in the meadows. What was that country? . . . Heaven. Fairyland. The land beyond the sunset. The land above the stars where the great multitude which no man can number stands before the throne, clothed with white robes and palms in their hands. The land behind the tree-trunks where Queen Mab and her fairies leave the track of their passing in flowers upon the grass. Raleigh's land, where birds of white and carnation perch in tall cedar trees, where the stones are of gold and silver and the rivers fall down crystal mountains with the noise of a thousand bells clanging together . . . They gave it so many different names, but he supposed it was the same place and that the spirits of some lucky people, saints and little children and dreamers like Raleigh, could follow the road of loneliness until they reached their home . . . But for him, if he opened his eyes, there would be nothing but the darkness of the musty-smelling old porch.

He opened his eyes and found himself gazing straight at a blazing star. His blood tingled through his veins and he felt himself gripped by a strange excitement. Was this his star whose face he had thought was turned away from him? Was it at last pointing upon him graciously? It shone so brightly straight into his eyes that for a moment he put up his hand to cover them. It was surely speaking to him. It said, "Come."

He got up and looked at it intently. It was hanging low over a gabled roof and beneath it was a tall chimney like a pointing finger. He knew that roof and that chimney. They belonged to the Crosse Inn, next door to Tattleton's Tavern where he had supped with Joyeuce . . . Surely once before upon Christmas Eve a star had hung low above the roof of an inn . . . The young man who stepped out of the porch of Saint Michael's at the North Gate into the clamour of Cornmarket was no longer lonely and unhappy. His cap was set at an angle and his cloak was flung back from his shoulders as though the wind took him. He was Saint Nicolas, the Christmas saint, come down from heaven, or Oberon, king of the

104

fays, or a sailor sailing towards the sunset. He was caught up in a fairy-tale and the glory of it swept him along as though his feet were winged.

Yet he was still sufficiently upon the earth to notice that the crowd in Cornmarket had grown considerably while he sat in the porch of Saint Michael's. And they were all going one way. They were all flowing in under the great archway of the Crosse Inn into its galleried courtyard. They, too, were bound for the inn. What was happening at the inn? "The Players!" cried voices in the crowd. "The Christmas Players! The Players are here!"

Bands of travelling players still journeyed up and down the country, playing the old Morality Plays in the inn yards and at the market crosses, and their coming was still one of the events of the year at Oxford. Scholars were strictly forbidden to attend theatrical performances in the inn yards, lest they should catch diseases or have their morals contaminated by the crowd, but this prohibition had never been one to which Nicolas thought it necessary to pay any attention; least of all to-night when he felt himself star-led to his destiny.

He was only just in time, for as he flung himself into the crowd that streamed in beneath the archway the clear note of a trumpet told him that the performance was about to begin. The rough wooden stage was set up in the middle of the courtyard, as though at the heart of the world, lighted at each corner by lanterns and decked with holly and evergreens, with the gaily dressed trumpeter standing upon it with his trumpet to his lips; and all round it surged the jolly Christmas crowd, fighting to get up to the best seats in the gallery that ran round the courtyard, or, failing that, a place on the wooden steps that led up to it, or, failing that, an inch of room in the packed space below. Aldermen and citizens with their fat wives and rosy children were there, apprentices and pretty girls, rogues and vagabonds and dirty little urchins all pushing and kicking and scrambling, but brimming over with humour and goodwill. They knew how to enjoy themselves on Christmas Eve, did these people of Oxford, and they were doing it. Nicolas had hard work to gain the spot which he had marked out as his own, a place against the gallery balustrade where he would get the best possible view of the stage, but he got there at last, wedged himself in between two fat citizens and a horde of apprentices and dirty little boys, and settled down to watch.

105

They were playing an old Nativity play to-night, followed by the story of Saint Nicolas, and he was no sooner in his place than the trumpeter stepped down, the lights in the gallery were hidden, and in a sudden silence, that fell upon the noisy crowd as though the shadow of the angel's wing passed over them, the first figures of the Christmas story stepped upon the stage.

It was very crude and at some other time Nicolas might have been moved to mirth, but he was not so moved to-night, neither he nor a single man, woman or child in that densely packed throng. It was Christmas Eve, and the same stars shone above them as had shone upon the fields of Palestine some fifteen hundred years ago. They sat in a deep and lovely silence, their eyes riveted upon the rough wooden stage where the figures of shepherds moved, and angels whose dresses had shrunk in the wash and whose wings and haloes had become a little battered by so much packing and un-packing, and a Virgin Mary whose blue cloak was torn and whose voice was that of a young English peasant boy who had not so long ago been taken from the plough.

Wedged against the balustrade of the gallery, Nicolas watched and listened in that state of heavenly concentration that leaves the human creature oblivious of himself. He was not conscious any more of the apprentices who pressed upon him, or of the smell of unwashed human bodies, or of his own empty stomach that had been presented with no supper this evening. He was only dimly aware of the crowd as a great multitude that he could not number, watchers in the shadows who had been watching there for fifteen hundred years. The Christmas story itself absorbed him. Though it was so old a story, one that he had known as soon as he was cap-able of knowing anything, it seemed to-night quite new to him. "Glory to God in the highest . . . A child is born." The old words he had heard a hundred times over seemed to cry out with the triumph of new and startling news. The figures that moved before him, Mary with the child in her arms, Joseph and the shepherds, Gabriel and the angels, Herod and the Wise Men, that he had seen so many times pictured in stained-glass windows and on the leaves of missals, moved now in this tiny space at the heart of the crowd as though they had come there for the first time . . . The love of God is with man . . . That, Nicolas knew suddenly, is the news of the far country, the mystery like a nugget of gold that men travel so far to seek, the fact that is stated but not explained,

106

by all the pictures that have been painted and by all the music and the poetry that has been written since the dawn of the world. It was as easy as that, and as difficult.

The Nativity play ended with a flash and a bang as the devil in black tights appeared to fetch away Herod to where he belonged. No one considered this an anticlimax; on the contrary they were all suitably impressed; this might happen to them if they were not careful. They groaned and shivered and were glad when the lanterns which had been hidden beneath cloaks were uncovered and the auditorium shone out into brilliance again. This was the interval between the two performances and a roar of voices broke out as though a river in spate had been let loose. Nicolas found that he, too, was shivering, not with fear but with the very intensity of his feeling, and looked round upon the noisy crowd with sensations that were entirely new. He felt so at one with them. A feeling of superiority had always been one of the most familiar of his pleasures, but now it had entirely gone from him. Those burly perspiring merchants, fat matrons, laughing girls and jolly apprentices, these rogues and vagabonds who pressed about him, seemed as much a part of him as his own body. He did not care that a beery citizen was breathing heavily down the back of his neck or that two filthy little boys were holding themselves steady in a kneeling posture by clinging to his legs. In fact it was a pleasure. He loved them. All of them together were the men whom God was with. He wondered vaguely what he would be feeling like in a few days' time, whether he would be again the old superior sceptical Nicolas ... Perhaps ... Yet he would never be able to forget what he had felt to-night. He prayed God that he would never forget.

The trumpet sounded once more to give warning that the second part of the performance was about to begin. The lanterns in the galleries were hidden again and the roaring voices dropped away to an indistinct murmur, then to silence, and Saint Nicolas stepped upon the stage in a red robe, a long white beard, and a most genial, fatherly expression.

Nicolas de Worde knew the history of his patron saint well – too well – for it had been dinned into his ears by every nurse he had ever had, so it was with a certain detachment that he listened to Saint Nicolas telling the audience the story of his early piety; as a new-born baby plunged into his first bath he had frightened everyone into fits by standing upright in the basin in an attitude of

107

ecstatic adoration. Having thus early shown his aptitude for spiritual things it was but to be expected, so he informed the listening audience, that he should now have attained to his present position of Archbishop of Myra under Constantine the Great. And now, he said, he was upon this cold winter's night waiting to receive a visit from three little boys, children of a friend of his, who were travelling to Athens to school and were to stop at Myra on their way to receive his blessing; for he loved children and cared for their happiness and their welfare more than anything else upon earth. Then he hitched up his red robe, adjusted his white beard, which was slipping a little sideways, waved a hand to the children in the audience and stepped down from the stage. His place was taken by a most villainous looking red-headed man, accompanied by the devil bearing a large wooden tub, who announced in flowing couplets that the stage was now an inn and the red-headed villain the innkeeper, and the tub was intended for the storing of murdered guests to the inn, whom it was the innkeeper's habit to slay for their valuables and later to sell at a profit as pickled pork; children, he said, being juicy and tender, pickled best. A shiver of horror shook the audience, and the children in it squeaked aloud, their squeaks rising to cries of warning as three little boys were seen to be moving out of the shadows towards the lighted stage, two older boys with dark hair and one minute little fair-haired boy clasping a woolly lamb with tin legs in his arms. But the three doomed children took no notice of the warning cries, and failed to see the devil hiding behind the tub. Confidingly they mounted the steps to the stage, and confidingly they piped out, "Innkeeper, Innkeeper, please will you give us lodgings for the night? It is too late now to disturb the good Archbishop. Innkeeper, Innkeeper, is there room for us in the inn?"

"Come in, my little dears," cried the Innkeeper, rubbing his hands together in horrid glee, and suddenly seizing the foremost boy by the scruff of the neck he whipped out a huge long knife and waved it in the air so that it flashed about his head like lightning. The audience moaned and cowered, and afterwards they were all ready to swear that they had actually seen those three shrieking little boys cut up into small pieces and stowed away in the tub; the fair little boy being cut up last and his lamb pitched in after him as a final tit-bit.

Having thus bestowed the little boys to his satisfaction the innkeeper sprinkled salt over them, stirred them about with a wooden spoon, and then settled himself on the floor with his back propped against one side of the tub, the devil being upon the other, for a well-earned night's rest.

But no sooner were their snores ringing out triumphantly upon the frosty air than Saint Nicolas came hurrying along to the scene of action. He had had a nightmare, so he told the audience in breathless couplets as he climbed the steps to the stage, in which the fate of the little boys had been revealed to him by Almighty God with such a wealth of detail that every separate hair upon his white head had stood completely up on end. At this point he reached the innkeeper, fell upon him and shook him with a violence surprising in one so aged. "Villain!" he shouted. "Awake! Repent! The day of judgement is at hand!" It is a well-known fact that a criminal startled out of sleep will, if charged with his crime, acknowledge it, and the innkeeper was no exception to the rule. He awoke, yelped at finding himself shaken by an Archbishop, fell upon his knees and made a full confession. Seeing him so repentant the saintly Archbishop prayed loudly for his forgiveness, banished the now awakened and peevish devil with a wave of the hand, and concentrated on the tub. He made the sign of the cross over it, he prayed over it, he wept over it, he stirred its contents with the wooden spoon and prayed again.

Up popped a small dark head. "Oh, I have had a beautiful sleep," it said.

Up popped a second. "So have I," it said.

Then up popped a golden head and a tiny bell-like voice piped, "And as for me, I have been in Paradise."

The audience rocked and roared and cheered, and their cheering did not cease until the opening of the second scene, when the three little boys, dressed now as three little girls, sat at the feet of a sorrowing father – the red-haired villain only thinly disguised by the addition of a black wig – and were told that because of his poverty they could have no dowries . . . They would in all probability have to be old maids . . . At this awful threat the three little girls wept most pitifully, with their fists thrust into their eyes so that they did not see Saint Nicolas peeping over the edge of the stage, and did not see him take three little parcels from his red robe, throw them in, and then creep away chuckling to himself . . . But they heard the thud as the parcels fell at their feet; they opened their eyes and picked them up; and they were three purses of gold.

The crowd cheered again and Saint Nicolas reappeared and came to the front of the stage, his genial white-bearded face beaming like the rising sun and his red robe shining gloriously in the lantern light. "Go home, all you little girls and boys," he said, "and before you go to sleep tonight put out your little shoes beside your beds, and it may be that Saint Nicolas, who loves little children as dearly today as he did all those hundreds of years ago, will come in the night and put presents for you in them." Then Saint Nicolas beamed and bowed again, and the performance was over.

Nicolas thought afterwards that it had been his detachment that had made him so acutely conscious of the little fair-haired boy with the woolly lamb with the tin legs. He had been one of the principal actors from the beginning. He had trotted at the heels of the shepherds as a little shepherd boy, clasping his lamb. He had knelt at the foot of the manger in Bethlehem as a little cherub, with his halo slipping sideways and the lamb still clasped to his bosom. He had been one of the innocents slaughtered by Herod and had died beautifully in the middle of the stage with the lamb still clasped to his chest. And then, with the lamb still apparently an inseparable part of his person, he had been one of the little boys saved by Saint Nicolas.

And in this story the other Nicolas had noticed him as a person for the first time. Before, he had been part of the Christmas story, one of the gleaming facets of this jewel at the heart of the world, but in this he had been a little boy acting in a play and as such Nicolas had not been able to take his eyes off him; and was surprised at himself, for as a rule he took not the slightest interest in children. The little boy's hair was smooth and fair, and shone in the lantern light as though his shapely little head were encased in a cap of gold. His face, grave and absorbed as he performed to the best of his ability the task that had been set him, was small and delicately heart-shaped, and the little bare feet that pattered so obediently over the hard boards of the stage were shapely and slender as those of a fairy's child. Nicholas could not see his eyes, but he was sure that they were blue, a deep violet blue that would turn to the colour of rain when sorrow clouded them. Surely this was no child of a strolling player . . . If Joyeuce were

110

to have a son, thought Nicolas, with a sudden constriction of the
throat that hurt him, he would have just such a smooth fair head,
just such a flower-like delicacy and grave absorption in his duty
. . . Possessing such a son, thought Nicolas, the cares of father-
hood would not seem heavy.

3

The play had ended and the actors and their stage had disappeared as though by magic. The lights shone out again and the
chattering multi-coloured crowd flowed down the steps from the
galleries and out from the benches beneath them, filling the well
of the courtyard as though wine had been poured into a dark cup.
The stars were still blazing in the square of sky that rested on the
gabled roofs and the Christmas bells were ringing. Nicolas found
himself caught up in the singing crowd and carried bodily towards
the archway that led back into Cornmarket, and the normal world
that he had left behind him when he had stepped into the porch
of Saint Michael at the North Gate. He pushed his way towards
one of the wooden supports of the gallery, seized it and clung
there and let the crowd surge past him, for the time had not come
to return to the normal world. His star had not finished
with him. He knew that as certainly as he had ever known anything.
"Will you come inside and take a tankard of ale, pretty master."
The crowd was thinning and Nicolas looked down into the face
of a pert little serving wench, with lips as red as holly berries and
a snowy apron tied over a flowering gown. Since he had known
Joyeuce he had rather lost his taste for serving wenches, but he
smiled and chucked her under the chin and followed willingly
enough. He was waiting upon events and her invitation seemed
the next one in the sequence.
He followed her through a stout oak door into the main room
of the inn, where a great fire of Christmas yule logs blazed on the
hearth and was reflected in a ruddy glow in the faces of some two
score of good citizens who were drinking ale, laughing, shouting
and singing in an orgy of good fellowship well befitting the festive
seasons. The air was thick with the fumes of the ale and the smoke

111

from the fire and it was impossible for even the loudest-voiced to make himself heard under a shout. Yet through the haze there loomed the great bulk, and above the tumult there sounded the bellow, of Master Honeybun, mine host of the Crosse Inn, as he heaved himself this way and that refilling tankards, quelling disputes and getting the best of every argument with a playful blow upon the chest and a pat upon the head that were like to be the death of those so favoured. But in spite of his multifarious duties he espied Nicolas and greeted him with a roar of welcome like to the roaring of a hundred bulls, for Nicolas was of the quality, and the quality was more likely to be found at the tavern next door than at the humble Crosse.

Nicolas, his sense of unity with all mankind still powerfully with him, felt himself instantly at home. He seized the proffered tankard and was soon laughing and talking with these ruddy-faced gentlemen as though he had known them all his life. The players were among them, he discovered, no longer angels and shepherds but English vagabonds of the road with weather-tanned faces and worn jerkins. But they showed themselves to be artists, messengers of another country, by little eccentricities of dress and manner that aroused the mockery of the rollicking apprentices drinking beside the fire; one wore a gay yellow sash on his shabby jerkin, one whose clothes were in rags, brandished a perfumed handkerchief of crimson silk, another wore heavy gold rings in his ears as though he were a seaman, and all of them had deeper voices than ordinary men, more graceful bodies, and gesticulating fingers and sparkling eyes that could convey in half a second the meaning or emotion that an ordinary man could not have expressed in twenty minutes of laborious speech; but Nicolas in his new mood found their unconscious striving for beauty and their lovely ease of communication matter for reverence rather than mirth.

"That is a lovely child of yours who played tonight," he said to him of the rags and the perfumed handkerchief, a slim boy who had played the part of the angel Gabriel.

"Which child, master?" asked Gabriel.

"The fair child. The one with a woolly lamb."

"Oh, that child. He's not one of ours. He's a gypsy's child who is staying at the inn. Our boy is sick and this child took his place. A clever child; it took only a couple of hours to teach him his part." A wicked grin spread over the face of the angel Gabriel and his slim fingers gripped Nicolas's arm. "Come and let me introduce you to his father."

The ruddy apprentices by the fire surrounded a group of older men, rough men from the poorer part of the town, a travelling tinker and a few gypsies, and into this group the angel Gabriel propelled Nicolas. "Here, Sampson," he cried, "here's a gentleman would like to meet the father of the infant prodigy."

Nicolas stared in amazement at the drunken giant of a creature who confronted him. He looked at the great broad shoulders, the dark matted beard, the coarse crimson features and the blood-shot green eyes that twinkled at him rather angrily, and in spite of himself he recoiled a little at the sight of the man's great hairy chest showing through his torn jerkin, and the reek of drink and sweat that assailed his fastidious nose. The recoil and astonishment were momentary, but they were seen, and a huge red hand shot out and gripped Nicolas by the front of his exquisite leaf-green doublet.

"So my young cockerel thinks I can't be the father of that damned child, does he?" bellowed Sampson in a maudlin indignation, shaking Nicolas as a terrier a rat. "The little whey-faced puling brat! So I'm not capable of fathering it, eh?"

"I never said so," remarked Nicolas breathlessly, but with humour. "I consider your worship capable of fathering any number of brats." His feet slipped on the floor, and his teeth clashed together as he rocked this way and that in the ruffian's grip, but he managed to continue, his eyes merry in his empurpled face. "It is merely that in the case I do not consider the family likeness very remarkable."

A great roar of laughter went up, for it seemed this was not the first time that the paternity of Sampson had been called in question, and it seemed this particular subject was a sore point with him for he let go of Nicholas and hit out with blind rage at the circle of mocking faces that hedged him in.

"Eh, Sampson!" shouted the tinker, a great bully of a man almost as vast as Sampson himself. "Can you give a name to the father of that boy? Can you give a name to the father of the child Sara's brought to bed with at this moment? Cuckold! Cuckold!"

Suddenly the affair that had begun as a coarse jest turned ugly. Sampson hit the tinker and the tinker hit Sampson. The laughter turned to a tumult of shouts and curses. Mine host bore down upon them and with one huge hand plucked Nicolas out of the hubbub as he would have lifted a chestnut from the fire.

And then somehow the whole crowd of them were out in the courtyard, under the starry sky, and there was a fight on. Sampson and the tinker, roaring drunk and mad with rage, were fighting each other in the centre of a ring of men whose faces were alight with a bestial eagerness to witness blood and suffering that was hideous to see. Now and then they yelled encouragement to the fighters and their cries were animal cries. Lanterns were held aloft that they might see the better, and the stars looked down.

Nicolas, with the boy who had played Gabriel grave-eyed beside him, stood on the outskirts of the crowd, and he felt sick. He had witnessed fights before, and always with keen enjoyment. He had fought himself, and felt the better for it. He had even attended several hangings and derived pleasure from the titillations of horror that ran up and down his spine on those occasions. But tonight he felt sick. Only a short while ago, on the very spot where those two brutes were fighting, the loveliest story in all the world had been enacted. Only a short while ago, in this very place, he had learnt so to love the men around him, that they had seemed a part of his own body . . . And now, because he still loved them, he had to stand here and watch the degradation of his body . . . "*Deus, propitius esto mihi peccatori,*" he murmured. The boy beside him looked at him, uncomprehending, but the sorrow in his eyes was an Amen and the stars seemed to press down a little lower, brighter and more pitiful.

It was soon over. The tinker was the less drunk of the two, and he got the best of it. A yell came from the crowd as Sampson crashed over backwards, then a sudden silence in which they could hear the voices of the Christmas waits singing far off in the town, and then an outbreak of shocked incredulous murmurings.

"What has happened?" demanded Nicolas, and pressed a little nearer.

Sampson was dead. He had fallen with his head on a projecting cobblestone and his magnificent great body was now as worthless as a heap of rubbish. Nicolas caught one glimpse of him, with his head lying in a pool of blood and his sightless eyes turned towards the stars, and then turned away in misery and horror . . . For he had done this . . . With a word spoken in jest he had started the whole tragedy. And somehow he had rather liked that coarse bully.

114

There had been something attractive about him; his rage had been swift and splendid, as elemental as a thunderstorm or the onslaught of a tiger, and his twinkling green eyes had stirred some vague memory in Nicolas that was as sweet as it was elusive. He was sorry that the man was dead.

4

They picked him up and carried him away and gradually the sobered crowd dispersed and went home. Loneliness possessed the innyard. There were no lights but the few that shone from the inn and the stars that glittered overhead, no sounds but the soft chiming of the bells and the faraway singing of the waits. But Nicolas still lingered. There seemed nothing that he could do, but he still lingered, pacing up and down over the soiled and trodden snow, his cloak wrapped tightly about him and his heart heavy.

A touch on his arm made him look round. It was the pretty little serving wench, shivering with the cold, her face white and frightened.

"Yes?" encouraged Nicolas, but she seemed to have nothing to say, and only huddled herself the closer in the shawl she had thrown about her shoulders.

"What ails you, my dear?" asked Nicolas again, and turned up her face to the starlight with one finger beneath her chin.

At this she recovered, and her dimples peeped. "I must tell her," she confided, "and, sure as I live, I've not the courage."

"Tell whom?" asked Nicolas.

"Sara. Sampson's wife. Sampson brought her into Oxford two days ago, for she was taken very bad and he wanted to get the physician to her."

"You mean that she is here? At the inn?"

"Yes. She often comes here to amuse the company with her fortune telling, and so she came here in her trouble and Master Honeybun took pity on her. He's a kind man, Master Honeybun. We made a bed for her in a part of the stable that we don't use. The babe died yesterday, and now she's likely to die herself."

"Then need you tell her?" asked Nicolas.

"Master Honeybun said I was to," she said, and looked down, twisting her shawl round her fingers.

"I'll tell her," said Nicolas suddenly. She looked up again, her eyes two round ohs of amazement, and Nicolas himself hardly knew what possessed him. Afterwards he thought it was a sense of responsibility for the death in the innyard that drove him to make what amends he could.

The girl was so thankful to have him relieve her of her duty that she allowed him no time to change his mind. She hurried him forthwith across the courtyard to a door on the far side. "In there," she whispered.

Nicolas lifted the latch and walked in. He was at the far end of the great inn stable, in a little space partitioned off from the rest by a rough curtain. A lantern hung from the raftered cobwebby ceiling and a small fire in a brazier brought a little warmth into the bitter air. A broad rough bed spread with old blankets and soft hay stood against the wall and in the glow of the lantern and firelight he could see the outline of a woman lying upon it, with another smaller figure curled up beside her. He stopped, his heart beating, aware that death was here, too, not the sudden death that had struck like lightning in the courtyard outside but an invisible brooding spirit whose presence seemed to set this little room at a great distance from the rest of the world. For a moment all memory fell away from Nicolas. He, this woman, the unseen child and the angel of death were alone together, enclosed in a little circle of light that hung like a star between heaven above and the unseen earth far away beneath them. When it was shattered the four of them would go their ways to where they belonged, but for the moment they were alone together in a unity so deep that understanding would need few words.

The hay on the far side of the bed rustled softly and a little gold head popped up. Nicolas, moving forward, found himself looking straight into a pair of blue eyes, a deep violet blue that would turn to the colour of rain when sorrow clouded them . . . Somehow he had thought that this child would have eyes like Joyeuce . . . He smiled and a merry little answering smile tilted up the corners of the child's mouth and set sparks in his eyes. He seemed to like this visitor and he turned and poked his mother with his toy lamb that she, too, might wake up and like him.

She stirred and moaned a little, a sound that was half question

116

and half plaint, and Nicolas came to her side and stood looking down upon her. He had expected to see a rough-looking woman, the feminine counterpart of the man who had died outside, and he was amazed at what he saw. Sara was dying, and sickness had robbed her of much of her beauty, yet even the remnant of it roused his homage. He bowed his head as he looked at the fine bones of her face, showing like ivory beneath the tightly stretched skin, at the mass of night-dark hair and the deep eyes, clouded with mystery, that looked up into his.

"So it was he who died outside!" she whispered.

"Yes," said Nicolas. As he had thought, few words were needed.

She moved her head a little restlessly on the pillow, but she gave no sign of grief. Perhaps, thought Nicolas, she had not loved him, or perhaps she was too near death to have any care now for anything that might happen on earth. But even as he thought this he knew he was wrong, for she turned her head and looked at him as though he himself were of extreme importance to her. She looked at the gallant picture that he made, standing straight and slim in his fine doublet and hose of dark green, the colour of holly leaves, with his scarlet-lined cloak flung back from his shoulders. In reverence for her he held his cap in his hands and the lantern light shone upon his crisp dark hair and the face with the mocking eyebrows, smooth girlish skin and strong mouth that in gravity could look so lovely. She looked at him appealingly, hungrily, as though he were not only a man who could help her but a symbol of something that she had intensely desired. She put out a hand and felt the fine stuff of his cloak as he stood beside her. "I wanted him to be like you," she whispered. "That was why I did it."

Nicolas did not understand, but he saw that she had something more to say to him and he bent over her, smiling reassuringly into her eyes. He felt no fear, now, of sorrow and death, only desire to succour. "I will do anything I can to help you," he said, slowly and clearly so that she should understand.

"Where do you come from?" She spoke so low that her whisper was a mere breath.

"From Christ Church," said Nicolas.

She made a little motion of her head towards the boy beside her. "Then take the child with you. Take him back where he belongs," she said, and sighed in relief and weariness as her eyes closed and her head rolled weakly back into the dented hollow on the pillow.

"Where?" asked Nicolas, but even as he asked her he knew it was no use. Her dark lashes, lying on the dark hollows below her eyes, trembled a little and then lay motionless. He knew that they would not lift again. He put his fingers gently on her wrist and felt the tiny flutter of the pulse, and even at his touch it was still.

He straightened himself and held out his arms to the little boy who was kneeling up in the hay staring at him. He had thought there would be tears and protestations, but there were none. Grave-eyed and obedient the child, too, held out his arms, his lamb clasped by a hind leg in one hand, and let himself be lifted across his mother's body.

As Nicolas, with the boy in his arms, lifted the latch of the door, he could have fancied that he heard the flutter of dark wings. The little circle of light in which the four of them had hung above the earth was shattered now and they were going their different ways, two to death and two to life.

The girl was still lingering in the courtyard and Nicolas paused only to send her inside to Sara before he made tracks for home. Now and then, as he strode down Cornmarket and across Carfax into South Street, he looked down at the boy. The little face looked very pallid in the starlight but there was always the flash of an answering smile when Nicolas looked at him, and his golden hair shone like a gallant cap of gold. His bare feet and legs were cold as ice and he was shivering, but he made no complaint. Nicolas, who had thought he did not care for children, held the little body close to his own to warm it and tucked his cloak round more firmly. He had no doubt at all as to where to take this child . . . To Joyeuce, for a Christmas present.

5

And meanwhile Joyeuce sat in front of the parlour fire with the children grouped around her, and her father and Great-Aunt in their big chairs one on each side, and listened to Faithful laboriously reading aloud from Foxe's *Book of Martyrs*. It was long past the children's bedtime but they had not wanted to go to bed and she

118

had let them stay up. Even the little ones felt the sorrow that hung over the house, this first Christmas after Giles's death, and they shrank from their dark cold bedroom. It was more cheerful in the parlour, where the log fire sparkled and crackled and a most extravagant array of candles shone all round the room.

But even then it was not particularly cheerful, for Great-Aunt, who had the indigestion, kept heaving great sighs, their father sat with his head sunk on his breast, rousing himself heroically now and then to make forced cheerful remarks that were more depressing than silence, and Joyeuce stitched away at her embroidery with a sort of desperation, as though she dared not let herself think. Grace, the boys and the twins stared sadly and a little sullenly into the fire, for they felt that happiness was their right at this season and they could not but feel bitter against the fate that had snatched it away from them. Diccon sat curled up on the floor at Joyeuce's feet, his curly head resting against her knees, and was still a prey to his secret sorrow, his poppy mouth drooping and his green eyes staring mournfully at the tips of his little pointed scarlet shoes. All the rest of the family were in black but he wore elfin green, with the scarlet shoes and a knot of cherry ribbons at his breast. Sitting there in the middle of them, so bright and fair to see, Joyeuce thought he was like the spark of unconquerable hope at the heart of sorrow. It did her good to look at him, even though he was so sorry a little boy.

All the time, muted by the closed windows and the drawn curtains, they could hear the bells ringing and the waits, bands of poor scholars who were allowed by the Vice-Chancellor to sing and beg at the houses of the rich, singing as they passed up and down the snowy streets. Sometimes a band of them passing up Fish Street would stop and sing under their window, and then their singing was hard to bear. "Unto us a Child is born. Unto us a Son is given." To-night the words seemed nothing but a mockery.

6

It was after one such visitation that Faithful decided he had better read aloud to his adopted family, and fetched his beloved *Book of Martyrs*. It had accompanied him through all the many changes and chances of his own life and he had always found it an unspeakable comfort. Not only was the example of the martyrs so uplifting, but it was really impossible to think of one's own woes when absorbed in blood-curdling descriptions of other people being burnt alive. There is nothing like the troubles of other people to distract one's attention from one's own.

But to-night, knowing Joyeuce to have a squeamish stomach and Great-Aunt's indigestion to be by no means a thing of the past, he concentrated upon the milder stories of Master Foxe. Finally, he read them the account of the riot in Saint Mary's church at Oxford in the year 1536, when Bloody Mary sat upon the throne of England and persecution was at its height. A certain poor heretic, a Cambridge M.A., was sent to Oxford that he might recant openly, bearing his faggot in the church of Saint Mary the Virgin upon a Sunday, in front of the whole congregation of Doctors, Divines, Citizens and Scholars. It was felt, apparently, that to make a fool of himself before Oxford University would, for a Cambridge man, be the final humiliation; it was thought, too, that it would give pleasure to Oxford to see him do it, and would be a great warning to such of the scholars as might be heretically inclined . . . The church was packed to the doors and in the middle stood the Cambridge heretic with his faggot on his shoulder.

But no sooner was Doctor Smith, the preacher, well away into his sermon, denouncing the poor heretic with the full force of his lungs, than from the High Street outside came a cry of "Fire! Fire!" Somebody's chimney was on fire, it afterwards transpired, but the crowded congregation had but one thought; sympathetic heretics and demons had fired the church. "Fire! Fire!" they yelled, and in the space of five minutes pandemonium had broken out, the panic-stricken congregation fighting like wild beasts to get out of the church. "But," said Master Foxe in his narrative, "such was the press of the multitude, running in heaps together, that the more they laboured the less they could get out. I think there was never such a tumultuous hurly-burly, rising so of nothing, heard of before, so that if Democritus, the merry philosopher, had beholden so great a number, some howling and weeping, running up and down, trembling and quaking, raging and gasping, breathing and sweating, I think he would have laughed the heart out of his body."

Now "in this great maze and garboyle" there were only two who

120

kept their heads, the heretic himself, who hastened to cast his faggot off his shoulders and bring it down hard upon the head of a monk who stood near by, breaking the head to his great satisfaction, and a little boy who had climbed up on top of a door to be out of the way of this seething horde of lunatic grown-ups.

Sitting up there on top of the door, the little boy wondered what he should do, for though he was not frightened he thought it would be rather nice to go home. Then he saw a great burly monk who was fighting his way to the nearest exit with more success than most. He wore his monk's habit and had a big cowl hanging down his back and he was coming quite close to the little boy. The urchin waited until the monk was right underneath him and then he slithered down from the top of the door and "prettily conveyed himself" into the monk's cowl.

The monk got out and made tracks for home, and being a very burly man, and the little boy being such a very tiny little boy, he did not at first notice anything out of the ordinary. But as he turned from High Street into Cornmarket it struck him that his cowl felt heavier than usual, and he shook his shoulders in some annoyance . . . Then there came a little whispering voice in his ear . . . Terror seized him like an ague, and he was more frightened than he had been in the church, for he had a guilty conscience and he had no doubt at all that one of the demons who had fired the church had jumped straight into his cowl. "In the name of God, and All Saints," he cried, "I adjure thee, thou wicked spirit, that thou get thee hence."

But there was no crashing of thunder, no searing of blue flame as the demon took his departure, only a little voice that whispered, "I am Bertram's boy. Good master, let me go." And then the long-suffering cowl suddenly gave way at the seams and the little boy fell out and ran away home as fast as his legs could carry him.

7

It was a cheerful story and everyone felt the better for it except Diccon, and Diccon most unaccountably began to cry. He did not roar and bellow, he just sobbed noiselessly in that devastating way he had when his heart was breaking. Everybody was most upset and gathered round to soothe and comfort, while Joyeuce, pressing his curly head against her knee, implored him to say what ailed him.

"I want that little boy," he whispered at last. "I want that little boy. I want him now."

As it had been with the ruby in the window of the aurifabray, so it was with the little boy; he must have what he wanted or he could no longer support life. Why, he seemed to ask, was I born into this cruel world? Whose fault was it that earthly life was given to me? Why was I dragged from the realms of celestial glory, where the angels gave me the comets to play with, to this earth where I stretch out my empty hands in vain for my heart's desire?

"But you can't have the little boy, my poppet," explained Joyeuce. "He's only a little boy in a story."

Diccon knelt up on the floor in front of her, his hands laid on her knees and his tear-stained face raised imploringly to hers. "He's a real little boy," he hiccuped, "and Diccon must have him."

"He was a real little boy years ago, when Master Foxe wrote that story," explained Canon Leigh, "but he is not a little boy now."

Diccon shook his head and choked, the tears running out of his eyes and dripping off his pointed chin on to his cherry ribbons in a positive cascade. "A real boy," he insisted, "just so big." And he stretched out his arms to show his own minute height. "Just so big as me. He has fair hair. Diccon wants him." And again he raised his imploring face to Joyeuce who loved him and always gave him what he wanted.

Joyeuce was near tears herself. Was this his sorrow? Was he so lonely? The twins were older than he and he had no one but Tinker to play with. She had heard that lonely children often invented imaginary playmates to be with them. Perhaps he had imagined his little fair-haired boy and was heartbroken that he could not turn him into flesh and blood. She shook her head helplessly and Diccon, his hands still resting on her knees, shook her lap almost angrily . . . It was Christmas Eve and seated upon it she should have had for him a little fair-haired boy.

The door opened and they all looked round in astonishment. Standing there smiling at them was the gallant figure of Nicolas de Worde, dressed like Diccon in the Christmas colours of scarlet and green and carrying a little fair-haired boy clasping a woolly lamb with tin legs. He walked across to them and deposited his burden in Joyeuce's lap.

There was a moment's pause of utter astonishment and then a chorus of ecstatic cries.

"It's Baa!" shrieked the twins and Will and Thomas. "The little boy has Baa!"

"It's Joseph!" shouted Faithful.

"It's a little Christmas angel," cried Grace.

"Tilly-vally! Angel indeed!" ejaculated Great-Aunt in some displeasure. "Some filthy child out of the streets!"

Diccon, with the tears still wet on his cheeks, clasped Baa's tail with one hand and Joseph's left foot with the other and laughed and laughed, his dimples peeping and the whole of his pink tongue exposed to view, while Joseph, curled up on Joyeuce's lap as though it were his proper home, seized his foster-brother's dark curls with both hands and laughed too.

As for Joyeuce and Canon Leigh, bewildered, incredulous, yet with a queer new joy struggling through their bewilderment, they found themselves gazing down into a little face that was the exact counterpart of that of the wife and mother they had both adored.

Nicolas leant against the mantelpiece, his eyes upon Joyeuce. "I was lonely and unhappy," he told her. "And so I went up into the town. And so I found him at the inn." Her eyes fell before his and he said no more, but watched the family group with smiling satisfaction. Without understanding yet what he had done, he knew that he had done something good, and something, too, that would bring him into the very heart of this family. Moreover he found the picture of Joyeuce with Joseph in her arms as satisfying as he had expected it to be.

The Christmas bells were still ringing and the waits were singing under the window. "Unto us a Child is born. Unto us a Son is given." There was no longer any mockery in the Christmas message.

123

Christmas with the Children

1

IT seemed to Jocelyn in anticipation that the hours until tea, Felicity and the story would be a howling wilderness of impatience, but it proved not to be so, for on his first Christmas Day since his own childhood that he spent with children he found himself recapturing a glamour that he thought had vanished completely.

For years Christmas Day had been for him a day when one ate too much so as not to disappoint cook, stifled a great many yawns and made a lot of silly jokes to hide an inner sadness that was both a lament for romance and belief that had faded and a vague sense of unsatisfied expectation.

But to-day, in company with Henrietta and Hugh Anthony, romance and belief and satisfaction were vicariously his again. He stood in the cathedral during morning service with the children one on each side of him and sang, "Hark the herald angels sing," aware that Henrietta, whose eyes were beaming with joy and whose muff was swinging from side to side like a pendulum as her figure swayed in time to the music, was seeing a starlit sky full of wings and a manger with a baby in it, and seeing them with her. Hugh Anthony on his other side was singing the tune a semitone flat with the full force of his lungs, but he looked happily distrait and his left hand was plunged deep in his pocket; it clutched, Jocelyn knew, the knife with two blades, a corkscrew and a thing for getting stones out of one's horse's hoofs (if one happened to have a horse that got into this predicament) that had been in his stocking . . . Jocelyn seemed to feel the delightful outside roughness of the knife against the fingers of his own left hand and knew the sensation of satisfaction that it brought.

Beyond Henrietta was Grandmother. She was sitting down with her eyes shut because she was tired with the Christmas preparations, but her mind was thankfully fixed upon the face of God made man. She was too practical, of necessity too concerned with the details of daily living, to be romantic in her religion like

Henrietta, or quixotic like Grandfather, but her faith was the strength of her strong-minded life.

As she sat there she was in that state of detachment and tranquil concentration that brings one mind very near to another, and Jocelyn could distinctly feel her sober certainty reaching him through Henrietta's stars and wings, as though what she and her like believed was the thread strung through the lovely bead of things that Henrietta and her like imagined, giving them form and value.

During the Dean's sermon Jocelyn's thoughts wandered, for the Dean's remarks never brought conviction to sceptical minds . . . Yet today he was almost persuaded by the silence of others, Grandfather, Grandmother. Henrietta and the small, thin Bishop who sat opposite him on his throne. It struck him as he meditated that if these four, whom he held to be his superiors, were believers, then their belief was more likely to be true than his own unbelief. The Bishop, a distinguished scholar with a mind far more able to test and probe than his, Grandfather with his artist's perceptiveness, Grandmother, with her everyday common sense and Henrietta, sensitive and romantic, playing so happily with the toys of religion and finding reality through them, had arrived through their different avenues of approach at the same place and who was he, in the face of their evidence, to say that the place did not exist?

2

The Christmas dinner, too, seemed because of the children to take on a new value. The turkey was a noble bird, brought overnight by Father Christmas in his sledge, and the flaming plum-pudding, that they had stirred laboriously in its earlier stages, was alight with the wishes they had wished as the spoon went round.

And then came the ecstasy of present giving, and then a short walk to assist the processes of digestion, and then, at last, it was tea-time and they were sitting in the drawing-room and waiting for Mrs. Jameson and Felicity.

"I'll go down and meet them," said Jocelyn with extreme casualness, as soon as the garden door was heard to click.

"Me too!" yelled the children, but Grandfather quite unaccountably seized one by the slack of his jersey and the other by her sash and seemed not to want to be left.

Jocelyn went downstairs and out into the garden. It was quite dark, with stars burning frostily, and the lantern that Felicity carried swung very gently on its chain, backwards and forwards, as Henrietta's muff had swayed in church, accompanying her singing, as the pendulum of the clock moves, measuring time, as the tides swing in time to the measured movement of the moon . . . And love too has its rhythm, its parting and its reunions, its time of waiting and its times of movement . . . And love to-night was on the move. Jocelyn standing still, and Felicity coming a little nearer with every swing of her lantern, both seemed to themselves to be drawing together without any volition of their own.

They were suddenly together in the lighted hall without any very clear idea as to how they had got there. As Jocelyn sat her down on the oak chest and took off her fur coat and goloshes Felicity chattered as a bird sings, joy being with her a thing that must be instantly expressed lest she burst, but Jocelyn did not speak, it being with him a thing that silenced. He took as long as possible over the removal of each golosh so that he could quietly verify all Felicity's high-lights . . . Her sunflower hair and tawny eyes, her laugh and her gaiety were mercifully unchanged . . . The velvet frock that reached to her ankles was a warm brown and she was not so unaware of her own charms as to forget to lift it a little now and then so that her orange satin petticoat could be enjoyed by an admiring world.

"I can't undo this safety-pin," complained Mrs. Jameson from the shadows.

Their joy had been like four walls that shut out all remembrance of an outside world but at the sound of her voice they jumped up in compunction and hurried to help her, unwrapping the five white shawls that hid the glory of her festival snow-white velvet dress and icy, sparkling diamonds.

The two women made a strange contrast as they followed Jocelyn and his lighted candle up the dark stairs, the one looking as though she were carved out of the same wintry grief that had paralysed her mind and the other in her brown and orange as palpitant with life as the crocuses when they spear their way through spring earth.

"Henrietta says you're going to tell us a story," said Mrs. Jameson.

"A story?" said Felicity. "What story?"

Jocelyn on the top stair turned to face her and their eyes met. Between them the candle-flame danced like a live thing, reflected in two pin-points of excitement in Felicity's eyes.

3

Henrietta never forgot that Christmas tea-party. Grandmother had lit twelve wax candles all round the drawing-room and there were twenty tiny candles on the small Christmas-tree that stood in the centre of the tea-table. The room seemed full of stars and all the stars were singing, like those that sang to the young-eyed cherubim when Lorenzo and Jessica sat on the bank where the moonlight slept . . . At least Henrietta thought they sang but perhaps what she heard were the bells ringing for the evensong that no one had time to go to on Christmas Day because of the cake having to be cut.

Hugh Anthony cut it, with Jocelyn applying a little pressure in the background, and it was all that it should be, white icing and fruity inside and all, though the latter was a little plainer than was customary because of Henrietta's weak digestion.

It struck Henrietta as she ate, biting it all up very carefully as Grandmother bade her, that they were all looking extraordinarily beautiful, Grandmother in her lace cap, Mrs. Jameson in her diamonds, Felicity with her lovely petticoat, Hugh Anthony with his flaming hair and Jocelyn smiling with his eyes in the way that she liked. Even Grandfather looked beautiful, with his snowy beard, and his bald head reflecting the candlelight so merrily . . . How safe they were, she thought. In this warm, cosy place nothing could hurt them . . . Outside it was cold and frosty but the cold could not get in to them.

The choirboys' annual Christmas party always took place on
Holy Innocents' Day and was a great event, for the entire Close,
as well as the choirboys, came to it. It took place at the Palace
and not at the Deanery because the Bishop liked giving parties for
small boys and Lady Lavinia did not. It was regarded by all as
an act of reparation made to the choirboys by Torminster. Other
small boys tasted the joys of leisure at Christmas-time but these
sweet innocents were obliged by the exigency of their profession
to work harder than ever. Christmas Eve, Christmas Day, Saint
Stephen's Day, Saint John the Evangelist's and Innocents' Day
followed close upon each other's heels with that singular lack of
proportion in the matter of festivals displayed by Mother Church,
who might surely have spaced them out a bit, and on all of them
the poor children had to attend at the cathedral twice daily and
shout themselves hoarse in anthems, carols, hymns and special
psalms . . . It was hard.

But the party, a gargantuan one, made up for it, and how fitting
it was, said those who never came into close contact with the
choirboys, that it should take place on Holy Innocents' Day . . .
All those sweet little boys with their round cherubic faces, guile-
less eyes and clean white collars . . . It was noticeable that those,
such as the organist and the headmaster of the choir-school, who
did come into contact with the cherubs, never expressed an opinion
on the matter.

The party began soon after three o'clock and lasted for five hours.

Henrietta and Hugh Anthony began dressing for it at twelve
o'clock. They wrestled with underclothes from twelve till one,
when they had lunch with overalls over the underclothes, and
from two onwards, with the assistance of the entire household,
they coped with the parts that show.

The underclothes of the young at that period were no light
matter. The amazing amount of heat that is stored within the
bodies of little children was not perhaps realized and it was considered that they must be kept warm. Henrietta wore immensely
thick woollen combinations, a woollen liberty-bodice, a woollen
vest, a flannel petticoat, a silk petticoat and finally her winter party

frock of blue velvet trimmed with fur. Hugh Anthony was not quite so overburdened with clothes, though his pants were tremendous, because Grandmother did not consider the bodies of the male young to be so tender as those of the female of the species, but his brown velvet suit with its frilly collar nearly drove him mad.

"I look a fool," he growled to Henrietta. "Why can't I wear Etons?"

"Grandmother says you can when you've worn out that," said Henrietta. "And I think you look sweet . . . Like Bubbles."

Hugh Anthony made a rude noise in his throat and hurled his shoes across the floor.

Yet when it was time to go his philosophic temperament had come to his rescue. What cannot be helped must be endured and he was not without hope that some untoward accident at the party might ruin his detested suit for ever.

Grandfather, Grandmother and the children started off together, the children carrying their party shoes in brown holland bags and all of them swathed to the eyes in coats and shawls and mufflers.

For it had turned very cold. The stars that had shone so brightly on the evening of Christmas Day had been the first torchbearers in a procession of sparkling days and nights. Every morning the sun rose out of a glowing bed of fire and slowly climbed a sky of cold, brilliant blue. There was not much warmth in the sun, though he was so bright and gay, and he seemed a little aloof from the earth that loved him, but at midday he unbent a little and graciously touched the frosted trees with his fingers so that each grey twig was strung with diamonds. Then he withdrew again, flinging as final largesse an orange glow like a veil over the roofs of the city and painting the shadows of the elm-trees deep blue across the snow. Close at his heels the stars came marching and the moon blazed over the cathedral towers like a round shield carried on the arm of a giant.

As the four of them crossed the Green the world was at that moment of pause between day and night. Henrietta had already noticed that there was always a haunting, unearthly beauty about this time of transition and that it was very varied. On grey, stormy days it was a gradual strange darkening that blotted out familiar shapes and divorced sound from its cause in a way that terrified. On sunshiny summer days it was a gradual intensification of colour and scent that came near to ecstasy. On other days

132

it was a sudden blaze as of fire, on others a hard, bright flatness as though the earth was a painted picture.

It was this last today. The bare branches of the elm-trees were strokes of paint laid on sharply against the primrose wash of the sky. The cathedral towers stood out hard and black against the sheeted gold of the west and the snow-covered grass stretched smooth and pure. Here and there a sudden speck of colour burned as the painter's brush touched the flat surfaces; an orange square of lamplight leaping out in a dark house, a flash of colour on the snow as a robin hopped across it, a gleam of blue and green as a child in a gay muffler ran home from school. As always on these days when the earth is a painted picture it was very still; the cawing of a rook and the chime of a bell fell sharply as pebbles dropped in a deep well.

They crossed the Green and came to the market-place, then turned to their left under the great archway that led to the Palace. Here they were overtaken by Mrs Jameson and Felicity, accompanied by Jocelyn, who had found someone to take charge of the shop till closing time . . . Grandfather had noticed before that when Felicity was in Torminster Jocelyn found it perfectly easy to leave the shop but when she was not it was a sheer impossibility.

They crossed the drawbridge and passed under the portcullis into the courtyard beyond. In front of them the old walls of the Palace rose majestically, quiet and withdrawn in the evening light, only the windows lighted. They paused to look at it for a moment, for it was very lovely, then scurried hastily to one side as the Dean's carriage and pair swept by them bearing Lady Lavinia in grey velvet, with a purple boa, and the Dean in a new top hat.

"Do they want to run over us?" inquired Jocelyn with irritation.

"We're not carriage folk," explained Felicity.

5

There was no need to ring at the front door, for it stood hospitably wide open, and Peppercue and Barleycorn, who always assisted the Bishop's decrepit old butler Baggersley on festive occasions, were hovering about to help them off with their coats. The huge stone-floored, vaulted hall was very cold and they parted with their wraps reluctantly. "There are two fires lit in the gallery," whispered Baggersley, with intent to cheer, and totteringly led the way up the lovely carved staircase.

Baggersley was very old, looked like a tortoise and was not of the slightest use. His dress clothes, green with age, hung loosely upon his withered old body and he could not now remember anyone's name, but suggestions that he should be pensioned off were not favourably received by him so the Bishop kept him on . . . "A disgrace to the place," the Dean said. "A – er – disgrace."

"Archdeacon Jones and family," quavered Baggersley at the gallery door and the Fordyces, Mrs. Jameson, Felicity and Jocelyn trooped smilingly in.

The Bishop, whose sight was poor, had a moment of confusion until Grandfather whispered hoarsely, "'Smee, Bishop," when he identified them with relief. The shortness of Baggersley's memory, together with the shortness of his own sight, made the arrival of guests something of a strain.

Few lovelier rooms were to be met with at this time in England than the gallery of the Bishop's Palace at Torminster. It stretched the whole length of one wing of the Palace and was perfectly proportioned for its length. The polished floor shone like dark water and the linenfold panelling on the walls roused the students of these things to ecstasy. At each end of the gallery a log-fire was blazing, its glow reflected on floor and walls, and in the centre was a Christmas-tree, its top reaching to the ceiling and its branches laden with twinkling candles and presents done up in coloured paper. The choirboys stood in an excited group near the tree, looking terribly clean in their Etons, their faces shining with soap and their eyes with expectation, while near them stood the dignitaries of the Close with their dependants, smiling with the urbanity of those who feel themselves to be in the position of benefactors but yet have no bother with the preparations. It was certainly a great occasion, and from the walls of the gallery the former bishops of Torminster looked down upon it from their portraits, the flicker-firelight playing queer tricks with their painted faces so that some of them seemed to smile at the happiness, and some to frown at the frivolity, while one gentleman at the far end of the room was distinctly seen by Henrietta to raise a hand in blessing.

The choirboys' presents were given first. Peppercue and

Barleycorn mounted two rickety step-ladders and cut them off the tree, calling out the boys' names in stentorian voices, while Baggersley trotted round in circles calling out instructions to Peppercue and Barleycorn, after the manner of those who while doing no work themselves see all the more clearly how it should be done. Paper and string strewed the floor and happy squeals greeted the appearance of knives, watches, whistles, blood-curdling books about Red Indians and boxes of those explosives which, when placed beneath the chairs of corpulent relations, go off with loud and satisfying reports . . . The Bishop always insisted upon this type of present, disregarding the complaints of the Dean and Lady Lavinia who maintained that they were in no way calculated to improve the morals of the dear boys. "No one," said the Bishop, "wants to be bothered with morals at Christmas"; which the Dean and Lady Lavinia considered such an outrageous remark that they were careful not to repeat it . . . Delight mounted higher and higher, reaching the peak of ecstasy when the tree caught fire and Barleycorn fell off his step-ladder, Baggersley remarking with acid pleasure that he had said so all along.

Grandfather took advantage of the confusion and howls of joy that ensued to press little packets into the hands of his young grandchildren. He remembered from his own childhood how difficult it is to watch other children receiving presents when you do not get any yourself. You may have a toy-cupboard at home stocked with good things, you may be going to a party every day for a fortnight, but it does not make any difference, for in childhood there is no past and no future, but only the joy or desolation of the moment. The tight, polite smiles that Henrietta and Hugh Anthony were maintaining with difficulty changed in the twinkling of an eye into happy grins as knobbly parcels were slipped into their hot palms from behind . . . Surreptitiously they opened them . . . A tiny china teapot and a box of pink pistol-caps numerous enough to turn every day of the next fortnight into a fifth of November.

Looking over their shoulders they saw Grandfather standing with his back to them, gazing with an appearance of great innocence at a portrait of an eighteenth-century bishop with a white wig and sleeves like balloons . . . They chuckled.

The fire put out and Barleycorn smoothed down they all went downstairs to the banqueting hall for tea.

135

The original banqueting hall, where kings and queens had feasted, was now a ruin standing out in the Palace grounds in the moonlight, but its name had been transferred to the sombre great room below the gallery, where damp stains disfigured the walls and where the wind always howled in the chimney.

Not that this worried the choirboys for the Bishop's cook had surpassed herself. They sat themselves down round the groaning table and they did not speak again.

But at the buffet at the far end of the room, where the grown-ups balanced delicate sandwiches and little iced cakes in their saucers, there was a polite hum of conversation. Extraordinary, thought Hugh Anthony, and Henrietta, who had to-day to be perforce counted among them, how grown-ups talk when they eat. Don't they want to taste their food? Don't they want to follow it in imagination as it travels down that fascinating pink-lined lane to the larder below? Sometimes Henrietta tried to picture that larder. It had shelves, she thought, and a lot of gnomes called "digestive juices" ran about putting things to rights . . . Or sometimes, unfortunately, forgetting to.

"Please," said Henrietta plaintively to Felicity, "could you hold my cup while I eat my cake? It's so dreadfully difficult, not sitting down."

Felicity, who had finished her own tea, was most helpful. She held Henrietta's cup in one hand and with the other she held the saucer below the cake so that Henrietta should not drop crumbs on the carpet.

"Shall I hold yours, Hugh Anthony?" asked Jocelyn, for Hugh Anthony's cup of milk was slopping over into the saucer in the most perilous way.

"No thank you," said Hugh Anthony, and his eyes were very bright because he had just had a brilliant idea.

Putting it into immediate practice he placed himself and his cup behind the Archdeacon, who was holding forth to Mrs. Elphinstone about total abstinence. Now when the Archdeacon held forth he had a curious habit of stepping suddenly backwards when he reached his peroration. He did it in the pulpit, frightening everyone into fits lest he should fall over the edge and kill himself, and he did it on his own hearthrug so that in winter his visitors had to keep a sharp look-out and make a dash for it when his coat-tails caught the flames, and he did it now. "Temperance, my

136

dear lady," he said to Mrs. Elphinstone, "is the foundation stone of national welfare," and stepped backwards on top of Hugh Anthony.

Everyone rushed to pick the poor child up. He was patted, soothed, kissed, and the milk that had spilled all over him was mopped up, though it was distressingly evident that his velvet suit was ruined.

The courage with which Hugh Anthony bore the pain of his trampled feet was much admired by everyone but Henrietta, for Henrietta, standing grave-eyed and aloof, knew quite well that he had done it on purpose.

6

"And now," said the Bishop, when the boys could eat no more, "I'm afraid we must go to evensong."

This was not the end of the party but only an interruption to it, and it was not even necessary to go out of doors, for a covered way led from the Palace to the Cloisters and the Cloisters led directly into the cathedral.

A silence fell upon them all as they entered the Cloisters, for the Cloisters always imposed silence. They were built round three sides of a square, the fourth side being occupied by the cathedral itself, and in the square the dead were buried; those very same bishops whose pictured faces had smiled and frowned upon the Christmas party, together with deans and canons whose names on the headstones had been washed out by wind and rain. It was bright moonlight now, with a blaze of stars, and the headstones showed up black and sharp against the snow. The feet of the living clanked harshly as they passed and all unconsciously they tried to go on tiptoe. Mr. Phillips, the organist, had gone on ahead with Peppercue and Barleycorn so that when the others came into the cathedral the candles were already flowering in the darkness and the organ playing softly.

They began with a hymn, "Once in royal David's city", after which evensong pursued its accustomed course until they got to the anthem, and it was here that Felicity and Jocelyn, who had never before attended evensong on the party day, had a shock, for it was Steggall's anthem, "Remember now thy Creator in the days of thy youth."

It was always sung on the party day and Grandfather considered it a most depressing choice, and had said so more than once at Chapter meetings, but was not listened to because what always had been done at Torminster always was done, suitable or not, and would be till the Day of Judgement, but Felicity and Jocelyn were not concerned with its suitability so much as with its beauty.

Felicity had always considered the twelfth chapter of Ecclesiastes the most haunting poem ever written. She found in it the same beauty, tinged with a feeling of eeriness, that years later she was to find in the poetry of Mr. Walter de la Mare. "Remember now thy Creator in the days of thy youth, while the evil days come not, nor the years draw nigh, when thou shalt say, I have no pleasure in them; while the sun, or the light, or the moon, or the stars, be not darkened, nor the clouds return after the rain." A boy's clear treble rang out in the great cathedral, where the candlelight fitfully shone on shadowed faces and carved stone and wood dark with age, while above them the pillars soared into darkness and all around them the night pressed in. A strange mutter of voices, quiet but very ominous, took up the next verse. "In the days when the keepers of the house shall tremble, and the strong men shall bow themselves, and the grinders cease because they are few, and those that look out of the windows shall be darkened." This lament for the fate of man, for the passing of his youth and joy and the coming of old age and death, was very queer and frightening, all the more so because one was not quite certain what it was all about. "Vanity of vanities, saith the preacher, all is vanity . . . The mourners go about the streets . . . The wheel broken at the cistern." Was that the end of the matter? "The spirit shall return unto God Who gave it." In that word "return" Felicity suddenly found comfort. The fate of man in this world was certainly a thing to be lamented over, a thing of uncertainty and loss and pain, and no amount of easy optimism could alter the facts of the case, yet in death he "returned" to his starting point of sun and moon and stars that are not darkened. Her mind wandering, she thought that the writer of this poem, when he chose sun and moon and stars as the supreme givers of joy, must have felt as Ferranti had done that man can best understand the meaning of perfection when he takes as its symbol a circle of white light. They were very

138

akin, Ferranti and this writer whose name she did not know . . .
Suddenly she started and touched Jocelyn's arm as he sat beside
her. The mist of sorrow that was in his eyes cleared away as he
looked at her and whispered the thought that was in both their
minds. "The answer . . . Our play must be presented as a great
lament."

The anthem ended and they knelt down to pray, their lowered
eye-lids shutting out even the faint candlelight so that each of
them was alone in darkness. To Jocelyn, even more deeply depressed than Felicity because depression came more naturally to
him, it seemed that the darkness of human life was too great to be
endured. The words of the prayers flowed on unheard by him as
he sank deeper and deeper into desolation. It seemed that he had
touched rock-bottom when Felicity, wise through that knowledge
of his thoughts that had come to her through love, put out a hand
and gently touched his side. Instantly his spirits rose a little and
opening his eyes he saw the candlelight. So often in his experience
the minor miseries of life had been eased by the touch of human-
ity; would the great miseries, when they came, be eased by God's
touch? One would have to be old to know and the old, he had
noticed, and not the young, were more often the men of faith.

They sang a last hymn and filed silently out of the dark cathedral
and through the moonlit Cloisters. Safely back in the Palace any
eerie feelings that might remain were dispelled by Mrs. Phillips.
"How those boys can sing like that after all that tea," she said,
"beats me."

7

After the pious interruption the party became secular again.
There was snapdragon in the darkened banqueting hall and races
in the gallery, followed by the giving of prizes to the winners of the
races and a few speeches. It was one of the habits of Torminster,
a habit to be deplored, that upon every possible occasion it spoke.
There were speeches at the choir-school prize-giving, speeches at
the annual missionary sale of work, speeches at drawing-room
meetings, speeches at concerts in aid of charity and, as if that was
not enough, speeches at the party. Why there should be speeches

at the party no one knew, but there always had been speeches at the party and so there always must be.

When the races had all been run, the orange-and-teaspoon race, the three-legged race, the wheel-barrow race, the hopping race and all the others, they sat down, the boys on the floor and the grown-ups on chairs, and the Bishop said a few words.

He made them as brief as possible, hoping that others might follow his example. He merely told his guests what a delight it was to entertain them at the Palace – at this point Baggersley who sometimes, like Grandfather, spoke his thoughts aloud, began to say something forcible to the contrary but his remarks were drowned by a very loud fit of coughing on the part of Barleycorn – hoped the boys had enjoyed themselves and congratulated Binks Major and Minor, Hopkins Minor and Jenkins upon carrying off the prizes. Then he sat down and the Dean got up, clearing his throat and grasping the lapels of his coat in his beautiful hands.

With the light shining on his silvery white hair and whiskers he looked magnificent. His coat was without a crease and on his gaiters every button was done up. His diamond ring sparkled and the toes of his boots, just showing below his gaiters, shone like glass . . . Torminster glowed with pride. Not every cathedral city, it thought, had a dean like theirs. You could have put him down anywhere and within two minutes he would have looked as though he owned the place.

"Dear friends and dear boys," fluted the Dean. This party, he felt, always had too worldly a tone – out of the tail of his eye he could see the prizes the Bishop would soon bestow on Jenkins, Binks Major and Minor and Hopkins Minor were boxes of fire-works and water-pistols – and he always did his best, in this speech, to raise things to a higher level. He did so now for a full quarter of an hour. He told the boys how grave and noble a calling was that of a choirboy. He likened them all to the infant Samuel serving in the Temple. He went on a long time about the infant Samuel. Then he warned them very seriously, with a sidelong glance at the fireworks, of the pernicious effects upon the char-acter of frivolity. In the midst of life, he said, we are in death, and we should not allow pleasures to lull us to forgetfulness of our sins.

Then he sat down amid loud and prolonged applause, for really, the boys thought, the old boy had looked splendid while he gassed, and dear old Canon Roderick, the senior canon present – for it was

140

impossible to get Canon Elphinstone's bathchair up the Palace stairs – tottered to his feet. Everyone loved Canon Roderick for he had a face like a rosy apple and he never saw a child but he gave it sixpence. Moreover, he always made exactly the same speech, both at the prize-giving and at the party, so that you knew exactly where you were and could applaud automatically in the right place without having to listen too hard. He always related the histories of his own sons – now elderly men – for he found, he said, that young people always like to hear about other young people. They began with Tom and followed his career through Eton and Sandhurst and into the army, went with him to India where he won distinction in a frontier skirmish, scurried at his heels to South Africa, where he won the V.C. – terrific cheers – and finally settled down with him in Hampshire where he was now, would you believe it, a retired general. Loud cheering, and they passed on to James, a sailor, following with deep interest and for the twentieth time as he climbed from midshipman to admiral and greeting his final elevation with a storm of cheering that nearly brought the roof off. Charles, a doctor, was a rugger blue – loud cheers – and Thomas, a schoolmaster, was a double first – rather subdued cheers. Henry was a leading barrister and last of all Edward, the baby, was actually a bishop. At this point, the company being what it was, the applause became deafening. Cheers, claps, and even stamping greeted the achievement of Edward. Canon Roderick, was helped to his seat, with his rosy face beaming with pride, and the Archdeacon rose to take his place with one of those speeches without which no prize-giving, not even a tiny one, is complete.

He began by saying that people who make long speeches are a great nuisance. Then for ten minutes or longer he explained why it is that they are a nuisance. Then he spoke a few words of congratulation to the boys who were to receive prizes, then a few words of consolation to the boys who would not receive prizes – conveying the impression that on the whole it is better not to receive prizes – followed by a few words to the grown-ups, followed by a peroration during which he suddenly stepped backwards on top of some potted plants and sent them flying.

The choir-school headmaster seized this opportunity to get up and begin his speech, which was always the last to be made at the party, hoping by this ruse to prevent anybody else from saying anything, for time was getting on and the longer they were over the speeches the longer it would be before his wife could get the boys to bed and there would be a little peace. On behalf of the choir he thanked everyone for their kindness and sat down.

It then seemed that Canon Allenby was going to make a speech, for he began to pant and grunt and heave his large person forward in his chair, and the headmaster cast a glance of anguished entreaty at the Bishop, for there was no reason whatever why Canon Allenby should make a speech, and once he started he never stopped . . . The Bishop got up hastily, while Canon Allenby was still heaving and grunting, and called upon Binks Major and Minor, Hopkins Minor and Jenkins to come and receive their prizes . . . Henrietta felt unhappy, and she could see that Grandfather felt unhappy too, for it was obvious that Canon Allenby was put out, and the old ought not to be put out. Let the young be put out, thought Grandfather fiercely, for the self-adjustment necessary to getting in again is so good for them. Then both he and Henrietta felt happy once more for they saw the Dean give Canon Allenby a glance of commiseration behind the Bishop's back and Canon Allenby, who adored the Dean and felt exactly as he did about the Bishop, was comforted.

The four boys received their prizes amid renewed applause and it was time for hide-and-seek all over the house.

The ardour of the grown-ups now began to cool a little and those of them who only liked children within reason gradually melted away, leaving behind those who after four hours of a party still liked children; on this occasion Mr. Phillips, Felicity, Jocelyn – though perhaps he only stayed because he liked Felicity – Hugh Anthony, Henrietta, Grandfather and the Bishop. The two latter, when hide-and-seek was well started, sank into chairs before one of the fires in the gallery, stretched their feet to the blaze, folded tired hands and meditated silently upon the amazing vitality of the young.

At eight o'clock the dishevelled children, their heated faces smeared with dirt and their Etons ornamented with cobwebs, were assembled in the banqueting hall and again fed, after which they all went home . . . It had been a grand party. The Bishop and Baggersley, as they saw their guests off at the hall door, could scarcely stand, while Grandfather did not refuse Jocelyn's offer of an arm home.

142

Felicity walked behind with the children.

"I've milked my front," said Hugh Anthony triumphantly, "and torn the seat of my trousers."

"You're a wicked boy," said Henrietta, "and your suit will have to be given to the poor . . . I'm not milked or torn," she continued with pride, and opened her coat for Felicity to see.

It was quite true. She was one of those fortunate people who are never untidy. Whatever Henrietta might do, and to-day she had fished raisins out of the snapdragon, slid down the banisters and hidden in corners that the Palace housemaid, having no mistress, consistently overlooked as a matter of principle, she always emerged at the end of it with unruffled hair and spotless dress. At this moment, in her blue frock in the moonlight, with her opened coat held out like wings and her eyes stars in her tilted face, she looked as much like a little angel as makes no difference.

"Oh, but I love you!" cried Felicity, and the garden door of Number Two the Close being now reached she gave way to that extravagance of action which so annoyed those who did not like her, went down on her knees in the snow and flung her arms round both children. "Don't ever go away from me," she implored them. "Never. Never." Hugh Anthony, kissing her chin politely, wriggled and went away but Henrietta remained, pressing closer.

8

The day after the party was the day chosen by Grandfather for the children's annual lesson on the connection between Faith and Works, and it was a black day. Faith, as understood by Henrietta and Hugh Anthony, was saying your prayers and going to church and this they had no objection to, but Works was giving away your toys to the poor and that was another thing altogether. What connection was there, they demanded indignantly of each other, between kneeling in your nightgown at the side of your bed at night and saying "Our Father-witchard-in-heaven", followed by "Now-I-lay-me", and parting next day from the dolls' perambulator and the tin helmet? . . . There seemed none.

The giving away of the toys always took place in the afternoon, and in the morning, as soon as breakfast was over, Grandfather and the children withdrew to the little room half-way up the tower where the toy-cupboards were kept. They toiled up the stone stairs, carrying two large baskets and the oil-stove that was to warm them during their melancholy employment, in a depressing silence.

The little room had been given to the children because it was like a room in a fairy tale. It was nearly at the top of the tower and its mullioned window, set in the thickness of the wall, had a lovely view of the cathedral towers, the Tor and the jumbled roofs of the city. It was quite empty, except for the children's treasures, and in it they were never required to tidy up.

They had a cupboard each whose state, Grandfather thought, was typical of their owners. In Henrietta's cupboard her dolls, together with their garments, furniture, crockery and cooking utensils, were laid out in neat rows on the top shelf. Her books were on the second shelf and boxes of beads were on the third shelf. You could see at once where everything was, and what it was, and when you opened the cupboard door nothing fell out.

With Hugh Anthony's cupboard it was not so, for as soon as the door was opened an avalanche descended. Jumbled up among engines with their wheels off, cricket bats cracked in the middle, headless soldiers and a moth-eaten golliwog who had seen better days, were chestnuts, bits of silver-paper, birds' feathers, the skin of a defunct snake, a mangel-wurzel and, most horrible of all, a baby chicken with two heads which had been preserved in a bottle of spirits and given to Hugh Anthony by Bates two Christmases ago . . . Hugh Anthony with his scientific mind adored this chicken and could never understand why everyone else averted their eyes when it was produced.

Having lit the oil-stove Grandfather sat himself down on the old rocking-horse and proceeded to superintend. Each child was required to fill a basket but they were not required to give away anything they had received this Christmas. They chose themselves what they should give away and Grandfather only interfered when he considered the choice unsuitable.

The cupboards were opened, the avalanche fell and work began.

Hugh Anthony always started by picking out the things that he really did not want, the heads of the soldiers, for instance, and the moth-eaten golliwog, but Grandfather's voice would thunder out behind him. "No, Hugh Anthony! Rubbish must not be given to

144

God's poor!" Then Hugh Anthony, after getting no answer to his "Why not?" which Grandfather considered a rhetorical question unworthy of answer, would be obliged to choose instead the soldiers that were very nearly intact and the least beloved of his engines, pistols and bricks. The things that he cared for most deeply, such as the two-headed chicken and the skin of the snake, Grandfather mercifully considered unsuitable.

Henrietta was the stuff of which martyrs are made, for when she had to give away she always gave what she loved best. Grandfather, as he watched her dark head bent sadly over the basket and her dainty fingers slowly placing her treasures side by side inside it, understood her and suffered agonies. Yet he never interfered with the suggestion that Gladys Hildegarde, the least-loved of Henrietta's dolls, would do just as well to give away as Irene Emily Jane the worshipped and adored . . . No . . . For who knew what spiritual strength and beauty might not pass from Henrietta to the sawdust bosom of Irene Emily Jane, and from thence to the little girl to whom she would be given?

But the sacrifice of this lady had taken place a year ago and she was now forgotten, for time heals even the worst of wounds. Henrietta had this year, so her conscience said, to part from the snowstorm that Miss Lavender had given her on her birthday. It was an incomparable toy. It consisted of a glass globe inside which a red man in a yellow hat stood on a green field. His cottage stood in the middle distance while to the right was a fir-tree and to the left a dog. This in itself was amazing, for how in the world did the red man, his cottage, his dog, and the fir-tree get inside the globe? But there was a greater marvel yet to come for when the globe was held upside down it began to snow. First a few flakes fell, then a few more, then they fell so thick and fast that the man and his house and his dog and the fir-tree were hidden from sight. Then you turned the globe right way up again and the storm ceased . . . It was amazing . . . Henrietta took it out of the cupboard and held it in her hands, her head bent. Then for the last time she held it upside down and watched the snow fall. Then she placed it in the basket and turned her back on it.

Grandfather watched her with painful attention and her action seemed to him to take on a mystic meaning. The globe was the world itself, containing all creation, trees, animals, man and his works, the earth and the sky, and Henrietta, it seemed, was one of those rare beings who, like Catherine Earnshaw, are prepared for love's sake to see "the universe turn to a mighty stranger".

After she had parted with the snowstorm it seemed to Henrietta quite easy to part with other things; with her necklace of blue beads, her set of drawing-room furniture made by herself out of chestnuts, with pins for legs and pink wool twisted round more pins for the backs of the chairs, her toy sewing-machine and her Dolly Dimple, a cardboard person with twelve sets of cardboard underclothes and ten hats.

When the baskets were packed they went downstairs and Grandfather read to them to cheer them up, and after that there was a rather penitential dinner of boiled cod and rice pudding at which Hugh Anthony did not behave well.

"Will you have skin, Hugh Anthony?" asked Grandmother, for she did not make the children eat milk-pudding-skin if they did not want to.

"No," said Hugh Anthony shortly.

"No, what?" asked Grandmother, who was punctilious about "thank you" being inserted in the proper place.

"No skin," said Hugh Anthony.

9

After dinner they started out, carrying the baskets and watched with disapproval by Grandmother. It was not that she disapproved of self-sacrifice, in fact she approved of it within limits set by herself, but in this case she feared its after-results. At the worst visiting the poor led to whooping-cough and at the best it resulted in the bringing home of insect life.

It had been snowing and the children insisted upon walking behind Grandfather so as to tread in his footsteps, for he was Good King Wenceslas and they were the page who, they decided, was really a twin.

"Couldn't you walk with me?" asked Grandfather, who felt a bit lonely by himself.

"No," they said, but they did not explain why such a thing was totally out of the question so he went on feeling lonely. They looked very odd, going up the street treading in each other's footsteps, but then Torminster was used to Grandfather and the children looking odd, and took no notice.

Beyond the Close a steep street wound uphill and here lived those people referred to by the Dean as the Lower Orders and by Grandfather as God's Poor. The part of the city where they lived had a fascination for the children because in its own way it was beautiful. The street knew, as the streams know, that it looks ugly to come down a hill in a straight line, and it wound about with stream-like winding so that you never knew what was coming round the corner. The cottages on each side were old, with weather-stained walls and flights of steps leading up to their front doors, and their crinkled roofs made a lovely pattern against the sky. No street that climbs a hill can be unattractive, Henrietta used to say in after years, the irregular line of the climbing roofs sees to that, but an old street on a hillside is one of the loveliest things on earth.

Today the curious white light of snow was over the world and a stinging cleanliness was in the air. The sky, emptied now of its snowflakes, was a pale grey with jagged rents torn in it through which one saw the blue behind; aquamarine just over the hills, turquoise higher up and sapphire overhead. To their right the trees that covered the Tor showed to perfection the softness of their winter dress. The bare twigs seemed by their interlacing to create colour, the brown of them melting into blue and red and purple. The Tor looked like the breast of a bird, Henrietta thought. It was hard to realize that if you came close to the trees their softness would melt into hardness and their colour into stark black and brown.

Firelight shone ruddily from windows and open doors and in spite of the cold the elder children were sitting on the steps that led to them, while the babies peered over the wooden boards put across the doors to keep them from hurtling down the steps. Inside the rooms busy mothers could be seen moving backwards and forwards, their figures dark against bright-patterned wall-paper and shining pots and pans.

It was, of course, difficult to know which cottages they ought to go to, for they could not go everywhere. The only thing to do, Grandfather had said when he first started the annual lesson on Works, was to begin at the bottom of the street and stop whenever they saw children, and next year to begin where they had left off

147

the previous year. There were bound to be complaints, of course, in the cottages where they did not go, but he was primarily concerned with the characters of his own grandchildren so he tried not to think about them.

"Last year," said Henrietta from the rear, "we stopped at the cottage half-way up on the left-hand side where the wicked little boy showed Hugh Anthony how to make a long nose."

Grandfather remembered the regrettable incident, as indeed he might, for Hugh Anthony had been making long noses ever since, no amount of spanking curing him of the habit. That was the worst of Hugh Anthony. The wrong things seemed always to make an indelible impression on him while sweet and good influences ran off him like water off a duck's back . . . Or so it seemed . . . Grandfather could only hope and pray that future years might prove it otherwise.

"We'll go and see that little boy again," said Hugh Anthony.

"We will not," said Grandfather firmly. "We will go to the first house beyond him that has respectable-looking children."

The wicked little boy seemed out and they passed the danger point in safety. Beyond were several cottages where there were no children but after that things began to happen.

They began well.

Three little tow-haired girls sat on a flight of steps one behind the other. They wore stout boots and mufflers crossed over their chests and tied in bows behind. The dirt on their faces was only surface dirt, for their necks in contrast with their black faces were white as snow, and they had the eyes of children who have been loved from the beginning. Large handkerchiefs were attached to their persons with safety-pins and they were eating bread and jam . . . A delightful family . . . A family after Grandfather's own heart . . . He smiled at them and they stopped eating bread and jam, wiped their mouths with the backs of their hands – the handkerchiefs being apparently intended for nasal use only – and smiled back at him. Then shyness seized them; they cast down their eyes and squirmed.

But Grandfather had seen behind them a clean, fire-lit kitchen, a cheerful mother and two tow-haired boys, and he led the way in, patting the heads of the girls as he climbed over them.

Inside, in an atmosphere of welcome, he was utterly happy. He sat himself down in a windsor chair, placed his hat on the floor

148

and talked to the cheerful mother as though he had known her all his life. He felt as though the hard, happy days of his parish work were back with him again, those days when he had not felt conscious, as he was always conscious in the Close, of living a segregated life. He hated segregation, inevitable though he knew it to be. He hated the barriers of time and age and class and language. He longed for the time when all the different lights carried by man in the pageantry of life should glow into one.

But his ease was as yet impossible to Henrietta and Hugh Anthony. They stood side by side, stiff and miserable, subjected to the unwinking stare of five pairs of eyes; for the tow-headed little girls had now joined the little boys in a group as far removed as possible from their visitors. The whole width of the kitchen separated the well-dressed from the ill-dressed and it was the well-dressed, weighed down by numbers, who felt themselves at a disadvantage. What makes one feel uncomfortable, they discovered suddenly, is not what one has got or has not got, but being different.

But gradually the situation eased itself. First Henrietta took a step forward, then one of the little girls, and then before they knew where they were the chestnut chairs with the wool backs had been set out on the stone floor, becoming in a flash mahogany upon a marble pavement.

After that the giving of gifts was easy. Hugh Anthony parted almost willingly from an engine with three wheels and a box of soldiers, and Henrietta added to the chestnut chairs her blue bead necklace and Dolly Dimple.

"Isn't 'Arold going to 'ave nothink?" asked the eldest little girl.

"Who's Harold?" asked Grandfather with benign interest.

"My eldest," said the woman. "Upstairs with the measles." She sighed, glancing at the youngest little girl who was sniffling. "They'll all 'ave it now. There's Rosie sneezing already."

Grandfather's eyes popped a little behind his glasses, but he was careful to go quietly on with the conversation until the end, when he rose and thought they ought to be going. A picture book was found for Harold, mutual good-byes were said and they departed.

"I think," said Grandfather, when they were out in the street again, "that it would be better not to mention the measles to your dear Grandmother."

"Why not?" asked Hugh Anthony.

149

"It would distress her," said Grandfather, "to think of the poor little boy being ill."

"Oh no, it wouldn't," said Hugh Anthony.

Henrietta privately agreed with him for she had noticed that Grandmother and Clara enjoyed hearing about other people's ups and downs. Whenever anybody's chimney caught on fire, or cook gave notice, or appendix had to come out, Clara would come running to tell Grandmother and Grandmother would say, "Dear me, Clara, you don't say so!" and look almost bright and interested.

They went on up the street, giving toys to the children whom they saw and sometimes going inside their homes, and all went well until they turned a corner and came upon a dingy-looking house from which no firelight shone. The broken window-panes were stuffed with rag, a most unusual sight in Torminster, and over the board across the door there peeped a dirty baby with a cold in its head, and no handkerchief. Grandfather, seeing the cold, would have passed on but as the children were still in single file behind him, treading in the footsteps of Good King Wenceslas, he had no control over them and before he could stop her Henrietta had darted across the pavement to the baby.

She had never seen such a pitiful baby and the sight of it made her feel dreadful. It was dirty all over, from its matted hair to its bare toes, and its poor little upper lip was terribly sore because no one had ever blown its dribbling nose. In a flash Henrietta climbed over the board and blew the nose on her own clean handkerchief, then picking up the scrap in her arms she staggered with it into the gloom beyond.

Inside were dirt and evil smells and dead ashes in the grate. A horrible-looking old woman, the grandmother perhaps, with greasy strands of grey hair escaping from a man's cap, was peeling potatoes and shouting raucously at the children who seemed swarming all over the place. Henrietta, unseen, stood still and stared, for the children had not got faces like the children she was accustomed to. They had old faces and their eyes did not seem to look at anything steadily. When the old woman hit out at two of the little ones they ducked cleverly, and without fear, but their cunning was somehow horrible. Then they saw Henrietta and came boldly crowding up to her, shouting out things that she did not understand, though she knew they were mocking things. She recoiled a little and found to her relief that Grandfather was just behind her.

"Give them some toys," he said quietly, "and then come away."

But before she had time to do anything a door burst open and a drink-sodden brute of a man was upon them, a man as repellent as it is possible for a human creature to become upon this earth. It was lucky for Henrietta that in her fright she did not see him very clearly, or understand anything of the torrent of abuse that he hurled at Grandfather, except his last shout of, "I'll have none of your damned charity."

"I have no wish to inflict it on you at the moment," said Grandfather sternly, and he moved to the door, pushing Henrietta and Hugh Anthony in front of him and quite unmoved, apparently, by the flung boot that missed his head by inches . . . This was not the first time in the course of his ministry that boots had been hurled at his head and he supposed it would not be the last, for with the vicar's permission he intended to visit this gentleman again.

Out in the street Henrietta suddenly dived under Grandfather's arm and ran back. When that terrible man had come in she had seen the children all cowering back, as they had not shrunk from their grandmother, and the sight had awakened in her some queer agony of understanding, for these were children who were not wanted. Deep down in Henrietta's mind was a half-formed memory of a time when she herself had not been wanted. It was not a real memory, like the memory of her singing mother, it was only a shadow that spread itself behind the figure of her mother, not emanating from her but from someone else, and faintly darkening those days at the orphanage when she discovered that her mother was dead and that no one would tell her anything about her father . . . Someone, at some time, had not wanted her, that was all she knew . . . The horrible man had disappeared again, but the children were still cowering in their corner. She pushed fiercely in among them and took the snowstorm from her basket. "Look!" she cried, and held it upside down. "Look at the snow falling."

Suddenly they were crowding round her, kicking and scuffling, fear and hatred forgotten and their eyes and mouths "ohs" of amazement. One of the boys seized the globe rudely from her and hit out indiscriminately at all the others so that he could have this treasure for himself. His hard fist caught Henrietta in the chest and nearly winded her, but she did not mind. Backing out from among them she ran back to Grandfather at the door, momentarily happy again.

But the swift changes of mood possible to childhood were not possible to Grandfather and he was by no means happy. He had had no idea that Torminster possessed such a family, and he was terribly sorry that the children should have seen it . . . Henrietta, he knew, would never forget . . . And he was grieved, too, that she should have parted with her snowstorm when she did, for he had not the slightest doubt that within two hours it would be at the pawnbroker's. Well, for two hours, for the first time and probably the last, those wretched children would possess for their own the world and its beauty, earth and sky, a tree, a cottage, a dog and a red man in a yellow hat.

They visited no more houses that afternoon for there was no more spirit left in them. They trailed rather sadly home, giving away the few toys that were left to the children they met.

When they got to their own garden door the light was fading and the shadows were long across the snow. The Tor woods had lost their colour and the bright patches of blue sky were swallowed up in the grey.

Henrietta and Hugh Anthony ran straight upstairs to Grandmother in the drawing-room, where the warm fire gleamed on dark panelling and coloured china and where the smell of the fresh chrysanthemums was clean and pungent. Grandfather went to his study, shut the door, fell upon his knees and prayed that the dear children might not catch the measles . . . They did not.

Christmas With The Three Grey Men

1

THE small village tucked away in a fold of the Devon Hills was a long way from anywhere, and in the reign of King Charles I did not concern itself much with what was going on in the great world beyond the West Country. It was a world to itself, this West Country world, and the rest of England might have been at the Antipodes for all that the villagers bothered about it, its inhabitants lumped all together as "foreigners" and dismissed from their attention as unworthy of it. Why should they bother themselves with what went on beyond the confines of their lovely land? They were self-supporting. Their rich red earth grew corn in abundance, the cattle grew fat in their green pastures, the orchards that in the spring filled the valleys with a froth of pink and white blossom seemed to flower afresh in the autumn, so bright and rosy were they with their burden of apples. Blackberries and elderberries and sloes for wine were rampant in the hedgerows, and the honeybees hummed all summer-time among the honeysuckles and carnations of the old gardens. There were herbs for simpling in the gardens, too, and pumpkins of enormous size, and raspberries and currants for preserves and cordials. Cropping the sweet turf of the round green hills were sheep in plenty to give their wool for spinning and weaving, and in the deep sheltered lanes grew plants for dyeing the wool all colours of the rainbow. And if the women could weave and spin and dye, could bake and brew and distill wholesome waters, the men could plough and sow and reap, could make their own furniture and build their own cob houses and thatch them with golden straw. And if through sickness or bereavement they fell upon evil days there was the squire (in the manor house upon the hill, that ancient manor house that had once been a monastery) to turn to for assistance, or Old Parson in the whitewashed parsonage. And when in the mating and birth and death, at the gathering of the harvest, at the time of the mystical hushed pause of midwinter, and the time of the re-birth of the world a sense of the mystery of things quickened their heartbeats and made them a little afraid, they

155

turned to the old grey church. It had a tall tower that reached like a pointing finger to heaven, a peal of bells that on festival days could be heard miles away, even beyond Paradise Hill, the great green fairy hill with its wishing well that rose up beyond Wildwoods and protected the village from the west winds that in winter could blow so coldly from the moors. The bells all had names, beautiful names such as Sweet Marie, Gabriel, Douce and John, and when they had been hung in place in the great grey tower the Bishop had anointed them with oil and salt and wine and signed them with the sign of the cross, just as though they were living people; which, in the eyes of the men who rang the merry peals, they certainly were. The whole village loved these bells, and scarcely less precious in their eyes were the other treasures of their church: the beautiful stained glass windows, the ancient golden cross upon the altar, and the fine set of vestments that had come from the monastery, woven in bright colours of gold and emerald, sapphire and amethyst and rosy red. Perhaps the village people scarcely realized how deeply they loved their church and its treasures, but if it had not been there to give them the assurance of the providence and bounty of God, it would have seemed to them that existence was a nebulous thing without firm ground for the feet.

And in this particular village the church provided not only the setting for those festivals by which the adults gave to the mystery of things some concrete form, but for the children's games as well. It was for the children a nursery full of playthings. It was supposed to be kept locked on weekdays, but the Reverend Obadiah Wilmot, always called Old Parson, put the key behind the mounting block at the lych-gate, and the children knew where it was. And Old Parson knew that they knew; in fact, he had himself pointed out to them its hiding place, and on dark winter days, when not much light came through the stained glass windows and he thought the shadows might make them a little afraid, he would join them at their play and light the candles and tell them stories. He liked children. Indeed being close on eighty, and having had strange fancies in his head ever since that night when his horse had thrown him as he rode through the stormy darkness to a dying parishioner at an outlying farm, he was more than half a child himself. Men tapped their foreheads significantly when Old Parson was mentioned, and the women sighed pityingly and said, "'The poor old soul!" when he was suddenly taken with some strange new freak of fancy, such as decorating the churchyard yews with coloured balls to amuse the angels at Christmas, or setting out tempting little meals of honey cakes and elderberry wine on the tombstones for the fairies on midsummer eve. And a few weakly persons confessed themselves afraid of the old man when they met him striding along the lanes in his tattered snuff-stained cassock, his white hair streaming in the wind, talking to himself, cracking his fingers and laughing as though he were having a good joke with someone whom no one could see. "A regular old scarecrow!" was the contemptuous laughing comment of those younger folk who had not known him in the days before his fall, and certainly when his tall gaunt figure was viewed from a distance the simile was apt. But the older people, who remembered him in the old days when his manners and appearance had had a grace that echoed the rarity and sensitiveness of his spirit, did not laugh, and they would rejoice in all that was still left to Old Parson of his old pre-eminence among his fellows. For, eccentric though he might be, he remained a fine artist. No one in the countryside round about could play the fiddle like Old Parson, and no one could carve wood as he did. There was nothing he could not make out of a bit of wood: a spinning-wheel for an old woman, or a cradle for a child; a carved pulpit, or a top; he could still make them all with those fine hands of his. At sight of some lovely thing his eyes would still shine with the old appraising fire, and his voice was still as deep and resonant as ever when from the pulpit he thundered forth the praise of God Who made the world so fair. And he had lost none of his country love, either. He was still wonderfully handy with sick creatures. Shepherd Joseph, who was the best lambing shepherd in the neighbourhood and spent most of his life in the shepherd's hut on Paradise Hill, always sent for Old Parson to come and help him when his beasts were ailing. Shepherd Joseph had known Old Parson longer than anyone else in the neighbourhood, for he was even older than Old Parson, so old that his white beard reached to his knees, and he never spoke to anyone except to Old Parson, in whom he saw nothing odd whatsoever.

And neither did the children. Like Shepherd Joseph, they were perfectly at home with Old Parson and neither mocked nor shunned nor pitied him. That was because for him, as for them and Shepherd Joseph, a certain door was open and their mutual use of it made them akin. When a child began to laugh at Old Parson, or run away at sight of him, that was a sign that the child was ceasing to be a child, that the door was slowly closing. Old Parson would go away and weep wildly when a child whom he had loved just turned away from him; it was not for himself that he wept, but for the child.

The playthings in the church would have had few attractions for the modern child, but for these village children, with no nurseries, and few toys, they were a continual marvel. There were not many of them, so that attention was acutely focused, and they were so simple that they left plenty of room for imagination. Instead of the modern nursery wallpaper with its myriad pictures there was in the church only one – a portrait of Saint Nicholas painted in oils upon a wooden board – but so darkened by the smoke of the tallow candles that unassisted by imagination one could make out nothing except the dim sweep of a crimson cloak and the suggestion of a smile upon a bearded face. Then for dolls there was in a niche in the wall, near the wooden pulpit that Old Parson had carved so beautifully, a small statue of the Madonna with her Baby in her arms, so worn by time that the Mother's face was almost worn away and the Child's hand, upraised in blessing, had had two fingers broken off; and a pulpit cloth of cherry velvet embroidered with a small winged cherub with a darn on the nose. And instead of Teddy and Panda there were the dogs on the Crusader's tomb, and these were the best of all, so good in fact that they have a paragraph all to themselves.

They lay at the head and the foot of the tomb. One of them formed a pillow for the Crusader's head and against the other were propped his crossed mailed feet. They were very small dogs of no known breed, for the sculptor who had created them had been a man of humour and imagination and had thoroughly let himself go. The one at the head of the tomb, whom the children called Todd, had a fat, smooth, round body like a sausage, ornamented at one end with a smiling, pop-eyed, snub-nosed, pug-like face, and at the other with a long tail with two twists in it. His legs were not quite hidden by his fat body, but his plump little paws peeped out engagingly fore and aft. Percy, at the Crusader's feet, was quite different. He had a fine leonine head, and a grand furry ruff round his shoulders. His body was long and lean, showing all the ribs in a rather painful manner, and he had a bedraggled tail like a moth-eaten ostrich feather. His long front legs, with huge claws on the paws, hung rather dejectedly over the edge of the tomb, but the back ones were folded up very neatly beneath his tail. His eyes were half-closed, weary and sad, as though he still mourned for his master. His was the faithful heart, it was obvious. In real life he would have liked best to lie at his master's feet of an evening, where he lay now, while Todd would have been scurrying round the room chasing the two twists in his tail, or yapping at the door to be let out to his dinner. It was pity for restless little Todd, pinioned beneath his master's mailed head, that had in the first place led Old Parson to spend so many long hours with hammer and chisel, working away until he had got Todd loose, but the delight of the children had been so great when Todd could be lifted out from the tomb and set on the floor and played with, that he had set to work to free Percy too, even though he had realized that freedom was not desired by Percy . . . For Percy had clung so firmly to the tomb with his hanging forepaws that it had not been possible to chisel them free, and now when he was lifted down he was lifted down without his front legs . . . Old Parson had grieved deeply over this maiming of poor Percy, until he saw how it endeared him to all the little girls of the village. They were passionately devoted to Percy, loving him if possible even more than they loved the little cherub with the darn on its nose. They would sit beside him for hours, talking to him and scratching him behind the ears, and smoothing his mane with gentle fingers. The little boys, on the other hand, were fonder of Todd. They would take him ratting round the church and knowing his weakness for good living they would bring him apples and nuts, or little bits of pork cracklings saved from their dinners.

Saint Nicholas appealed equally to both boys and girls. The mysterious darkness of the picture made it a subject for endless conjecture. Was there, or was there not, something hidden under his cloak? And why was he smiling? Was it because he had some splendid secret to keep? What secret? Had he got it hidden under his cloak? Old Parson wouldn't tell them, however insistently they appealed for information . . . They'd know all in good time, he said.

The children never played with Mary and the Baby in quite

the way they did with Percy and Todd and the cherub, although the little painted wooden statue would have been quite easy to lift out of its niche in the wall, because Old Parson had taught them that this Mother and her Child were holy and not in the same class at all with dogs or even cherubs; but they loved the statue very dearly, and every day the little girls brought nosegays and put them in the niche at Mary's feet. Even in midwinter they always found something they could bring, for the winters were mild in this West Country and there always seemed plenty of scarlet haws on the old thorn tree beside the wishing well on Paradise Hill, and periwinkles or tinted leaves in the deep lanes. And on those rare days when there was snow on the ground they would bring sprays of holly or sprigs of yew. And they would make daisy-chains for Mary's neck, or a necklace of rose hips strung together. And they would bring playthings for the Baby – a chestnut, or a jay's feather, or scarlet moss-cups clustering upon a mossy stick. And taught by Old Parson, who accompanied them most sweetly upon his fiddle, they would sit at Mary's feet and sing lullabies to the Baby.

And of course when Old Parson was up to his crazy tricks, when he was setting out dainty meals for the fairies upon the tombstones or hanging coloured balls upon the yew trees, he always had the enthusiastic co-operation of the children. And at the seasons when the grown-ups were having their games (only they didn't call their festival services games, and drew a sharp distinction, which the children found difficult to understand, between themselves singing hymns in the church on Christmas morning and their offspring singing lullabies to the Baby on ordinary days) the children and Old Parson made the church such a bower of beauty with sheaves of corn, or holly wreaths, or daffodils, or bridal lilies, or whatever the occasion might demand, that people would come from miles round just to look at it. More and more as the years went by the church became an object of pilgrimage for the countryside, and that not only because of Old Parson's eccentricities, but also because of that open door of his; through it a radiance shone that soaked into the very structure of the building where he prayed, so that others liked to pray there too. For old Parson had always been, would always be, a great man of prayer. And his prayer had never taken the form of asking for things, it was simply worship. Artists never do want to possess – only to give.

160

2

And so, for one reason or another, this church had achieved a certain fame, and the Parliament men chose it to make an example of. For alas, if you want peace and quiet it is not enough to ignore the outside world, as the village had always done; the outside world has to ignore you also, and this it is not always disposed to do.

Upon a cold grey winter's morning, heavy and still with the coming of snow, only a week before Christmas, when Old Parson was shut up inside the church playing with the children, there rode into the village three grey-faced men dressed in grey garments, with tall black hats. They were ugly men, and about them and their clothes there was a dusty sort of look, as though they had journeyed a long way across some arid desert. Yet tired and dusty though they were they held their heads proudly, as though their tall hats were crowns, as though they knew a lot, or thought they did, and they had about them that unmistakable kingly look that comes from the possession of authority. This suggestion of power, of glooming heavy wisdom, was so blighting that when they dismounted at the pump in the centre of the village and the leader climbed upon the horse-block there to make a proclamation, the usually light-hearted villagers headed by an unrecognizably grave-faced squire, gathered to hear it in a sober silence.

They had an inkling of what the proclamation was to be about because uninterested though they were in the affairs of "foreigners" they had yet lent an inattentive ear to the reports circulated by travelling pedlars about the goings-on in London lately. They knew that the King and Parliament had fallen out about many things, including religious matters. The King loved the old traditional ways of Catholic worship, the easy colourful ways that were part of the very earth of the easy colourful countryside of England; but Parliament was dominated by men called Puritans who had adopted the teaching of the Dutchman Calvin, a double-dyed "foreigner" in that he was not only foreign to the soil of the West Country but to the soil of England also. Yet those Puritans preferred this way of serving God – a way that condemned every kind of festivity, that ceased to extol the bounty of God and concerned itself only with the terror of hellfire – to that of their fathers, and they had become strong enough to impose the will of Parliament upon the King. Last Michaelmas, by order of Parliament, it had been commanded that from every church in the land there be removed all deceitful idols, whether pictures, images or painted glass, all coloured vestments, and that no village be permitted any longer to observe the old religious holidays . . . But who among them had expected that these hated Puritans, who would root out all singing and laughter, all colour and festivity and joy from life, would have thought it worth their while to come all this way to submerge with their dusty greyness this remote fairyland, and to read out their hateful law from the village pump?

Yet so it was. In silence they heard out the proclamation, in silence they gazed balefully at the sour faces of the three Grey Men, and up at the winter sky that to-day was as drab and cold as the way of life that these men desired to force upon them, and then they sighed and turned homeward again. They did not argue the point. The West Country folk have always been peaceable folk, with a hatred of sharp words. Besides, the Grey Men had the power of the law behind them, and better to lose the few gew-gaws out of the church, old and precious though they were, than to risk the lock-up or the stocks. So they just melted away, all except the squire, who thought it politic to stay behind and offer the travellers a mug of ale at his house . . . But he did not offer it with any great show of hospitality, because when he had been a little boy he had beguiled the tedium of many a long sermon by telling himself stories about what Saint Nicholas had hidden under his cloak.

They accepted his offer, but first they demanded to know where they might find the parson. They had not noticed him among the men who had listened to the proclamation and they wished to enforce upon him personally the necessity for obeying the law with thoroughness and dispatch; for on the afternoon of Christmas Eve it was their intention to return and see if their commands had been carried out, and if they had not it would be the worse for the parson and the squire and the whole village. The squire heard their threat and nodded towards the church. "You will find the parson in his church among the so-called idols," he said curtly. "I will await you here." And then he smiled grimly as the three Grey Men walked up the moss-grown path under the old yews whose

162

branches to-day spread dark and glooming like a starless night sky . . . For what in the world would they make of Old Parson? Or he of them?

When they entered upon him, Old Parson was sitting on the steps of the pulpit and at his feet were gathered all the children of the village listening enthralled to the story he was telling them, the story of the flight into Egypt of Mary and her Child. Because it was one of those grey days that made the church dark, he had lit the candles in the big branched candlestick beside the pulpit, and the circle of thin light illumined a scene so lovely that it must surely have melted a heart made of any substance less hard than iron. "Ironsides" was a name that the Puritan men had not yet earned, but in the future they would earn it, and deserve it, because it was in them to look upon a scene like this and not be moved to mercy by it.

Candle-light was always kind to Old Parson. In its radiance his white head shone like silver and his aged face might have been carved out of old ivory. His dark eyes, that at times looked so vacant, were pools of wisdom when he told tales to the children by candle-light, and the expressive gestures of his fine thin hands were an integral part of the telling of the story, as though he painted the scene as he described it. The children, with their bright heads and bright clothes lit by the candlelight, made a glowing mosaic of colour at his feet. Curly golden heads, tousled tow-coloured heads, sleek chestnut and carroty heads, jerkins of russet and green, skirts of rose and blue, of scarlet and primrose and lavender looped up over gay flowered petticoats – it was as though midsummer bloomed again in mid-winter. It was not surprising that the cherub with the darn on its nose seemed to smile as it hovered over the scene, and that the Madonna in her niche in the wall beside the pulpit seemed to be holding up her Babe a little higher than usual in her arms, that he might bless it. She too seemed to be smiling, and no wonder, for the children had hung a necklace of holly berries that gleamed in the candle-light blood red like rubies round her neck. Percy and Todd had been lifted down from the Crusader's tomb and sat with the children, enthralled as they were by the astonishing adventures (unrecorded in holy writ) of Mary and Joseph and the Baby on the way to Egypt. Saint Nicholas was half out of the lighted circle, his cloak billowing more mysteriously than ever. It was so dark beyond the

163

circle of the candle-light that the stained-glass windows and the cross upon the altar shone beyond the towering pillars and the interlacing arches like the lights of some distant city seen at dusk through the branches of a forest. Theirs was a faraway celestial beauty but the loveliness within the circle of candle-light had a homely charm that would have sent a truly wise man tiptoeing away back where he came from, lest he disturb the rhythm of a perfect moment.

But the three Grey Men were wise with the wisdom not of the heart but of the brain, and it did not even occur to them to let this moment swing on through time to its perfect completion in eternity. They took it and broke it and flung the broken fragments of it round about them like the petals of a torn flower. They knocked over the candlestick and extinguished the light, so that the cherub and the Madonna and Child and Saint Nicholas fled away into the shadows and the children scattered in fright to the farthest corners of the church, and they seized Old Parson by the arm and pulled him up to stand before them like a criminal in the dock. They had left the door open behind them when they came in, and the cold air blew icily through the church.

Then, one of them prodding him insolently in the chest, they delivered to Old Parson the commands of Parliament, as they had dictated them to the squire and the villagers at the pump: the stained glass must be removed from the windows, the cross from the altar, and all vestments and idolatrous images must be taken away and destroyed. And they themselves would return on Christmas Eve to see if their commands had been obeyed. And when they spoke of idolatrous images they looked about them and saw the children's toys, and one of them tweaked the cherub's nose with a contemptuous finger and thumb, and another snatched angrily at the necklace of holly berries round the Madonna's neck and broke it, so that the berries rolled down upon the floor like drops of blood, and the third, the man who had prodded Old Parson, kicked poor Percy and struck Saint Nicholas with the riding-whip that he carried, and made a dent in the scarlet cloak . . . But Saint Nicholas made no movement when he was struck, and he did not reveal what he had hidden beneath his cloak and the Child in his Mother's arms did not cry when the berries fell, nor did the dogs bark or the tweaked cherub so much as flutter its wings in outrage, and Old Parson, when prodded and dictated to, neither

164

moved nor spoke. And the children in the shadows were as silent as mice – more silent, for they did not even squeak.

It was intimidating, this silence, and so was the blazing scorn in the eyes of Old Parson, and for the first time that day the three Grey Men showed slight signs of discomfort. They blustered a bit, but their blustering was swallowed by the deep silence of the church like a stone thrown into deep water, the angry words lost as soon as uttered. One of them rubbed his long nose, and a second coughed, and then they turned on their heels and clanked out of the church rather hurriedly, as though the silence was a physical force pushing them out. When they had gone Old Parson picked up the candlestick, restored it to its place and lit the candles. Then he sat down on the pulpit steps and went on with the adventures of Mary and Joseph and the Baby in Egypt exactly where he had left off, and the children came flocking back from the dark corners to listen to him . . . But it was not exactly as it had been before, because the Madonna's necklace of holly berries lay broken on the floor and the children all had pale faces . . . In the days that followed Old Parson did not remove the holly berries; he left them lying there, like accusing drops of blood, telling how something had been hurt in this place.

3

But that negative action was his only protest. To the squire's astonishment, and secret relief, for he knew the old man's high spirit and had expected some instant explosion, Old Parson made no difficulties when the squire brought skilled workmen to remove the stained glass from the windows; he only asked, humbly and gently, that he himself might be entrusted with the removal of the golden cross and the vestments and the idolatrous images. The squire, looking the old man sympathetically in the eye, nodded. It was his intention to bury the stained glass very carefully in the manor house garden until this tyranny should be over-passed, and it was just as well that they should not have all their precious eggs hidden in the same basket. Old Parson made his request one evening at sunset, when the promise of snow had been fulfilled and the light white flakes were whirling down like goose feathers from the grey sky, and by sunrise the next morning the church looked as bare as Mother Hubbard's cupboard. Everything had gone, even Todd and Percy. Nothing was left except the cross on the altar, and Old Parson promised that that too should have gone by the afternoon of Christmas Eve.

The children wept at first when they saw their empty nursery, but they were cheered by a cryptic remark of Old Parson's. "Remember," he said, "how the Holy Family ran away into Egypt." They did not understand this remark but they found it comforting because in the story Old Parson had told them on the day the three Grey Men came the Holy Family had been having great fun in Egypt. And early on the afternoon of Christmas Eve, a day of sunshine and blue sky and sparkling crystal frost upon the light fall of snow, they almost forgot their grief for their lost toys in the excitement of being summoned by Old Parson to assist him as usual with the Christmas decorations.

"But will the Grey Men like us to have decorations?" asked Prue, the daughter of the innkeeper. She spoke anxiously, for she was the eldest of the children, old enough to understand that when the Grey Men came back this afternoon they might make it very unpleasant for everybody if they considered that their commands had not been obeyed.

"Holly wreaths are not idolatrous images, Prue," said Old Parson. "We shall decorate as usual this afternoon, and when we have finished we shall praise God by singing in the church just as we always do."

But they did not decorate as usual, for, driven by Old Parson's fiery zeal, they decorated more gloriously than ever before. It was an exceptionally good year for holly and mistletoe and Old Parson had collected masses of it in the church, together with branches of yew and fir, and many strings of the coloured ornaments that he made yearly to hang on the trees in the churchyard to amuse the angels. There were so many this year that the children guessed Old Parson had been up all night every night for a week making them. They were made of inflated bladders, coloured red and blue, and gilded fircones, and the hard outside shells of small round striped pumpkins, and, hung among the green wreaths inside the church, and the yew branches in the churchyard, they were the gayest things imaginable. In the course of the decorating, grown-ups came hurrying along to protest, for like Prue they were afraid that

166

the Grey Men might not like these goings-on, but once they had arrived upon the scene of action their protests died upon their lips and before they knew what they were doing they also were helping with the decorations. They didn't quite know why. It was something to do with Old Parson's compelling power. They got caught in its beam, as a benighted traveller is caught by the finger of light shining across the dark road through an open doorway, and cannot leave it because it is so warm and glowing. And once caught they worked as though their lives depended on it, turning both church and churchyard into a bower of beauty to the glory of God, and when the last holly wreath had been adjusted and the last coloured festoon hung in its place, and Old Parson standing in his tattered cassock at the chancel steps had tucked his fiddle under his chin and struck up the tune of the first carol, men's basses and women's trebles mingled with the voices of the children in the merry air, and the whole village seemed standing shoulder to shoulder within the church . . . It was only then that the squire, standing close to Old Parson with his head thrown back and his mouth wide open bellowing like an amiable bull, noticed with dismay that the cross was still on the altar.

And a minute later, in the tiny pause between the ending of one carol and the beginning of another, he heard the unmistakable sound of the clip-clop of horses' hoofs on a hard, frosty road. Old Parson heard it too and their eyes met, and the fanatical fire in those of the old man caught up the other into a state of blind obedience that he was never afterwards able to understand.

"Take the cross from the altar and lead straight out of church," Old Parson commanded the squire. "Lead through the village and up through Wildwoods to Shepherd Joseph's hut on Paradise Hill. Go at an easy pace, suited to the eldest and the youngest here." And to the people he cried out in a loud voice, "Follow the cross, good people. Listen to the tune I play and sing glory to God in the highest, and on earth peace. Goodwill towards men."

When the sun shines in the West Country it seems to shine more brilliantly than in other parts of England. Especially is this so on clear, frosty December days, when the deep blue sky, the clear crystal light, the brief glow of warmth and the powdering of snow on the hedges give the illusion that May-time has suddenly blossomed in mid-winter. The three Grey Men, not natives of this country, found themselves queerly dazzled by the shining splendour as they rode down the hill to the village. Every rut in the road had its slither of sparkling ice, every humblest weed its diamond crown, every bush its exquisite flowery burden of purest white, and the blue air was shot through with silver and the stillness and the silence held the land so entranced in beauty that time stopped. The Grey Men trotted on bemused, hardly aware of where they had come from or where they were going, or what they were supposed to do when they got there. It was merely mechanically that they dismounted at the lych-gate and passing into the churchyard stood gazing stupidly up at the old yews that were no longer dark and glooming as on the day of their first visit, but silvered with the frost and festooned with spheres of coloured light like a night sky all aglow with the stars and planets. "There's not the smallest orb which thou beholdest, but in its motion like an angel sings." The music was all about them as they stood bemused upon the path, and it was not until the singing procession was almost upon them that they realized that it was not the trees themselves that were carolling so blithely. They looked up and gaped, and so bright was the dazzle of sunshine upon the golden cross the squire was carrying that they faltered, and stepped aside to let it go by.

And before they could recover themselves Old Parson also had gone by playing his fiddle, passing them with a nod and smiling glance that seemed to hold no memory of past injury, but was just the casual greeting of a fellow wayfarer upon the same road. And then the crowd of singing children behind him parted and gathered them in, and as a strongly flowing stream picks up three insignificant straws, so were they picked up and borne onward by the singing village by a way that they did not know to a journey's end that was wrapped in mystery. It was the strangeness of it all that kept them silent, that and the bemusement of the bright light, and the unfamiliar outflowing of goodwill that brought a strange peace to their hearts. By the time they came to themselves a little they were outside the village, and winding along a narrow, deep lane towards the woods, and to have stopped and protested would have been merely to make fools of themselves. Better to go on and see what happened. Besides, they could scarcely do anything else, for they were imbedded in singing children like three black flies in golden honey.

4

And so they came to Wildwoods, where the pines and larches grew so thickly together that the sunlight reached them only in shafts of silver piercing like lances through the interwoven branches. They went more slowly now, for they were going up-hill, but they did not cease their singing, and the way was easy to travel because the walk through Wildwoods to Paradise Hill was a favourite one with the villagers and the path was well-trodden. Paradise Hill had got its name because of the spring of clear water that bubbled up beneath an old twisted thorn tree that grew half-way up the hill. A legend of the countryside said that this was a holy spring, and all the villagers treated it as a wishing well. Long ago a shepherd pasturing his sheep upon the hillside had felt the need for a more conveniently placed water supply than was provided by the dew-pond at the very summit of the hill, and had prayed to the holy angels to supply the deficiency, and because he was pure of heart they had heard his prayer, and now the well on Paradise Hill never failed even in the longest drought. Because of it Paradise Hill had never come under the plough, but had always been used for the folding of sheep, and at lambing time small white specks were dotted all over the green grass like daisies, and the small bleating voices made such a noise when they called out all together that they nearly drowned the music of the stream purling down over the stones. There was a shepherd's hut roofed with pine-branches near the bottom of the hill, facing east towards Wildwoods, and Shepherd Joseph spent a large portion of his time there. The traveller who had fol-lowed the path through the larches and the pines saw his hut as soon as he emerged through the trees, and looked up beyond it to the glorious slope of Paradise Hill towering against the western sky.

The village folk were familiar with the looks of Paradise Hill at sunset, for it was generally on a fine evening, when the day's work was done, that they came to stand beneath the old thorn tree and wish for what they wanted – a good harvest or a fat baby or a silver thimble or whatever it might be – and they were familiar too with Shepherd Joseph's hut and the attractive picture it made against the hillside when one emerged from Wildwoods. But the three Grey Men were from a far country, and what they saw when the larches and pines drew back behind them and they were in the open again gave them a shock from which they never afterwards recovered.

When the singing procession came out from Wildwoods the sun was just setting, and Paradise Hill, clothed in a dazzling crystal mantle of white snow, towered up against a sky that passed through every gradation of colour from saffron to rose, and from rose to pale aquamarine that deepened gradually through azure to hyacinth blue, and when the blue was deepest, just above the summit of the crystal hill, one star was shining, and exactly below it upon the hillside Shepherd Joseph's hut was illumined with light from within. The light shone out through the open doorway and made a path of gold over the snow that reached as far as the feet of the Grey Men. A few steps more and they were treading this path of gold, and they were no longer Grey Men weighed down by the foolish wisdom of the spiritual desert where they had been living, but children again walking once more in the light from an open door that they had imagined had shut behind them long ago for ever. They were suddenly young, as young as Shepherd Joseph, young as Old Parson, or as King David when he suddenly let go of his years and dignity and went capering along before the Ark, playing his harp; young as the youngest child in the procession, little Jane the blacksmith's child, riding upon her father's back.

But young though they were, they could not bring themselves to enter the lighted hut, as did those who were children in stature as well as in heart and went crowding in with shouts of glee, tumbling one over the other like ecstatic young puppies for sheer joy that they had found their nursery again. The Grey Men stayed outside with the other grown-ups and looked in through the windows and the door at the heart-warming sight within.

The Virgin and Child might have had to flee away from their home in the church because of the persecution of foolish men, but they were now very much at home in exile, comfortably settled upon a wooden shelf upon the wall that Shepherd Joseph had made for them. His brazier full of glowing coals stood to one side of them, keeping them warm and illuminating the whole hut with rosy light. Upon the other side of them stood Shepherd Joseph

170

himself, leaning on his staff, keeping watch over them as he had kept watch all down the centuries over the weak and helpless. In the straw near the brazier, where in the lambing season Shepherd Joseph put sick lambs to sleep, Todd lay, with Percy stretched out beside him in a most companionable manner. The cherub with the darn on its nose was there too, in reality fastened to the wall, but seeming in the enchanted light to be poised in flight like a real cherub. Indeed, to the children, and to the three Grey Men because a blow dealt by a scene of sudden and unexpected beauty had sent them staggering back into their childhood in an exceedingly dazed condition, the toys in the hut were toys no longer, but living breathing creatures of flesh and blood. If proof were needed of this it was given by Saint Nicholas, who was leaning against the wall beyond the brazier smiling to himself in a most mysterious manner, because his cloak was no longer billowing out over the something secret that he kept hidden beneath it, but lying in deflated folds, and on the floor at his feet was the thing that he had kept hidden – a huge bulging sack. With shouts of joy the children fell upon it because they knew it was for them, and tumbled its contents out upon the floor.

There was a present for every one of them, from the oldest to the youngest, from Prue to little Jane, wonderful toys all fashioned from wood. There were wooden dolls with painted faces and wonderful garments made of gay scraps of silk and velvet, whose colours were strangely reminiscent of the church vestments whose disappearance had been commanded by the Grey Men, wooden skittles for playing the beloved old game of ninepins, wooden figures of rabbits and field mice and little birds all in a row on a branch, wooden cradles for the dolls and wooden hobby horses with flowing manes of real horsehair, wooden tops and Noah's Arks and wooden pipes and whistles for playing merry tunes on. The children did not doubt that Saint Nicholas had had those things hidden beneath his cloak for many a long day, just awaiting a suitable moment for delivery to their rightful owners, but the grown-ups thought to themselves that Old Parson had surpassed himself this time, and no mistake.

When the hubbub had subsided a little, Old Parson, the only grown-up except Shepherd Joseph to enter the hut that night, took the golden cross from the squire and propped it against the wall of the hut beneath the Virgin and Child. "Come now," he said, "the moon is rising and the owls are calling out in Wildwoods that all good children should be in their beds by nightfall on Christmas Eve. You shall come here again whenever you like. This shall be your nursery until the tyranny be over-passed."

5

Afterwards the three Grey Men scarcely remembered how they got back to the village. They only knew that though Wildwoods had been very dark there had been no fear beneath the branches, and that where they had emerged into the lane the stars had shone most gloriously. By the time they reached the lych-gate the moonlight was so bright that they had refused the squire's invitation to spend the night at the manor house, for the way to the nearest town would be as clear as though it were day. Yet they lingered a little, loath to leave, and when at last they mounted their horses, the village folk had gone home to bed and they and Old Parson were alone together.

And then the oldest of them said an unexpected thing. "Forgive us," he said.

"There's no harm done," said Old Parson. "The other day you smashed a fine monument in the church yonder, but by God's help I put the pieces together again, and the children took no harm."

Then the second Grey Man, looking up at the fine old church with its soaring tower blocking out the stars, also said an unexpected thing; though the unexpectedness lay not so much in the actual words as in the sadness of the tone in which he spoke. "Empty windows and a bare altar," he said, "and no colour anywhere when you take the holly wreaths down."

"It will be for a short time only," Old Parson reassured him. "This joyless creed that you are forcing on us is contrary to the spirit of this country and will not endure. In a land where the spring woods are enamelled every colour of the rainbow, where lambs make merry in the meadows and the birds sing as loudly as the choirs of Paradise, you cannot permanently stop the people from following God's example and delighting in colour and music and festivity. Do you think I would have emptied my church of

172

beauty at your orders if I had thought the emptiness likely to endure? I would have died first."

And then the third Grey Man said an unexpected thing; though again the unexpectedness lay not in the words but in the questioning tone in which he said them. "Wassail at Christmas, the blessing of palms, the cross upon the altar and holy water in the stoup – just children's games?"

And now it was Old Parson's turn to surprise his hearers. "Just children's games," he agreed placidly. "Almighty God created us children with the whole wide world for our nursery, and you misunderstand Almighty God, my dear sirs, when you forget at whose command old Noah made the Ark."

And Old Parson was proved right, for though a bloody civil war had to rage over the land before his faith was justified, yet at long last men and women laid aside the grey garments and the gloomy faces and the hellfire creed that was so alien to the spirit of the land and Merry England was herself again, colourful and light-hearted, praising the bounty of God with the chiming of bells and a merry and cheerful singing in the churches that were filled once again with colour and fragrance and candle-light and toys for young and old.

"The Restoration" the world at large called this happy period, thinking of that day of jubilation when King Charles II came back to his own again, but the village was as uninterested as ever in what went on in London town, and to them the phrase meant the digging up and replacement of the stained-glass windows, the wearing and embroidering of new vestments, the triumphant return from exile in Shepherd Joseph's hut of the golden cross, the Madonna and Child, Saint Nicholas, the cherub with the darned nose, Percy and Todd, and the restoration of the children's nursery to its proper place inside the church.

Christmas in the Village

1

ARSON FRODSHAM was settling down to write his Christmas sermon. He groaned, shifting his great bulk from side to side in an effort to get comfortable in his not very comfortable chair; the stuffing was bursting through the splits in the leather seat and the back and arms were solid wood. He took his wig off and hung it on the back of the chair to cool his brain. Then he put on his spectacles, trimmed his quill pen, spat on his hand and gripped it. He dipped it in the ink and applied it to the paper, but it spluttered and ink went all over the virgin page. He dropped it and swore loudly. Then he wiped it on the disreputable old cassock which he wore in his study merely for warmth's sake, for he was not really a cassock-minded man, trimmed it once more and tried again.

"Dec. 24th, the year of our Lord 1735," he wrote at the top of the page. "Sermon preached by Benjamin Obadiah Frodsham in the Church of St. Mary the Virgin, of St. Gabriel and All Angels in the village of Gaysbarton in the county of Devonshire. The seventh verse of the second chapter of St. Luke's gospel, 'She brought forth her first-born son, and wrapped him in swaddling clothes, and laid him in a manger.'" So far so good. Parson Frodsham had a fine flowing handwriting with enormous s's and f's, and g's and y's with tails like sea-serpents, and this had covered quite a lot of the page. He lay back in his chair and looked at the ceiling. A bunch of herbs dangled from an old oak beam within a few inches of his nose and he sniffed appreciatively. Sage. Thyme. Gideon was at this very moment preparing the goose out at the back. His mouth watered. "God have mercy upon me a sinner," he groaned, "for I have too much respect unto my stomach." He leaned forward again and wrote, "Good people, once more we are assembled here upon this feast of Christmas."

Now why, Parson Frodsham asked himself, dropping his pen as though it were an adder, did he leave the writing of his sermon until Christmas Eve? He knew it took him a sennight of hard labour and yet always – always – he left it till the last moment. And why did he listen to this troublesome conscience of his, insisting that the Christmas, Easter and Whitsun sermons must be written by himself? Upon every other preaching occasion he merely grabbed a tattered book of other men's sermons which lay on the floor and preached whatever came to hand. It saved him hours of anguish and sent his tired congregation off to sleep just as well as his own efforts. But somehow on the great festivals he felt that God was asking of him his poor best. His best got worse and worse as the years went on, what with the screws, and being so fat and old, and so increasingly choleric in temper, and feeling the cold more than he did, but he did try to give it at least on the big days, the great days of God's glory when even he inside his rheumaticky mountain of flesh could feel something stirring like the sap in spring. "To adore the Babe of Bethlehem," he wrote, "and receive into our hearts his peace."

Now that was a fine phrase. He'd expressed that very well. He was so pleased with himself that he put his pen down again and rubbed his hands together. After all, he thought, he ought to be able to write good sermons for he was a literary-minded man. He read a great deal. There were so many piles of books on his study floor that it looked like a forest clearing full of tree-stumps, with upon every stump a dirty cup and saucer, mementos of the tea-drinking of many days past, the whole covered with a fine coating of dust and cobwebs. Parson Frodsham was a bachelor and his only servant was Gideon the mole-catcher, for if there was one thing he hated more than writing sermons it was women. Gideon did not believe in disturbing dust and Parson Frodsham always knew where to find everything. Moleskins were nailed out flat against the beautiful panelling of the room, for Parson Frodsham was as fascinated by the art of mole-catching as Gideon was. The two old men were very happy together.

"Good people, let us now consider the angels," wrote Parson Frodsham, not that he wanted to consider them particularly for a hatred of wood-pigeons and blackbirds made him not very partial to winged creatures, but he had to say something, and Gaysbarton was named after Gabriel. The angels. What could he say about angels? At least they did not despoil his garden. Their message, now. The angels' message. That was a part of Christmas. Where was it? He peered through his spectacles at the torn page of his old Bible and pinned the verse down with a horny forefinger.

178

"Peace on earth, goodwill towards *men*." He wrote it down and his pen, without his volition, made a spluttering but forceful line under the last word. He looked at it, finding himself for once entirely in agreement with winged creatures. Drat that woman! Drat the Widow Gascoigne. Gascoigne! What a name! And she liked to be called Madame, Madame Etienne Gascoigne, just because she, a Devonshire woman born and bred and christened Jane Cob in this very church, had married a heathen Papist as her second husband. More shame to her! If it was true, as the village said, that her second marriage to please herself had been even more disastrous than her first marriage to please her father he could only feel it was a judgement on her. Quarrelsome busybody! She had set the whole village by the ears. He was quarrelsome himself, always falling out with somebody, and then asking God to forgive him, but he never asked to be forgiven for quarrelling with the Widow Gascoigne, for his war with her was a holy war.

Every Christmas she insisted on bringing the Joneys into church and every Christmas he told her to remove them, and every Christmas she quietly refused, and her will being stronger than his every Christmas she won the battle. But this year, Parson Frodsham told himself, she would *not* win. If by any chance she smuggled those Joneys into church again without his seeing it he would take them out and they should go into his kitchen fire and roast his goose; and a fit end that would be for such heathen images. Roaring softly beneath his breath he moved his table and chair, himself and his sermon nearer to the window, for he had planned to spend the rest of the daylight hours writing his sermon and watching the village green that lay between the Widow Gascoigne's house and the church, so as to pounce on her and bar her passage as she and her sour-faced maid came along with the Joneys. In other years she had always got them into position inside the church without his knowing, and that had increased his difficulties. She had, he believed, chosen the moment when he was absorbed in his dinner, of which she knew him to be inordinately fond. He suspected the village of keeping a nose cocked for his dinner and betraying him to her, for the village loved the Joneys and in this holy war he had them all against him.

Eighty years ago the Widow Gascoigne's grandfather had been appointed the parson of Gaysbarton. He had been a Caroline high churchman and an expert woodcarver and he had made figures of Joseph and Mary and the Child, Gabriel and the shepherds, and had put them in the church every Christmas to delight the children who called them the Joneys, a Devonshire word for any sort of little image. Thirty years later his son, also a high churchman, had succeeded him and remained at Gaysbarton for forty years, dying there as his father had done, and during all that time the Joneys had come into church every year and had become a part of village tradition. Even during the years of the Commonwealth they had come in, for the village was so remote among its wild hills that authority took little note of what they did in such a tiny place. Ten years ago Parson Frodsham had himself come to Gaysbarton, preceded by a mere two months by Madame Gascoigne, coming home in her widowhood to spend the rest of her life in the place where she had been born, and determined that all things should be carried on at Gaysbarton as they had been in her father's and grandfather's day. Parson Frodsham, on the other hand, had determined differently, for he was a low churchman, as low as he could be without falling out at the bottom. The village was indifferent to churchmanship, high or low, but liked the Joneys. There had been war between Madame Gascoigne and Parson Frodsham from the first.

The old man surveyed the village green, empty at present. It was twelve o'clock of a frosty morning. There had been a light fall of snow during the night, the first of an open winter, and it sparkled in the sun. Parson Frodsham was not an aesthetically-minded man but he did think it all looked very pretty. The village, perched on a steep hill, was very old. The whitewashed thatched cottages were grouped about a green with a grey Celtic cross in the centre of it. The church was one of the loveliest in all that countryside of wonderful churches. Its tower soared up above the small village like the tower of a cathedral. From his little thatched house Parson Frodsham looked out over the village, and the wooded valley below, to the great bare moors. They were snow-covered to-day, streaked with amethyst shadows, and because the air was so clear they had moved nearer, their crests jewel-sharp against the brilliant blue sky. On other days they were misty and distant, and on other days again they disappeared behind sweeping curtains of rain. No two days were alike in this country but each day, even in bad weather, had its own incredible beauty. Looking out on the beauty, Parson Frodsham's pen slipped from his hand, even though he was not aesthetically minded.

A group of small children came running from the direction of the church all bunched up in their winter garments, rosy-cheeked and merry, and Parson Frodsham smiled benevolently as he watched them. Then clear high voices reached him through the closed but ill-fitting window. "The Joneys have come to church! The Joneys have come!"

He leaped to his feet, the table lurching so violently that the inkpot described a circle in the air and the ink sprayed out all over the cups and saucers on the piles of books, and the delicate counterpane of dust and cobwebs that covered them. He just remembered to clap his wig on his head but he did not stop to put his cloak on. Gathering his cassock up in both hands he shot his great bulk forth from his little front door and across the green in kangeroo leaps and bounds, for it was just possible that the Widow and her maid might still be in the church and he would catch them there. They must have taken the Joneys into church while he was absorbed in a late breakfast.

He was under the lych-gate in two strides and across the church-yard in six. He fumbled feebly at the latch of the west door, staggered into the church and collapsed in a pew, so winded that there was no more strength left in him. He sat forward with his head in his hands, breathing like a bellows. "Gross fat," he reproached himself. "Too fond of my belly. Lord have mercy upon me." He felt better, sat up and looked about him. The church was empty. The Widow had gone home long ago. But the Joneys were in church. There was a small disused chapel to the right of the chancel and within it he could see the straw-filled manger, and the figures of Mary and Joseph, Gabriel and the shepherds. Behind them, on the small stone altar, the Widow had placed a pot of holly and two candles. Every Christmas day she lit these candles and every Christmas day Parson Frodsham blew them out again. He looked at the Joneys miserably. It was difficult to take them out when they were arranged there with such loving care, but this year he must do it. But not for a minute or two. He must get his breath back.

Presently a familiar peace enfolded him, as it enfolded everyone who came to this church that was so old and holy. The pews of dark oak had carved pew ends, each one different. The flagstones were worn by the passing of many feet through the centuries, the feet of men and women who had gone up to the altar miserable and hungry in spirit and come down again comforted and satisfied. There was an ancient screen carved with the figures of our Lady, Gabriel and the angels. The old green glass in the windows was opaque but it let the sunlight through with heavenly alchemy. The old Parson sighed deeply.

Then there slowly came to him the conviction that he had been wrong in thinking he was alone in this church. There was another human presence here. Yet he could see no one; only the Joneys with the soft sea-green light streaming through the south window to illumine their blue and red and green, and Gabriel's golden wings. What was that? Parson Frodsham's heart gave a great lurch, for he saw a minute hand waving above the edge of the manger. He stared, but there was nothing. Of course there was nothing. There it was again, waving to him. He passed his great hand across his eyes and groaned. The tricks that indigestion could play on a man! It was not there when he looked again. Of course not. Yes, it was. Motionless now, blessing him. Not *blessing* him? Yes, blessing him. Stuff and nonsense. Gone now. There was nothing to be seen any more, but a thin angry wailing filled the church.

Parson Frodsham heaved himself to his feet and staggered up the aisle to the little chapel. Two worn stone steps led up to it and he tripped over them and stumbled to his knees before the manger. In it, instead of the usual beautiful bambino, pink-cheeked and blue-eyed, with golden curls and a seraphic expression, was an extremely ugly baby, its purple face creased up in fury, its fists flailing, bald as an egg, and wrapped up in an old shawl. Parson Frodsham passed through a moment of sheer terror and then he poked it, and found it damp. This, he knew, was invariably the case with babies, and was the chief cause of his objection to them. When he baptized a baby he clutched it, signed it, bawled its name over its head and handed it hastily back to its mother. He was not a baby-minded man. Nevertheless he soon knew that something had to be done about this one. It was very new, and if left in the cold church in its damp state would soon have frozen into a solid icicle. Murmuring a prayer for strength he picked it up. Then holding it in the crook of one arm he bent and looked under the manger. There, lying on the cold stone, was the real bambino. He picked that up too and put it back in its nest. Then he carried the baby out of church.

Carrying it through the churchyard he wondered what on earth he was to do next but once he reached the village green the matter was settled for him, for feeling the chill of the outer air on its bald head the baby set up a terrific wailing and instantly a window in every cottage surrounding the green was flung wide, including the parlour window of Madame Gascoigne's neat little house, and a female head shot out like a jack-in-the-box. "A baby has been abandoned in the church," he said, and stalked on with great hauteur towards the parsonage, every able-bodied woman in the village at his heels. In his study they steered expertly in and out between the piles of books on the floor, their skirts bunched close to them that they might not upset the cups and saucers, and in a moment were milling about him and the baby, whose wails were drowned in the piercing clamour of their conversation. The excitement was intense, for not only was there the baby, but every woman present had for years been longing to get inside the parsonage and get her hands on its disorder, and those who could not get near the baby were even now piling the dirty cups and saucers on top of each other and carrying them out into the kitchen. Parson Frodsham's head went round, he swayed, and the baby was gently taken from him. "I will take care of this child," said a firm, cool voice. "Sit down, Mr. Frodsham. Maria Larkin, get his reverence a cup of tea."

Parson Frodsham collapsed in his chair and mopping his face with a large torn handkerchief, said meekly, "I could do with something stronger, marm."

"Maria, a glass of brandy for his reverence," said the cool voice. "Doubtless you will find it in the cupboard in the dining-parlour."

In a moment the glass was in his hands. He flung his head back, tipped it over his nose and gulped once. The woman had put precious little in the glass, but it was enough to restore him to some semblance of his former self, and he was able to get the Widow Gascoigne into focus. She was a woman of perhaps forty-five or so, a pretty woman, small and neat, but the brilliance of her dark eyes and the line of her jaw showed great strength of character. She was dressed in a plain grey gown with a spotless white muslin fichu and a large white mob cap. (No woman present had stopped to put a cloak on but they did not seem to be feeling the cold.)

183

Under the cap the wings of her dark hair were becomingly touched with grey at the temples. The baby was in her arms. "I will take charge of this child," she repeated.

There was sudden silence and then an ominous murmur, and Parson Frodsham understood that every woman in the room had taken exception to this ruling and considered the baby to be hers by right. He heaved himself to his feet, compelled by the bright eyes that were fixing his like gimlets, waved his hand for silence and said as they commanded him to say, "Madame Gascoigne, as granddaughter and daughter of former pastors of this place, has charge of this baby. It is her right."

Before he could withdraw his hand it was seized. He looked down and saw that a minute fist had closed about his forefinger with a grip of iron. The baby had opened its eyes and it appeared to Parson Frodsham that they looked straight into his, and the grip tightened as though in the fellowship of profound dismay. Was this life? All these women surging about a man? Men must hold together or be lost.

"He's a fine boy," said Parson Frodsham hoarsely.

"I believe him to be a girl," said the Widow Gascoigne tartly.

"A boy," said Parson Frodsham with conviction, and then strengthened by the friendly sympathy of that grip he raised his voice and said, "Ladies, now that this matter is settled I should be grateful if the use of my study might be restored to me. I have my sermon to write. Good morning to ee."

2

Gideon, who had been skulking in the larder until the tyranny should be overpast, shut the front door on the last rustling petticoat. It was now found to be dinner-time. Parson Frodsham took a very long time over his dinner, so exhausted was he and so sadly in need of nourishment. Then, to get himself into the right frame of mind for tackling his sermon again, he helped Gideon skin some moles. When that was over a fiery sunset was burning itself out into a luminous green twilight. But Parson Frodsham did not at once turn to his sermon because all the time he had been skinning moles an insistent question had been slowly rising to the surface of his mind. He had tried to push it down several times but it had always come up again. Where was the mother of this child? Deep down in him, overlaid by age and fat and weariness, but in him, there was a true priest. He would, in the last resort, have given his life to save a soul. The child's mother might be a hardened and wicked woman, or she might be a weak and giddy young girl, but in either case she was a soul in danger, and where was she?

Parson Frodsham ate a couple of slices of plum cake to give him strength and said, "Gideon, I'm going out." Then he put on his cloak, lit his lantern and walked slowly and heavily down to the church. The moon was rising and a few stars were showing. Presently they would be brilliant in the clear frosty air, just as they should be on Christmas Eve. He went into the church and sat down, his large hands spread out on his knees, his lantern set on the stone floor near him. Its light glowed softly on the glorious carved pew ends, and there was a faint glimmer of moony light in the windows, but the rest of the great church was lost in deep shadow. Parson Frodsham could hardly be called a prayerfully-minded man, indeed "God have mercy upon me" was practically the only prayer he did pray, except on Sundays when he was bawling the prayers out of the prayer book, but whenever he was in a dilemma he came and sat in the church like this, his hands spread on his knees, and then his muddled mind began to clear. Now what, he asked himself after a while, had been the thoughts of this poor woman? Could he think of a similar case? He racked his brains but could only think of Moses in his rush basket. What had a woman done then? Hidden herself and watched, he remembered, until she saw the child taken to safety. In that case, he thought, the woman was not here now, for she would have gone away after she had seen him rescue the child. But would she? No one seemed to have seen her entering the church. She must have done it while they were all at breakfast, and hidden herself until she saw the Widow Gascoigne and her maid bring in the Joneys, arrange them and then leave again. She must have known about the Joneys, and in that case she had not come from far, and would not have far to travel to get home again. She would be able to wait to start back until the village was indoors and the curtains drawn. She might still be hiding in the church.

Parson Frodsham picked up his lantern and began a thorough search, unaware that the noise he was making falling over the

185

hassocks was more than enough to warn any stowaway of his purpose. He looked under the seats and behind the altar. He looked in the pulpit and behind the brooms in the corner, but there was no one there. He was just about to go away again when he bethought him of the little vestry. The door was shut but he pushed it open and went in. It was a small place, furnished with a cupboard, a table and a chair. The chair was a large one, for it was one of his own brought down from the Parsonage. Curled up in it was a child asleep. She had kicked off her shoes and they lay on the floor. Her hood had fallen back from her head and her dark hair lay on her shoulders. He put the lantern on the table and bent over her, but she was so deeply asleep that she did not stir. Long dark eyelashes lay in pools of shadow on her cheeks. Her lips were parted and the breath came evenly and sweetly between them. Her small nose had a dusting of freckles on it. But she was evidently dreadfully tired. Poor child, thought Parson Frodsham, poor child, and forgot all about the reprobate mother for whom he was looking. He put his hand on her shoulder and shook her gently and she awoke with a cry.

"There! There!" said Parson Frodsham, patting her shoulder. "There's naught for a little maid to be afraid of."

"Thomas!" she said, for she was only half awake.

"Who's he?" asked Parson Frodsham.

"My baby," she said, and thrusting her feet out from beneath her cloak she began feeling about for her shoes.

"*Your* baby?" ejaculated Parson Frodsham. "A little maid like you can't have a baby."

"I'm sixteen," she said petulantly. "Where's Thomas? I can't remember where I put him."

"In the manger," said Parson Frodsham drily, "and I think you be a naughty little maid."

She was fully awake now and she began to weep. "It was because of Moses," she sobbed.

"I thought as much," said Parson Frodsham, and then he repented him that he had spoken drily and made her cry. "There, there, child, put your shoes on. How are we to think what's to do next if you have no shoes on?"

Groaning, he bent and picked up her shoes. She held out her feet, very small feet in worsted stockings full of holes, and he put her shoes on them. They were icy cold to his touch, through the holes. It struck him, as with Thomas, that the first thing he had to do was to remove this child from the chill of the church before it froze.

"Come with me, maid," he said. "We'll get some hot milk inside you, and warm your feet at the fire, and then we'll see."

She came with him meekly enough, dragging her feet wearily as they crossed the village green, her sobs subsiding into hiccups. It was nearly dark now and no one saw them. It did not even occur to Parson Frodsham to take the girl to some woman of the parish. Instinct told him that this was something he could manage best himself. Also he and Gideon had had more than enough of women for one day. This child was not a woman. She was so small, as she shuffled along beside him, that he could not believe she was sixteen.

In his study he sat her before the fire and yelled for Gideon who, appearing, accepted the situation with astonishing ease after the first shock. Seated before the fire, a bowl of steaming bread and milk on her lap, her stockings off and her toes curling and uncurling in the warmth, the girl began visibly to recover. Colour returned to her face and a dimple to her left cheek. Watching her, Parson Frodsham could see that she was a pretty creature, and in good health probably wiry and strong. She had a brown little face, with a firm mouth, and her small hands looked capable. She finished her bread and milk down to the last drop, was given a boiled egg and an apple and finished those, more bread and milk and finished that. Then she asked who had Thomas and Parson Frodsham told her. "Will she be good to him?" she asked, and Parson Frodsham said she would. "For always?" she asked, and instead of answering Parson Frodsham produced a large pocket-handkerchief and sneezed into it, for he was not sure. The Widow Gascoigne had never had a child. He remembered her precise ways, the acidity of her maid and the exquisite neatness of her house. He believed the Widow's thoughts would turn to orphanages later on; especially as Thomas was not of the sex she had thought he was.

"I'll tell you about Thomas, sir," said the girl suddenly. She put down the empty bowl, folded her hands on her lap and turned and looked at the old man. Her hazel eyes were very direct in their glance. She was an apothecary's daughter, she said, but her father had died two years ago. Her mother had died in her babyhood

187

and she was their only child. She had to earn her living and she had gone to be stillroom maid at a big house ten miles away. Then came the usual story of betrayal, which she told frankly and steadily, and Parson Frodsham heard with inward fury, all the more fury because he was as a rule far more sympathetic to his own sex than the other. The housekeeper at the big house had paid out of her own pocket for her to go to a farmhouse nearby to have Thomas, but they would not keep her there. Then she had remembered Moses, and remembered being told about the Joneys at Gaysbarton, and so here she was, and Thomas.

"And what do you mean to do now, maid?" asked Parson Frodsham.

"I don't know, sir," she said. "I thought – perhaps I could do like Moses's mother and be Thomas's nurse – I thought – I didn't know what to do and I went to sleep in the vestry." He saw that in spite of the firm mouth and the direct glance she was a child still. Her father had died too soon. "I do miss Thomas," she finished lamely.

"Then put your shoes and stockings on and I'll take ee to Madame Gascoigne," he said.

But she began to cry again. "I want to stay here," she sobbed. "I want to stay here with you and Gideon. I could sleep here by the fire, with Thomas. Please, sir, will you fetch Thomas? I could be your housekeeper, sir, and live here with you and Gideon and Thomas always." Parson Frodsham's heart fell. A woman in the house! She was a child now but she'd be a woman in no time at all. But there was Thomas. All day he had been feeling the grip of Thomas's hand upon his finger. The girl looked up at him. "You see, sir," she said, "I don't like women."

He looked at her. He could see that she had suffered much from them. How had all those women at the big house behaved to her in her trouble? He reached for his cloak. "What's your name, child?" he asked.

"Penelope," she said.

"Stay here for to-night, then," he said, "and I'll fetch Thomas to ee."

It was years since he had been inside the Widow Gascoigne's neat little house, not since the mighty quarrel they had had about his pigsty, whose aroma she declared entered her parlour window when the wind was in the east. She had declared Gideon never cleaned it out, which was not true. He swilled the whole place out every Easter Monday without fail, and oftener if necessary. The sour-faced maid was so astonished to see him on the doorstep that she ushered him straight into the parlour before she realized what she was doing. Madame Gascoigne was seated in front of the fire but she was not looking her usual composed and immaculate self. Her cap was awry and her face flushed. She looked very tired. On her lap was Thomas, shrieking.

"Marm, he'll do himself an injury!" said Parson Frodsham in consternation. "What's the matter with him?"

Madame Gascoigne looked up at him, and she was near tears. "You see," she faltered, "this is a small village and just now there is no one —" Being a bachelor he failed to follow the drift of her thought. He was all at sea, and she had to come out with it. "We want a wet nurse," she said.

"Ah!" said Parson Frodsham, enlightened. "But I thought, in such circumstances, cow's milk could be used?"

"Yes," she said. "Diluted with warm water, and a little sugar. But he won't have it. He is a very obstinate and naughty baby. And he is a boy. I was so sure he was a girl."

"Don't you like boys, marm?" asked Parson Frodsham.

Into her tired eyes came a glimmer of the old fire. "After all I have suffered from two bad husbands I cannot endure your sex," she said low and bitterly.

Somehow Parson Frodsham had never liked her so well. He held out his arms. "Then give me the boy, marm," he said. "His mother is at the Parsonage."

She handed him the yelling Thomas and broke into tears of relief.

3

The next morning, after he had come back from the first service of Christmas day, Parson Frodsham, exhausted, could think of nothing but food. Gideon, anticipating his thought, had a gargantuan breakfast ready for him in the kitchen. After the edge of his hunger had been slightly blunted by four slices of home-cured ham and two eggs he looked up at Gideon and asked, "Where's the little maid?"

"Up the stairs," said Gideon, who was seated before the fire peeling potatoes. "She's sweepin' out the guest chamber. It'll make a nice little room for 'erself an' Thomas, so she ses." He gazed at his master. "She's stayin', so she ses. Our 'ousekeeper, so she ses."

Parson Frodsham brought his great hand down with a crash on the table. "Does she, indeed? *I* didn't say. She put it to me last night and never a word did I say in answer. What will you and I be doing with a woman in the house? Can you tell me that, Gideon?"

"What us be told," said Gideon. "But there's the boy. I could teach un to catch moles."

Parson Frodsham filled his mouth with ham. He could see that he and Gideon were in agreement. They could not turn out that pretty child. They hadn't the heart. And there was Thomas. He masticated and swallowed. "Where's Thomas?" he asked.

"In the study," said Gideon. "Good as gold, he is."

The word study reminded Parson Frodsham of something. His eyes widened in dismay and his two-pronged fork, loaded with ham, was lowered slowly to his plate. "My sermon," he said. "I've not written it."

"No time now," said Gideon easily. "But if ee'd not spent the 'ole of last evenin' watchin' the little maid with Thomas ee could 'ave written it easy. No matter. Preach one out o' the old book."

Parson Frodsham decided that he must do that. He relaxed, finished his breakfast in a leisurely manner, lit his clay pipe and stretched his feet to the fire. Upstairs Penelope went backwards and forwards, putting her room to rights. Her footsteps were light, quick, happy and very busy. It was a pleasant sound. The church bells were ringing for matins when he went into the study to find his sermon book. The first thing he saw was Thomas, asleep in a wooden box by the fire. He bent over him. It was the first time he had seen Thomas in a state of well-being. His face was less purple and creased than it had been. One small curved hand rested against his cheek. His right ear looked like a seashell. A nice little boy. It was a full five minutes before Parson Frodsham turned from him to look for his sermon book, which he knew to be the fourth book in the pile by the window. Then, turned, he saw the appalling thing that had happened. His room had been tidied.

Penelope must have been up with the dawn, and done it while

he was in church. All the books were back in the bookcases. There was not a dirty cup and saucer to be seen, nor a cobweb nor a speck of dust. For a short while Parson Frodsham stood motionless in misery. Then he took a grip on himself. He would get used to it. One could get used to anything. God helping him, he would get used to being clean and tidy. The bells were ringing more insistently and he turned to the bookshelves to find his sermon book. All his books were much alike, old, brown, torn, and with their titles worn away. He hunted up and down, opened this book and that, but he could not find his sermon book. The bells had changed to the one five minutes' bell and with despair in his heart Parson Frodsham put on his cloak, adjusted his wig and walked down to the church. Though he mechanically returned their greetings he scarcely saw his parishioners, streaming along in the same direction in their Sunday best, happy in the frosty sunshine. He had never preached extempore in his life, and his people expected a full forty-five minutes' oration. He tried to remember a text he knew, something about it shall be given you what you shall say, but he couldn't get it right. "God have mercy upon me," he prayed in the porch.

Inside the church he felt better. He always felt better inside his church. He was even able to say to himself that the Widow Gascoigne was not here yet, because the candles on the altar behind the Joneys were not lit. Then he saw that she was here. She was in her accustomed pew and she turned her head and smiled at him. He could hardly believe it. To please him she had chosen not to light the candles. He bowed to her, walked up to the little chapel, took his tinder box from his pocket and lit them. Then he bowed to her again and went to the vestry. The Joneys looked very bright and gay in the mingled sunlight and candle light, almost as though they knew that they would never now be banished.

The service that morning seemed even happier than it usually was at Gaysbarton on Christmas day. The choir in the gallery scraped at their fliddles and twiddled at their flutes with enormous gaiety, everyone sang hard, and people who had not been on speaking terms for ages were seen to be smiling shyly at each other, even as the Parson and Madame Gascoigne had done. But it all seemed like a confused nightmare to Parson Frodsham. "It shall be given you," he kept saying to himself, but when he got into the pulpit he couldn't even remember the text upon which he had meant to preach. But he remembered another and gave it out loud and clear. "Unto us a child is born, unto us a son is given." His flock waited in delighted expectancy, for they saw he had no sermon with him. He must have forgotten it. Would he go back home for it? Would he send Amos the clerk for it? Would he try and remember it? Hush, now, he was off.

Parson Frodsham preached no sermon in the accepted sense. It came to him just to tell them how he had found Penelope and Thomas. They knew far more about it than he did, of course, for the story had been all round the village, with a thousand embellishments, long before midnight, but they listened with kindly attention. Then he told them that this child was a Christmas gift to them at Gaysbarton. They must take great care of him, and of his young mother who was no more than a child herself. They must bring them up to be good servants of Almighty God. And then, suddenly, he began to speak of himself. He was a sinner, he said, he was a quarrelsome old sinner, and it was because of him that there had been so much quarrelling at Gaysbarton. He had set them a bad example. He asked them to forgive him. They couldn't have quarrelling now, not with this child here to be brought up in the peace of God. He spoke a little, stumblingly and shyly, about the peace of God, but he managed to end up with what he thought was a good phrase. "Let us adore the Babe of Bethlehem," he said, "and receive into our hearts His peace."

It was the shortest sermon Parson Frodsham had ever preached at Gaysbarton, ten minutes instead of forty-five, but it must have been one of his best because no one went to sleep and some of his congregation were moved to tears. Parson Frodsham was much moved himself and felt a need for a handkerchief. He plunged his hand deep in his cassock pocket and brought out a dead mole.

Christmas with the Angels

1

THIS is the story of an almost unbelievable humbling, nothing less than the story of the life that God lived when he came down from heaven and lived upon earth as a man. In a particular human body, born of a Mother belonging to a certain race of people, nearly two thousand years ago in the country of Palestine, God lived and died for us men and for our salvation. The fact of this humility is so glorious that it is beyond human understanding, but the limitations of race and time and place put a sort of picture-frame about the glory, so that we can look at it without being blinded. And we must look at it, because the picture in the frame is the most important thing in this world, or in any other.

Man had forgotten what God looked like. In the beginning God made man and loved him, and man looked up at God, and loved him also. God was at the centre of man's life and man looked at him, humbly worshipped him, loved and served him, and was happy. Man loved God of his own choice because God had given him free will. Unless God had given man the gift of choice he would have been incapable of love, because it is the nature of love that it cannot be compelled, but must be freely given. But now man did the most dreadful thing that he has ever done in the whole course of his history. He turned away from God and put himself in the centre instead of God. He chose to love and serve himself instead of God, and for a man to think himself more worthy of attention than God is pride, the most detestable of all the sins and the root of all the others. To serve God is to serve holiness and life eternal and to attain to them, to serve self is to serve sin and death and to die eternally.

To save man from his death the great love of God chose to do two things: to show himself to man all over again in his eternal beauty, and to lift up the great weight of sin that kept man a prisoner and carry it away, that man might be free to rise up and turn from self to God, and serve and love him as he used to do in the beginning.

And the way of God's choice was the way of this humbling. He came down to earth and lived as a man among men, that they might see and hear and touch eternal beauty, and he took upon himself the dreadful suffering and death that are the result of sin, though he himself was sinless, and in this way lifted the load and carried it away.

This great showing-forth and deliverance God accomplished for us in the person of his Son, who is one with him, the Word of God, the brightness of the everlasting light and the image of his goodness. The mystery of the Holy Trinity, the Father and the Son made one by the Holy Spirit of Love, Three Persons and yet One God, is beyond our understanding, but what we must understand is that the adorable beauty which we see in Jesus of Nazareth is the beauty of God himself, and that the suffering and death endured for us by him are the suffering and death of God.

But still he has left to us the power of choice. We need not look at him and love him unless we want to. We need not turn from ourselves to him unless we choose. But if we have once looked at him, even though we have seen him only dimly, we find we cannot do anything else but try our very hardest to put him in the centre of our lives.

This humbling began very far back in history, in God's choice of the people who should be especially his people. He did not choose to belong to one of the powerful nations of the world, or even to one of the cleverest or most civilized; he chose the people of Israel, a nomad shepherd people whose story, like his own, has much joy in it, but great hardship and sorrow too. But the people of Israel had one great treasure, and that was a truer idea of God than other nations possessed. Ever since that turning from God which we call the Fall, man has been like a lost creature trying to find the way home, and the religions of the world are his blundering attempts to find again the God whom once he saw and loved so well. And in this search the people of Israel came closest to the reality. They worshipped one God and they knew that he was the creator of the world, holy and just, not capricious and cruel like the many gods of other nations. And so it was to this poor and struggling nation who knew the most about him that God came.

For centuries before he was born they knew that he would come to them. Their prophets, men whose holiness gave them power to foresee the future, told them about him. They called him by many wonderful names – the Christ, the Messiah, the Deliverer, the Holy One of Israel, the Son of Man. But most of them imagined he would come as a conqueror who would deliver his people from their earthly enemies and establish an earthly kingdom. Very few realized that the enemy he was coming to fight was man's selfishness, that he would conquer by suffering and that his kingdom would be the spiritual kingdom of those who love God.

The bit of earth where the nomad people of Israel found a home at last is the narrow strip of land on the shore of the Mediterranean which to-day we call Palestine. It is a small country, and beautiful, but dry and mountainous and not very productive. And it is so wedged in between countries larger and wealthier than itself that throughout its history it has had little peace. Foreign armies have been perpetually marching across it, fighting battles on its soil, oppressing its people or taking them into slavery. Its history has been rather like the history of Poland in our own day, wedged in between Russia and the nations of Western Europe, and nearly crushed to death between them. And it is this small and oppressed bit of country that the creator of the whole immense universe called especially his own when he lived on earth.

The people of Israel enjoyed in their history a few short periods of freedom and prosperity, but God did not choose one of them in which to come among his people. Instead, he chose a moment when they were having a difficult time. Rome had conquered nearly all Europe, as well as Palestine, and we can visualize the people of Israel enduring much the sort of life that the French people endured after Hitler conquered France. Most of the men in high places had made friends with the enemy for the sake of the comfort and security that this friendship brought them, but the rest of the nation was heavily taxed and very poor in consequence. They were not badly treated if they did what they were told, and the Romans were efficient rulers, but the people of Israel have always been a proud and independent people and the loss of their freedom was bitter to them. In Palestine at that time, as in France during the last war, there was a vigorous underground movement. In France they were called the Maquis, in Palestine the Zealots. If the Romans caught the Zealots engaged in active rebellion they executed them, and their way of torturing and killing rebels was the dreadful way of crucifixion. It was no unusual thing in Palestine at that time to see crosses set up beside the road and men dying on them in agony. The outward life of the country, the tending of the vineyards and olive groves, the ploughing of the fields, the sowing and gathering of the crops, the lives of the farmers and shepherds and artisans and their families in the small villages perched upon the hilltops, went on normally enough, but underneath it was much hidden anxiety and grief and pain, and into the middle of it all came God. And, as we shall see as we follow this story, there was nothing of their life that he did not share with his people; and does not to-day share with us, because we are his people if we love him, and he is as close to us as he was to them, when they heard his voice and saw his face and put out their hands and touched him.

2

We have thought a little of his people, his country and his time, and now we come closer to him and think of his Mother.

She lived in a village called Nazareth, in Galilee, to the north of Palestine. We can imagine ourselves travellers approaching Nazareth on the evening of a day in early spring. All around is a scene of great beauty, for the February rains are just over and this country that for the greater part of the year is dusty and arid is now fresh and green. Behind us as we toil up the steep rocky path is the beautiful plain of Esdraelon, to the east are the mountains of Moab, while the snow-capped peak of Mount Hermon shines out against the sky. There were many trees in Palestine in those days. The lower slopes of the hills are wooded with cedars and oaks and ilexes, and all about us as we climb up to the village are terraces of vines and olives. Though it is such a steep climb up to Nazareth, the village itself lies sheltered in a hollow surrounded by steep hills. The white houses are small, the poorer houses roofed with branches, the larger ones with small stone domes. Some of the bigger houses have gardens about them planted with fruit trees, figs and citrons, almonds and pomegranates. The almond trees are just coming into bloom and here and there is a froth of pink blossom over a garden wall. The atmosphere is crystal clear and the sky a deep blue flecked with golden clouds. The colour on the hills is very wonderful, purple and rose and tawny orange, and the shadows sharp and dark; for this is a land of brilliant pure colour and vivid contrasts, like the life that we are going to try to follow.

We are in Nazareth now, walking up a narrow cobbled lane between the houses. The men have not yet come home from their work in the fields and the people whom we pass are the women and children. They are poor people and the women wear long dresses of blue and brown cloth that they have woven themselves on their looms, with white veils on their heads to protect them from the sun. But they have woven bright garments for their children and the little things run along beside them looking very gay, the boys with small round caps on their heads, or turbans bound round with a fillet in imitation of their fathers, and the little girls with veils like their mothers. Most of the women are going to the spring to fetch water, so that their husbands and sons can wash themselves before they sit down to the evening meal. Some of them carry their waterpots on their shoulders, others balance them on their heads. The water at Nazareth gushes out from the hillside, clear and very cold. You can see the same spring to-day and hear it called "Mary's Fountain".

The women linger here, exchanging village gossip with each other, sometimes lowering their voices to talk a little of the sorrows and dangers of the times. But as much as they can they like to forget these and talk of the small, happy affairs of the village that make up the brightness of their lives. They are pleased that Joseph-bar-Jacob the village carpenter is going to marry Mary the daughter of Anne. They like Joseph and they are talking about him as they stand by the spring, taking their turn to fill their waterpots. "He is a just man," they say of him. And they mean a good deal by that great word "just". They mean that Joseph is trustworthy, that when he has given his word he does not go back on it, and when he has undertaken a job of work he does it as well as he can right through to the end. And they mean also that he is a good man, whose life is clear like the mountain air and whose words and deeds are kind. Mary is lucky, they say, that he has chosen her for his wife, and Anne is lucky that she can give her daughter into such safe keeping. And then they pause in their talk because Mary herself is coming up the lane with her waterpot.

What does she look like? No one seems to have written down a description of her but we are told that she belonged to a tribe that in appearance was very like the modern Bedouin Arab. That means that she is olive-skinned and slender, with soft dark eyes. Girls married very early in Palestine in those days and she is about fourteen or fifteen years old. She wears a blue homespun dress with a white veil on her dark hair, and on top of her head is a pad with the waterpot balanced on it. She has trained herself not to touch the pot with her hands as she walks, and this has taught her to hold her back straight and her head high and to walk with the grace and dignity of a queen.

Out of all the women who have ever lived upon this earth, or who will ever live, this village girl is the one whom God chose to be the Mother of his Son, and so we know that she was as perfect as a woman can be, lovely in mind and in spirit as well as in body, and like all lovely people very much beloved. She must have been strong and sturdy too, like all country girls trained to hard work, and we know from all that happened afterwards that she was extraordinarily brave. So the other women were glad to see her at the spring, and she was glad to see them. They talked to her about Joseph, and teased her a little, and her cheeks flushed pink with happiness and her eyes were bright with laughter as she lifted her waterpot from her head and held it beneath the gushing water. She stayed and talked to them all for a little while before she turned to go home, one hand now holding the full pot steady on her head, walking very slowly and carefully so as not to spill the water, looking about her as she walked at the great beauty of the world and thanking God for it in her heart. The greatest moments of our lives often come upon us unawares and perhaps she did not know, as she walked home with her waterpot, that before the night had fallen upon this lovely land something would have happened to her that would have changed her from a girl into a woman, and opened for her a door into heaven that would never again be shut.

The great artists of the world have loved to paint pictures of the thing that happened to Mary. They have called it the Annunciation and they have all imagined that it happened while she was saying her prayers. Without being artists we too can paint a picture of it in our minds. Mary's home, like others in Palestine, was built round a small inner courtyard, with the chief windows and doors opening into it. The windows in the outer walls were mere slits, so that the noise and glare of the outer world was shut out. The room where Mary prayed was cool and quiet with no sound in it except the whisper of leaves from the fig tree growing in the courtyard. The Eastern people do not kneel to pray, they stand, and Mary stood with bent head and arms crossed upon her breast, and praised God and thanked him, and asked him to have mercy upon his handmaid. Perhaps she used her own words, or perhaps the words of the psalms of David that she would have known by heart. "Praise the Lord, O my soul," and "Have mercy upon me, O God, after thy great goodness."

It is not difficult to imagine the thoughts that were uppermost in her mind as she prayed. Day by day she heard the talk at the spring. She knew all about the suffering of her country, and being so loving a girl she must have carried the sorrow of it always with her. And like all her people she was watching day by day for the Holy One of Israel who would come to deliver his people. Perhaps as a little girl she had sometimes looked out from one of the narrow outward facing windows of her home, to see if she could catch a sight of him riding up from the valley below with his sword at his side, or run to the courtyard door at the sound of a strange footfall in the street, to see if it were he at last. Perhaps, now, like King David, she cried in her heart with the voice of all her people, "Thou art my helper and redeemer: make no long tarrying, O my God." But against this dark background of the sorrow and longing of her people the thought of her own joy would have sprung up like a flower; Joseph, and the children they would have, and their home where they would all live together. She would have prayed that it might be a happy home. And then perhaps through the door that opened on the courtyard the light of the setting sun streamed so gloriously that she looked up, and in that moment the door was no longer just the door into the court-yard but a door opening from earth into heaven.

And now we do not have to use our imaginations any more, be-cause Mary has left a record of what happened to her then. She thought that an angel came to her, stepping from heaven into her little room. Her people had always loved and reverenced those servants and messengers of God, the angels. King David had thought of the clouds and the winds as angels and had dared to imagine them carrying God himself across the sky upon their wings. "He rode upon a cherub and did fly; yea, he did fly upon the wings of the wind". Isaiah had seen the terrible six-winged seraphim who stand about the throne of God, great and awful presences who yet veil their faces with their mighty wings before the even more awful presence of God. Jacob had seen a ladder set up between earth and heaven and the angels passing and repassing upon it. Abraham and other holy men had spoken with angels as a man speaks with a man, and received from them the commands and the comfort and the strength of God. To four of these loving and lovely spirits, who sometimes at God's command humble themselves to stoop beneath the low lintel of the door of earth and come to us, the people of Israel had given names: Raphael, Gabriel, Cassiel and Michael. Mary believed it was Gabriel who came to her that day. She has left no description of what he looked like; perhaps, like the angel whom St. John saw on the Island of Patmos, "a rainbow was upon his head, and his face was as it were the sun", and the light blinded her. That is really all that people who have looked into heaven are able to tell us about it – that it is "light". But she knew what he said to her.

"Hail, thou that art highly favoured, the Lord is with thee: blessed art thou among women."

In this story of an almost unbelievable humbling this angelic humility takes its place, this coming in of Gabriel to Mary, this greeting of a young girl by a great angel with words of gentle courtesy. Some of the old painters have shown Gabriel kneeling before Mary, like a courtier before his queen, as he uttered those words that have always been called by the lovely name of "The Salutation".

What did Mary do? She says she was "troubled", wondering "what manner of salutation this should be". She must have been afraid, because Gabriel's next words brought her the comfort of God to the frightened.

"Fear not, Mary, for thou hast found favour with God."

Then she knew quite certainly for always that God loved her, and that whatever happened to her through the rest of her life she would never have to be afraid. This certainty steadied her spirit, made it calm and peaceful like a still pool, so that she was able to accept the amazing revelation of God that followed, as the quiet water is able to receive the reflection of the sky and stars above it. She was to be the Mother of the Holy One of Israel, for whom she had watched so long, the Mother of the Son of God. Her watching and waiting were nearly ended now. In a few months' time she would hold the Son of God in her arms, and he would be her Son too. She, Mary of Nazareth, a fourteen-year-old girl whom the great world had never even heard of, she and no other was to be his Mother. The angel told her this, and almost unbelievable though the revelation must have seemed to her, yet her quiet and loving spirit was able to believe it.

Yet though she was no longer frightened, she was appalled by the greatness and the mystery of this thing that she was asked to do. This child, her child, was to be the Son of the Lord God of Israel himself, not of Joseph. She was asked to be the Mother of God. How could she be? How could she do it? Who was she that this honour should come to her? She was not strong enough to bear it. "How shall this be?" she cried out to Gabriel. And we can picture her no longer standing but crouched down on the ground with her face buried in her hands. This is how humble men and women always feel when God calls them to do some great thing for him. How can I do it? How can I possibly do it?

The answer is always the same answer, the one that Gabriel gave to Mary. "The Holy Ghost shall come upon thee and the power of the Highest shall overshadow thee." Not in their own strength, Mary, do the servants of God do the work to which he calls them, but in his. What a man or woman cannot do by themselves they can do when God is with them, for with God nothing is impossible.

And so the second great certainty came to Mary, and she lifted her head and opened her arms and said, "Behold the handmaid of the Lord; be it unto me according to thy word."

She knew a third thing now, that she loved God who loved her and whose power would never fail her. She had nothing to give him but herself, and so she gave herself. She loved him so much that she wanted only one thing now, to do his will whatever it should cost her.

3

It was to cost her a very great deal. She was to have great joy in her life, but great suffering too, and both of them so piercing that only a woman as strong and stout-hearted as Mary would have been able to endure them without breaking.

Her worries began almost at once, for Joseph was deeply troubled when he found that she was to have a child who would not be his but the direct gift of God to her. He too, like Mary, had been watching and waiting for the Holy One of Israel, and he knew the prophecy of Isaiah that foretold that a virgin of Israel would be the Mother of the Messiah. But he had not expected this virgin to be Mary. It must have seemed as though this girl whom he loved had suddenly been taken away from him. He felt shut out. She was no longer the Mary whom he knew, but someone mysterious and strange whom he could not understand. He did not know what to think about it all, and in his unhappiness and bewilderment he felt that he could not now marry her.

And then one night, after he had lain awake tormented by his doubts, he fell deeply asleep and dreamed that the door opened into heaven for him too, and an angel came to him out of the light with the same glorious message that had come to Mary. "Fear not." He too, like Mary when the light shone upon her, received into his soul, to the utmost extent to which he was able to bear it, the knowledge that the Almighty and Eternal Lord God loved him, loved Joseph, the obscure carpenter of Nazareth, a poor and humble man, and had called him to be the foster-father of his Son. When he woke up there was no more doubt or bewilderment left in him. He wanted only to do one thing, and that was to obey the God who loved him and whom he loved. From that moment onwards he did not question anything, but just did quietly and at once what he was told.

About this time, perhaps while Joseph was so troubled and because she felt he would be happier if she went away, Mary paid a visit to her cousin Elisabeth who lived up in the hills in the country of Juda, southward from Galilee. Perhaps she travelled part of the way with friends who took care of her, and then parted from them at the foot of the hill upon whose summit was perched the small white town where Elisabeth lived.

It was later in the year now. The valleys were green with the waving corn and all over the slopes of the hills above them was spread the glory of the spring flowers. Those who have seen the flowers of Palestine say that their colour and beauty are almost unbelievable. There are scarlet and purple anemones, blue speedwell, blood-red pimpernel, yellow daisies, cyclamen and violets. Marigolds are a flame of gold under the sun, and the midday heat draws out the good smell of the aromatic things that Isaiah loved. "I will plant in the wilderness the cedar . . . and the myrtle and the oil tree," he wrote. "I will set in the desert the fir tree, and the pine, and the box tree together."

Mary in her blue dress, under the blue sky, must have climbed upwards among the flowers most joyously. Even though she was worried about Joseph she would have put the worry away from her, for this was a day made for joy. Pulling a sprig of Isaiah's loved myrtle, she would have remembered him and the glorious and glowing words in which he described the Son of God. "And his name shall be called Wonderful, Counsellor, The Mighty God, The Everlasting Father, The Prince of Peace." And this Wonderful One would be her child. God was giving to his people, through her, their Saviour. "Comfort ye, comfort ye my people, saith your God." Not much longer now. Soon God would stoop from heaven to lay his Son in her arms, and her arms would give him to the world. She must have marvelled at the humility of God. He could have given his Son to the world without her help. He could have sent him down from heaven in a blaze of glory. Yet he did not choose this lonely and lofty way, he chose to bend low and whisper to her, "You and I." Yet this, she knew, is always God's way, for God is love, and love is something that cannot exist at all if there is only an "I". There must be "you and I", the Lover and the Beloved, and the Lover honours the Beloved, even though the one is the great God in heaven and the other a peasant girl in a worn blue dress.

Mary must have spent the whole of the rest of her life thanking God for the way in which he had honoured her, and one of her songs of thanksgiving, the Magnificat, has been sung all down the centuries for love of her. Perhaps she began to make it up as she climbed the hillside, to fit a tune to her words and to sing it to the accompaniment of the wind in the pine trees. "My soul doth magnify the Lord, and my spirit hath rejoiced in God my Saviour. For he hath regarded the low estate of his handmaiden; for, behold, from henceforth all generations shall call me blessed. For he that is mighty hath done to me great things; and holy is his name."

And meanwhile in a small house in the town at the top of the hill Elisabeth was sitting at her window waiting for Mary, and she too was praising God because to her and to her husband, as well as to Mary and Joseph, there had come the great "Fear not", and to her too God had whispered, "You and I".

Elisabeth was married to a priest called Zacharias and they had grown old together serving God. They must have been happy people, for the servants of God are always happy, but they had one grief; they had no child. They had prayed long and earnestly to God to give them one, but the years had passed and they had grown old and still there was no child. So then after the foolish fashion of men and women they had imagined that God had not heard them. They had learned a good deal in a long life but not yet that God never fails to answer prayer. But he answers it in the way and at the moment that is best for everybody, and man who does not know all about everybody, and cannot see the wonderful pattern that God is weaving with the lives of all us, gets discouraged if the way is not to his liking and the moment delayed.

Elisabeth's baby had to be delayed because God had chosen her child to do a particular piece of work for him at a special time. It had been foretold that a great prophet should be born upon the earth who should prepare the way of the Christ. In those days, when a king decided to visit the cities of his kingdom, a messenger would be sent running before him through the wilderness to tell the people he was coming, so that they could prepare their city and make ready to receive the king. Isaiah had described this Forerunner. "The voice of him that crieth in the wilderness, Prepare ye the way of the Lord, make straight in the desert a highway for our God." And to Elisabeth and Zacharias God gave the great honour of being the mother and father of the Forerunner.

It was revealed first of all to Zacharias. He was in Jerusalem, the holy city of Israel. Now that he was old the time had come for him to give up his life's work of serving God as a priest in the Temple, and he was in the last week of his service there. The Temple at Jerusalem was very beautiful. King Solomon had built the first Temple, but it had been destroyed by enemy invasion, and then rebuilt, and now it was being rebuilt once more by Herod, the Jewish king who in obedience to the Roman Emperor ruled this conquered country for him. It was built of marble and white limestone, inlaid with beautiful mosaics, with great open courts grouped about the Inner Temple, the Holy Place and the Holy of Holies. Day by day the people gathered in the court outside the Holy Place to pray, but they did not go into the Holy Place, into which only the priests might go. They entered it in turn, perhaps only once in their lives, and burned incense there just as the dawn was breaking. Into the Holy of Holies only the High Priest might go, and he only once a year.

The day came when it was the turn of Zacharias to enter the Holy Place for the last time. Old and white-haired, dignified in his priestly garments of purple and white, he made his way through the Temple courts with two assistant priests on either side of him, and as he went he struck a gong to tell the people that the hour had come for the burning of the incense. The coming of man to God and God to man, their meeting and union, is a thing so full of mystery that man has always had to use symbols or pictures to help him to understand a little of the wonder of it. The smoke rising up from the burning incense was a picture of the prayers of the people rising up from their penitent hearts, and Zacharias burning the incense in the Holy Place was giving them to God.

When the assistant priests had made everything ready, they withdrew, leaving Zacharias alone to burn the incense. Standing before the altar in the Holy Place, he could see the door leading to the Holy of Holies. To many Israelites this small windowless room was the most sacred place in the world because it was the symbol of the presence of God dwelling with his people. Alone in the quietness Zacharias bowed his head and worshipped, as Mary had done in the quiet room at Nazareth.

And as the smoke of the incense ascended and he lifted up the prayers of his people to God, once more the door opened and the glory of heaven shone through. Zacharias saw an angel formed all of light standing at the right side of the altar and, like Mary, he was terrified. And then to him too there came the great "Fear not", and he was comforted, and as the turmoil of his terror quieted it seemed that he heard a voice telling him that his prayer had been heard. He was to have a child and he must call him John. "Thou shalt have joy and gladness; and many shall rejoice at his birth." The voice itself was glorious as light, each word falling like a flake of fire to lighten the darkness of his fear and drive it away. "He shall go before him . . . to make ready a people prepared for the Lord." The Forerunner. He was being told that he was to be the father of the Forerunner. But he could not believe it. He was old, and Elisabeth was old, and they had given up hope of this child so long ago. It was too wonderful to be believed. He wanted more proof than this light that blinded him and this voice speaking right inside his soul that might both of them be nothing but delusion. He could not believe without some sort of solid proof. Again came the voice in his soul, flooding it with light.

"I am Gabriel, that stand in the presence of God; and am sent to speak unto thee, and to shew thee these glad tidings."

But still he cried out for his proof, and the voice came again. "Behold, thou shalt be dumb, and not able to speak, until the day that these things shall be performed, because thou believest not my words, which shall be fulfilled in their season."

The light faded and the door was closed. Slowly he came back to himself. It seemed to him that he had been on a long journey and had been an immense time away. He remembered who he was, and where he was. Outside the Holy Place the people were waiting for him. He had offered their prayers to God and now he must go back to them and bless them. Staggering a little, because he was a very old man and he had just experienced great fear, great gladness and great doubt, he came out to them and saw the astonishment on their faces . . . So he *had* been a very long time away . . . He raised his hand and tried to pronounce the blessing that was always given at this time, "The Lord be merciful unto us and bless us, and lift up the light of his countenance upon us, and give us peace," but he could not, because no words would come. He had his proof. He was dumb. But it seemed to the people that blessing came to them from the light upon his face. Because of the light they knew that he had seen a vision.

He went home and as he could not speak he must have written out an account of what had happened for Elisabeth to read. But perhaps she knew already. Perhaps God had already said to her, "You and I. I will put your son in your arms and you shall give him to my people to prepare the way."

There was a light step in the courtyard and a voice called "Elisabeth! Elisabeth!" Looking through the window, Elisabeth saw Mary standing beneath the old fig tree which grew beside the well. She looked happy and eager yet shy and humble at the same time, for she was young and Elizabeth was old, and Elisabeth had known her all her life, had loved her like her own child, and now she must find it hard to believe that this child Mary had been chosen out of all the women of Israel to be the Mother of the Holy One. But Elisabeth did not find it hard to believe, because she was humble too, and like all the humble she had a great reverence for other people; even those whom she knew in and out, through and through, and had held in her arms when they were small. With her old face flooded with awe and joy she came to Mary and, holding the girl's hands in hers, she bent her head as though she did honour to her Queen.

"Blessed art thou among women," she said, "and blessed is the fruit of thy womb. And whence is this to me, that the Mother of my Lord should come to me? For, lo, as soon as the voice of thy salutation sounded in mine ears, the babe leaped in my womb for joy. And blessed is she that believed, for there shall be a performance of those things which were told her from the Lord."

Then Mary put her arms round Elisabeth's neck and kissed her and clung to her, not at all like the Queen whom Elisabeth had greeted but like the child whom she had always loved as her own. Then they went together out of the blazing sun of the courtyard into the cool dim house. Mary stayed with Elisabeth for three months, and we can imagine them sitting together and making clothes for their babies, and talking of the wonderful thing that had happened to them both. When she was alone Mary sang as she sewed, for now she had completed her song of praise and she thanked God not only that he had so honoured the poor and humble people of the world, in choosing a peasant girl to be the Mother of his Son, but for his faithfulness too. Men had wondered sometimes, as the long and bitter years went by, if he had forgotten his promise to send his Son to help them. But he had not forgotten. There is no forgetfulness in God. "In him is no variableness, neither shadow of turning."

"The dayspring from on high hath visited us," said Joseph, and Mary answered softly, "To give light to them that sit in darkness and in the shadow of death, to guide our feet into the way of peace."

Over their heads the night sky blazed with stars and the frosty road rang sharply beneath the donkey's feet. The donkey stumbled now and then, for it was just about dead-beat, and Joseph limped as he walked because his feet had got sore with so much tramping over stony hill-paths. It might have been thought that Mary had the best of it, warmly wrapped up in a thick cloak and sitting on the donkey's back, but she was really the most tired of the three. Her eyes looked enormous in her white face, and her voice as she answered Joseph was hoarse with weariness, yet when Joseph looked at her anxiously she smiled, and then he smiled too. Throughout the long and weary journey from Nazareth to Bethlehem they had both been extraordinarily happy, for they had given themselves utterly to do the will of God and now its movement was like a great wind that carried them along.

Mary and Joseph had wondered sometimes, during the first weeks after they were married, about the prophecy which had said that the Holy One of Israel would be born at Bethlehem. "And thou Bethlehem, in the land of Juda, art not the least among the princes of Juda: for out of thee shall come a governor, that shall rule my people Israel." And yet here they were at Nazareth, and the time for the baby's birth was coming near.

And then one day a Roman soldier had come riding into the village, and when he had gathered all the people together he had read them a proclamation. The government was going to hold a census, an official numbering of the population for the purposes of taxation, and each man must go with his wife to the city from which his family had originally come, to record their names and give an account of their circumstances. This meant that Joseph and Mary must go to Bethlehem, because he was descended from King David and Bethlehem was David's city. Their neighbours must have been horrified, for such a long journey in winter would be very bad for a young girl expecting her first baby. But Mary and

Joseph were not horrified, for they saw in this journey the movement of the will of God and they were not afraid.

Yet they must have needed all their courage. We are not told anything about their journey, and so it is only supposition that they kept up their hearts by repeating the hymn of praise that Zacharias had composed when his son John was born and his speech was restored to him again. Yet surely they did, because it was so lovely a prophecy of the coming of their child . . . The dayspring from on high. Light in darkness. The way of peace . . . They had only to reach their journey's end and it would all come true.

"Look, Mary!" said Joseph.

Mary straightened herself and looked eagerly in the direction in which Joseph was pointing. Bethlehem, like most of the old cities of this country, is built upon the summit of a rocky hill, and clear-cut against the sky they could see tall cypresses and squat houses black and white under the moon. The sight of it put new life into them and it did not seem long before they were passing beneath the archway in the city wall and entering the narrow streets.

Bethlehem to-night was full of bustle and noise. Roman soldiers guarded the gateway and the cobbled streets were crowded with the many travellers who had come, like Joseph and Mary, to register their names.

Joseph asked his way to the inn, but when they reached it his heart sank. The inns at that time were just a yard surrounded by a high wall and a colonnade, with rooms for the travellers under the arches. But the yard of this inn was full of camels and donkeys being unloaded, and jostling, tired, bad-tempered travellers, with the harassed innkeeper moving about among them, and one glance told him that the rooms all round were full too. "To guide our feet into the way of peace." He wanted peace for Mary, but it did not look as though he would find it in this inn.

We do not know who it was who suggested that they should go to the stable. Perhaps the innkeeper fetched his wife and she, seeing how ill Mary was, took her quickly to their own stable as the only quiet place she could think of. The old houses of Bethlehem are built over caves in the limestone rock. You can see them to-day, just as they were on this night nearly two thousand years ago, with the caves level with the street and the houses above

211

reached by a flight of steps. The poorer houses have only one room and the family live there all together, with their animals stabled at night in the cave below. The innkeeper's little house must have been already full of guests and noisy children, or his wife would have taken Mary there. She must have chosen the stable below as the quieter place of the two.

The cave at Bethlehem that has been reverenced all down the centuries as the cave of the Nativity is a small place, only fourteen feet long and four feet wide. We can picture the floor of trodden earth and the rough stone walls, and the trough or manger for the hay hewn out of the wall. There were a couple of iron rings in the wall and to these were tethered the old ox that the innkeeper used for the ploughing, and his donkey. Perhaps the dog was there too, asleep in the corner. The little place could not have been at all comfortable, but when the wooden doors fixed in the entrance to the cave had been shut it would have been very peaceful. The gentle beasts don't make a noise, like men do, they are always quiet, especially when they are sleepy. This hidden, hollowed place right inside the earth must have felt to Mary like the quiet heart of the world, and here the Creator of the world, God Almighty, our Lord and Saviour Jesus Christ, was born.

7

Not far away, in the quiet fields, shepherds were guarding their sheep. They had built a little fire within the sheepfold, for it was cold, and were sitting about it wrapped in their cloaks, and they were nodding with sleep. Christians have always believed that Our Lord was born at midnight, and the author of the Book of Wisdom wrote, "While all things were in quiet silence, and that night was in the midst of her swift course, thine Almighty Word leaped down from heaven out of thy royal throne." And so perhaps it was round about midnight that the shepherds suddenly woke up.

They were awakened by a great light, the light neither of their fire, nor of the moon or stars, but a light so glorious that it filled them with a great terror. It was the same light that had already shone upon Mary, Joseph and Zacharias, the light of the world beyond this one, and the words that came with the light were the same great words, "Fear not!" The terror passed as the assurance of God's love gripped them and held them steady, and they were able to receive, as Mary had done, the message of the great angel who stood there in the light.

"I bring you good tidings of great joy, which shall be to all people."

It must have seemed to the poor shepherds, kneeling there before the courteous angel, as though the joy and the light were reaching out through them to all poor men all over the world, a great multitude of poor men whose Saviour had come among them.

"For unto you is born this day in the city of David a Saviour, which is Christ the Lord. And this shall be a sign unto you; Ye shall find the babe wrapped in swaddling clothes, lying in a manger."

So he had come at last, their Christ and Lord, not born a rich young prince laid in a golden cradle, but a little poor babe lying in a manger. But no rich young prince ever had such music at his birth as this poor babe had. It seemed to the happy shepherds that the very stars were singing, each star an angel of the heavenly host. As the glory of heaven streamed out to the four corners of the earth, it seemed that the light was the music and the music was the light.

"Glory to God in the highest, and on earth peace, good will towards men."

Peace had come down to dwell with men for ever. No matter what the suffering, the fighting, the storms, the distress, nothing now could ever take from the lovers of God the gift of his peace. Men could never again doubt the good will of God towards them, for God had given his own Son to be born, to live, to die, for their salvation. God's good will was incarnate now as a little child lying in a manger.

The moment of vision passed and the door was shut in heaven. The night was quiet again, lit only by the moon and the stars and the flames of the fire. But the shepherds did not doubt the truth of what they had heard and seen. They did not even waste time talking about it. "Let us go now," they said to each other, and we are told, "they came with haste" to the place where their Saviour lay. We do not know how they found the way. Perhaps by the time they got to Bethlehem dawn was not far away and they saw

213

the morning star shining like a lamp over the roof of the little house that was built over the cave. They went in and found him wrapped in his swaddling bands, lying in the warm hay in the manger hewn out of the wall, with Mary and Joseph loving and watching him there, and the gentle beasts looking on in amazement. In the fitful lantern light they could see him like a flower in the hay, and they knelt down and worshipped and adored. They saw him with their own eyes and their joy must have been almost too great to be borne.

> *Light looked down and beheld Darkness,*
> *"Thither will I go," said Light.*
> *Peace looked down and beheld War,*
> *"Thither will I go," said Peace.*
> *Love looked down and beheld Hatred,*
> *"Thither will I go," said Love.*
> *So came Light, and shone;*
> *So came Peace, and gave rest;*
> *So came Love, and brought Life,*
> *And the Word was made Flesh, and dwelt among us.*
> LAURENCE HOUSMAN.

8

It is only a journey of five miles from Bethlehem to Jerusalem, and when their baby was still not many days old Mary and Joseph took him there that they might present him to God in the Temple. All the fathers and mothers of Israel brought their babies to God in this way, very much as we bring our babies to be baptized in church.

The scene is the same beautiful Temple where Gabriel came to Zacharias; and we can picture a priest dressed like Zacharias in purple garments standing at the top of a flight of marble steps, and the mothers standing at the foot of them with their babies in their arms. Mary among them, patiently waiting her turn to lay her baby in the priest's arms that the priest might bless him and offer him to God. Joseph was beside her carrying a wicker cage with a pair of turtledoves or two young pigeons in it, for when a baby was presented to God the father always offered a sacrifice.

214

To us it seems dreadful that worshippers coming to God's Temple should have brought live animals and birds with them, and that these should have been killed and burnt upon the altar of sacrifice in one of the great open-air courts. But all through the centuries of their history the people of Israel had offered sacrifice in this way. Just as the smoke from the incense was a picture of prayer rising up to God, so these sacrifices made a picture to them of their penitent souls offered to God in sorrow for their sins. When they saw the flames leap up they felt that God had accepted their penitence and that they were made one with him again. If they had no birds or beasts of their own they had to buy them, and it cost them something to offer this gift of their penitence to God. Well-to-do people could afford to sacrifice goats and sheep, but the very poor could only afford the turtle-doves or pigeons that Joseph brought.

Mary's turn came and she and Joseph went up the steps together and she laid her baby in the priest's arms, and then she and Joseph bent their head while the priest blessed their son and lifting him up offered him to God. Sometimes this is called the first sorrow of Mary, because this moment at the beginning of Our Lord's life, when she saw him lifted up and given to God, is a picture of the moment at the end of his life when she saw him lifted up upon the cross and given to God again. At both these moments, at the beginning and the end, he was taken from Mary. All she could do was to stand by and watch.

To the priest who blessed him, and to the other fathers and mothers, Our Lord was just one baby among all the rest, not very important because his parents had only brought two birds in a wicker cage as a sacrifice, but there were two people in the Temple that day who did know that their God and Saviour had come among them. Their names were Simeon and Anna, and they were old and holy people who were always waiting for the coming of Christ, and to Simeon it had been revealed that he should not die until he had seen his Saviour. He knew that day that this was the moment for which he had been waiting all his life, and he came to the Temple and was watching and waiting when the fathers and mothers came with their babies. He knew at once which of all those babies was his Lord and King, and with a cry of joy he held out his arms, and Mary, after one glance at his transfigured face, put her baby into them. And Simeon cried out aloud and blessed

God and said, "Lord, now lettest thou thy servant depart in peace, according to thy word: for mine eyes have seen thy salvation, which thou hast prepared before the face of all people; a light to lighten the Gentiles, and the glory of thy people Israel."

Then Simeon gave her baby to his Mother again, and blessed her and Joseph, and looking at Mary he said to her, "This child is set for the fall and rising again of many in Israel." He saw in that moment how the presence of the Christ among them would test men. The holiness of God would shine out from him and in that light they would see themselves for what they were. They would not like what they saw, and the proud among them would hate him for showing it to them and fall into the deadly sin of turning away from him, while the humble, hating themselves, would rise up out of themselves to him. And then looking at Mary in her youth and happiness it seems that he saw her as she would be when the time of the second offering came, and her youth had gone and her happiness had turned to anguish, for he said to her, "A sword shall pierce through thy own soul."

And then old Anna came. She spent all her time in the Temple praising God and praying to him. She knew, too, that this baby was her Lord, and bent her head and worshipped him, and praised God that she had lived to see him with her own eyes.

And Joseph and Mary took their baby back to Bethlehem, to the house where they were staying while Mary grew strong, and they marvelled at all these strange things that were happening.

9

When our Lord grew to manhood he said one day to the poor men gathered about him, "a rich man shall hardly enter into the kingdom of heaven," and perhaps he remembered as he spoke the story Mary had told him of the rich men who came to Bethlehem to worship him, and how bitterly hard the way had been for them.

This story is so strange and mysterious that we can go on thinking about it for ever and still find something fresh to think about. In the book of Isaiah there is a verse which seems to foretell their coming. "And the Gentiles shall come to thy light, and kings to the brightness of thy rising." And so because of this verse, and because of the splendour of the gifts that they brought, lovers of Our Lord throughout the years have thought of these men as kings, and they have thought of them also as representing the three races of mankind, the men of Asia, Africa and Europe, and they have given them names, Caspar, Melchior and Balthazar.

But all that St. Matthew actually tells us about them is that they were three wise men and that they came from the east. But those three words "from the east" tell us something about their journey. They must have crossed the desert of Arabia and the mountains of Moab, and it must have been a long and bitter journey during which they endured hunger and thirst, fever, heat and cold, and ceaseless danger from wild beasts and desert tribesmen. If they had not been men of great courage and determination they could not have endured and persevered. We long to know how it was that they set out upon their journey. When they reached Jerusalem they explained their presence by the one quiet sentence, "We have seen his star in the east and are come to worship him," and that is all we know. Yet from it we can learn a little. All through the ages wise men have loved to study the stars. The Greeks believed at one time that great heroes became stars when they died. Other wise men have thought of the stars as guardian angels, believing that people born in certain months are under the protection of particular stars. Shakespeare wrote in one of his sonnets,

> *Till whatsoever star that guides my moving*
> *Points on me graciously with fair aspect*
> *And puts apparel on my tatter'd loving,*
> *To show me worthy of thy sweet respect.*

The three kings must have been men of science, astronomers who studied the stars, and seeing a new light in the sky have believed it to be the protector of a great hero coming upon the earth. As this star was very glorious, so this hero also must be very glorious; he could be no less than a very great king. And so guided by the star they set out upon their long journey. And that is all we can know.

Yet in our own minds we can't help giving a name to that star of "fair aspect", and calling it Gabriel, who stands in the presence of God and brings men to that presence. Those poor and simple men, the shepherds, were in their humility so near to God that they could actually perceive the angel and accept his message as

217

the truth without a shadow of doubt in their minds. And their journey to their Saviour was a very short one. But the journey is not so easy for clever men. For them Gabriel is not the child's angel of intuition, near and swift and warm, but the angel of reason, cold and distant like a star in the sky. Long and difficult thought brings them to their Saviour, and the way can be hard and may take years.

But the kings came at last to the land of Israel and made their way, as was natural, to the chief city of the country, to Jerusalem. We can picture them riding through the city on their camels, travel-stained and tired, but majestic and awe-inspiring men whose strange appearance made an instant and startling impression upon the crowds thronging the narrow streets. And the question which they kept crying aloud as they rode was equally startling. "Where is he that is born King of the Jews?" They did not ask, where is he who will be king, but who *is* king. They were asking for no child born to a reigning monarch, who would be king one day, but for one who was king *now*, king at this very moment.

The expectation of the Christ was always like a living fire burning in the heart of every man and woman of Israel. They never knew when he might suddenly appear among them, and they so longed for him to come and deliver them from Rome that this expectation could easily flame up into revolt at any rumour of his coming. One man whispered to another, "They say he is born." The rumour flashed right through the city and reached the palace, and when Herod heard it "he was troubled, and all Jerusalem with him".

He was troubled because he did not want revolt. The birth of some child whom the people would believe to be the Christ would disturb the order he had struggled for years to maintain. He was called Herod the Great because he had succeeded in making his people live in obedience to Rome, and that had been a great achievement. He had crushed any attempt at rebellion with dreadful cruelty, but with success. He had been a very clever king, and now that he was an old and dying man he did not want failure at the last. He asked where it was prophesied that the Christ should be born, and when he was told it was at Bethlehem he sent for the three kings and questioned them about the star. Then he sped them upon their way to Bethlehem with words that sounded most kindly and courteous.

218

"Go and search diligently for the young child; and when ye have found him, bring me word again, that I may come and worship him also."

But behind the courtesy his words have a sarcastic ring. It is not likely that he believed in the Christ; but he wanted to find out if a baby had been born whom the people really believed to be the Christ, so that he could get rid of the child at once.

That evening the kings travelled the five miles to Bethlehem and to their joy the star went before them and brought them to the house where the baby was, burning low over the roof so that they could make no mistake. Perhaps the house to which Mary and Joseph had moved was the innkeeper's little house above the stable, perhaps another, but in any case it would have been a humble place, not accustomed to receiving visits from royalty. As the star was shining over the roof, it must have been already dark when the kings arrived. They would have left their servants and camels in the street below and climbed the stone steps with the starlight and lantern light glinting upon their swords and bright raiment and the rich gifts they carried so carefully. They were not taken aback at finding their king in this poor little house; they did not care where they found him if only they could come to him at last; they "rejoiced with exceeding great joy," as they knocked at the humble door and stood waiting with reverently bent heads.

Joseph would have heard the jingle of the camels' bells, and the sound of strange voices in the lane, and opened to them at once. The happy shepherds had praised God for the heavenly thing that had happened to them, and told everyone about it, so that by this time Joseph must have been quite accustomed to all sorts of men and women and children coming to see the baby; yet he must have been astonished to see those strange and magnificent foreigners standing there like figures out of a dream, looking at him so humbly and eagerly. As it was already dark Mary would have put her baby to bed some hours ago, but she had realized by now that though he was hers he belonged to everyone else too and she must share him gladly and graciously. So as Joseph bowed at the doors she smiled at the three kings, and lifting her sleeping son from his cradle sat with him on her lap to show him to them. All his life Our Lord was always at the mercy of everyone who wanted him and scarcely had a minute's peace, yet he never lost patience. So he was patient now and did not cry when the voices and bright

219

lights woke him up, though perhaps he stuck his small fists in his sleepy eyes before he opened them wide and smiled.

The three kings "fell down, and worshipped him", adoring him in the Eastern fashion with their foreheads touching the ground. And then they dared to lift themselves up and look at him, and knew a joy greater than anything they had ever dreamed of. To see him with their own eyes, to worship him, was worth all that they had suffered, worth the long journey, the weariness, hunger and thirst, the danger and the pain. It was so much worth it that in this moment of joy all they had suffered was forgotten as though it had never been. They poured themselves out in adoration before him and all that they had and were they laid at his feet.

For the gifts of gold and frankincense and myrrh symbolize the utmost that a man can give to God. The gold is our wealth: our money, our talents, our health and our strength. The frankincense is our prayer: our souls adoring God, our minds thinking about him, our hearts loving him, our wills resolved to serve him only. And the spice called myrrh, that is used in the east to embalm the bodies of the dead, is our pain: our griefs and disappointments, the aches and the illnesses of our bodies, and our death. In those three kings kneeling there we can see ourselves. They knelt there for us all. Yet though they gave, for themselves and for us, the utmost that a man can give, how little it is in comparison with God's gift to them and to us, the gift of his Son who is himself.

For God gives too to the utmost, and the greatness of God's gift, as well as the tiny content of our own, is symbolized by the gold and frankincense and myrrh. For Our Lord is our King, our Priest and our Sacrifice, who rules over us, prays for us and died for us. It was the greatest King who has ever reigned, the only utterly holy Priest, the only perfect Sacrifice, whom the kings saw in that child, and when they remembered this they bowed themselves in worship all over again.

They left their splendid gifts there and they looked their last on the child, yet not sadly, knowing they would see his face again when he and they had each died for the other; and they kissed a fold of Mary's shabby dress, and bowed to Joseph, and went away. But they did not go back to Herod, for in their sleep that night God told them in a dream to go back to their country another way, and not through Jerusalem. Their journey would have seemed easy this time, for they travelled light. They had given all that they had to God.

And Joseph and Mary were alone with their baby, and Mary "kept all these things and pondered them in her heart".

10

As we follow the story of Our Lord's life we shall see that there is nothing at all that men can suffer that he did not suffer too. One of the greatest miseries which men endure is that of banishment from their own country. Thousands of men and women and children were driven from their homes in the last war, and many have never been able to return to them, and the people of Israel have endured the wretchedness of exile over and over again all through their history. And the sorrow of exile was the first of the sorrows that came to Our Lord.

King Herod was a man who let nothing whatever hinder him from doing what he had decided to do. He had made up his mind that this child whom he feared his people might hail as the Messiah should be got rid of, and the fact that the kings did not return to Jerusalem to tell him which of all the babies in Bethlehem was the one they had worshipped did not turn him from his purpose. He gave the order that all the children in Bethlehem under two years old should be murdered. Such cruelty seems to us unbelievable, but Herod was a man so intensely cruel that he had murdered his own wife and children when he had suspected them of treachery. And he was an old man, and dying, and perhaps hardened and embittered by his pain. He gave the order and it was carried out. Yet it was only over the bodies of those children that Herod had power, and Paradise waited for their happy spirits. They were the first of the martyrs to die for Our Lord, and the only ones who actually died before he did. The company of his martyrs is past counting now, but when he himself passed from the martyrdom of his cross to Paradise it was just that little band of children who met him joyously at the gate.

King Herod was no doubt satisfied with what he had done, but the one baby whom he had wanted to kill was the only one who escaped. Joseph had another of his dreams, in which an angel of

God warned him of what was to happen, and told him to take Mary and her baby to Egypt and to stay there until it was safe to come back again. He obeyed at once, as he always did, though he must have felt something very like despair, wondering if he would ever again get back to his own village, and the work that he loved, and the quiet life with Mary in their own home that he longed for. And this journey down into Egypt with a young wife and a small baby would be full of danger and difficulty. And when they got there how would he support them, in a foreign country, among people who did not even speak his language? And then he remembered the great "Fear not", and the assurance of God's love that had come to him then. The despair passed and he gave himself once more to do the will of God.

Joseph and Mary and their baby must have followed the old caravan road to Egypt that Joseph travelled when he too went into exile. We know nothing of that journey except that it must have been full of danger and difficulty. Once again Mary would have ridden upon a donkey, aching with weariness, her arms numb with the weight of the child, and Joseph would have tramped beside her, tired and footsore. At first they must have been terrified lest Herod's men should overtake them, and kill their baby after all, and when that dread was left behind there would have been the fear of the unknown in front of them. For Joseph and Mary were mortal man and woman, and even the greatest of God's saints, who have experienced his love and given him their trust, occasionally have panic-stricken thoughts that don't quite keep pace with their faith. And when they had left their own land behind and entered Egypt there would have been the heat of the desert by day and the cold at night, the sudden dust storms choking them, and the fear of losing the way. There must have been days when they hadn't enough to eat, and the water in their water-bottles ran short. Joseph and Mary would not have minded so much for themselves as for their child. In Bethlehem they had rejoiced in the health and beauty of their baby, but now they had to see him weary and fretted. Small babies can be wonderfully patient when they are ill and miserable, but their very patience breaks the hearts of those who love them.

Somewhere in Egypt they found a place to live, perhaps in some small mud-walled house in a village by the Nile. Some Egyptian man and his wife, poor people like themselves, for the poor are always good to each other, were kind to them, and Joseph was put in the way of earning a living, and Mary given clothes for her child. It is strange to think that dark-skinned Egyptian women would have held Jesus in their arms and rocked him and sung songs to him. Perhaps they sung the song of the Pharaoh Aknaton, the song of the God who is One, and never knew that they held him in their arms. Yet Mary and Joseph must have felt very homesick, and when Mary sang to her child perhaps she sang the children of Israel's song of exile, "By the waters of Babylon we sat down and wept, when we remembered thee, O Sion." When we adore Our Lord for all that he suffered for our salvation we sometimes forget all that his father and Mother suffered too.

Yet the time passed, and was not as long as it seemed, and once more in his sleep the great angel stood by Joseph and told him that Herod was dead and that they might go home.